THE HAYLING ISLAND MURDERS

A gripping crime thriller full of twists

PAULINE ROWSON

The Solent Murder Mysteries Book 17

Joffe Books, London
www.joffebooks.com

First published in Great Britain in 2023

Cover art by Dee Dee Book Covers

ISBN: 978-1-83526-168-2

CHAPTER ONE

Tuesday 19 July

'What's that awful smell?'

'Well it's not me, guv. It's that.'

Horton dumped his leather jacket and crash helmet on the floor of his office and followed the direction of Walters's pointing finger. Not that he needed to. The obnoxious offender was planted squarely on his desk on a sheet of newspaper that Walters had at least had the initiative to place under it.

'It's a metal box.'

'I can see that.' Horton crossed to it trying, with difficulty, to ignore the sewage-like odour emanating from it. It was about nine inches high by fourteen wide and ten deep, and it was covered in mud, grit and green slime. Fastened to one of the side handles was a pair of handcuffs. 'Was it resisting arrest?'

'Ha ha. Those were on it when it was found.'

Unusual. 'Tell me about it.'

'Can't we do it somewhere else? That pong is making my stomach heave. It's putting me off my food.'

'I don't think anything will ever do that.' Horton pointedly eyed Walters's corpulent frame.

'You should smell my car.'

'No, thanks. And I agree we need to get it moved, but to where?' DCI Bliss's office sprang to mind. Wouldn't that just ruin her immaculate desk? Walters was clearly of the same opinion.

'We could shove it upwards.' He jerked his head.

'Not sure the boss would like that.'

'What wouldn't I like?'

They both started. Horton spun round to find the lean figure of Bliss in the doorway. He hadn't heard her high heels clipping across the floor. She must have tiptoed in. Either that or she'd had rubber soles fitted. More likely, they had been too distracted by the smell of the box. She had the uncanny knack of appearing the moment Horton arrived or happened to be talking about her. He'd often thought that his office was bugged. He wouldn't have put it past her.

'The smell, ma'am. DC Walters was about to tell me about it.'

She wrinkled her nose and glared at the offending item. 'Well, go on then and open the window.'

Horton did so, letting out the cool air-conditioning and allowing in a wave of stifling heat along with the roar of the traffic. The smell stayed just as strong. His mind ran through the possibilities of what the box might contain, and he didn't like what he was thinking.

Walters said, 'Havant police were contacted by a member of the Portsmouth and District Angling Society, who manage Sinah Lake — that's on Hayling Island.'

'I know where it is, Walters. I was stationed at Havant before my promotion,' Bliss curtly replied, stepping further back. Horton didn't blame her.

Walters rubbed his nose. 'They fish carp, tench, bream, roach, rudd and decent-sized pike.'

'Thinking of joining?' Horton asked.

'Nah, I prefer my fish in batter.'

Horton shook his head with a smile.

'Oh, do get on with it,' Bliss snapped, looking at her phone.

'On account of this heatwave, and no rain for weeks, the lake has been drying out to dangerously low levels for the fish, so it has been closed. To the fishermen that is, not the fish.' Walters's attempt at a joke fell on stony ground. 'The fish have been moved to higher levels, where there's more water, and the pond manager and secretary thought they'd have a bit of a tidy-up. The pond manager found that and called the police. Uniform scratched their heads, then called us because of the handcuffs on the box. They thought there might be something fishy about them.' Again, the pun went over Bliss's head. 'As I was the only one here, I thought I'd better take a look.'

And grab a burger on the way, thought Horton. Not to mention Walters slipping out of the office, even in the heat, to avoid answering the phone and working.

'Why call Portsmouth CID?' Bliss sharply asked. 'What's wrong with their own detectives looking into it?'

'Said they hadn't got anyone available.'

'They could still have taken it back to their own station.'

'Could have done, but I don't think they wanted that thing in their nice, sparkly clean police car. I didn't much fancy it in mine but didn't have a choice. With that stench I wondered if it might contain something dodgy, like that hand Inspector Horton and Sergeant Cantelli fished up in that plastic container last Christmas.'

'Fishermen fished it up, Walters,' Horton answered, recalling the investigation. But Walters was right. From the smell there could be something deeply disturbing inside the box.

Bliss scowled and flicked at her ponytail. 'Are they police-issue cuffs?'

'They were at one time.' Horton peered more closely at them. 'Hiatts, steel chain ones.' Not the rigid cuffs they used now. 'I think anyone can buy these off the internet.'

Bliss said, 'Well, get the box opened, and if there are no body parts in it, there will be no need for SOCO to get involved — or us. We have enough to do. Pass it over to Sergeant Wells to log as lost property.'

Wells would love that.

Her phone rang, and with it pressed to her ear she marched out saying, 'No, sir, not yet. Yes, sir, we're still working on it.'

'Working on what?' Walters asked.

'Everything including solving the mystery of the *Mary Celeste*, and the disappearance of Lord Lucan and Shergar. Leave the box where it is.' Horton made for the vending machine in the corridor, reaching for his mobile. He rang the forensic locksmith, Paul Leney, told him what they had, and asked if he could come and open the box.

'Sounds fascinating. Be there in half an hour.'

Then, despite Bliss's instructions, he called SOCO under the ABC principle of crime investigation, which Bliss seemed sadly to lack — accept nothing, believe nothing, check everything. Taylor answered.

Once again, Horton explained about the box. 'I'd like you to take some samples before Leney opens it. If, after that, it warrants further examination then you can send it over to Joliffe for a detailed forensic examination.' Taylor too said he would be over shortly.

Horton pressed the button for black coffee, no sugar. He could smell the tin box from out here and it was lingering on his shirt. It was going to take an age to get rid of the stench. He sincerely hoped its contents were innocuous, or that it was empty. But why the handcuffs? And how had it ended up in Sinah Lake? He couldn't see one of the angling club members ditching the thing there and spoiling something they enjoyed. But someone had. The sea would have been a much better choice and only a few hundred yards to the south of the lake.

'Hello, Andy.'

Horton spun round, his heart skipping a beat. Standing before him was the woman he had been dreading seeing for the last three months. Harriet Ames.

'What are you doing here?' He tried to make his tone light while holding her deep blue eyes in his gaze and fighting desperately not to let his churning emotions show. She looked thinner than when he had last seen her in April at a fogbound Southampton Airport when she'd been returning to the Hague, where she worked for Europol. She'd pleaded with him to tell her why he was so keen to speak to her father, Lord Richard Ames. He had declined because he didn't know what the outcome would be. But he had promised he would update her in time. It had been a foolish vow. The truth of his exchange with Richard Ames could never come out.

'Working.'

'You're on a case for Europol?' he asked, surprised.

'No. I've transferred to the Hampshire and Isle of Wight Police.'

His head swam with this news. It was the last thing he had expected or even wanted to hear. It would mean coming into frequent contact with her, and he wasn't at all sure how he'd handle that. There would be no avoiding her, and that would mean no avoiding the past.

'You didn't hear about it?' she asked, then hastily added, 'No reason why you should, it's a big police force.' She pushed back her fair hair, her eyes never leaving his. 'I'm in the Serious Case Review Team at Southampton.'

Only twenty-five miles west along the motorway.

'I've been assigned to review the Giles Priestley missing person case. Rather apt, given the circumstances, don't you think?'

He listened for the bitterness in her voice but there was none, only a faint hint of sadness.

'You know that my father's yacht was found with nobody on board.'

He had read of it three weeks ago. In fact, he had devoured every item about it online, including the speculation as to what had happened to the peer of the realm — some wildly weird theories involving time warps, others maliciously hinting that Ames's financial affairs were in disarray, while others suggested he had absconded with a lover. But the sensible and obvious conclusion was that he'd gone sailing, had been caught in the fog and suffered an accident or illness, then fallen overboard. No one knew about the gunshot Horton had heard on board that boat on the pontoon. And the fact that Richard Ames hadn't been alone but with his brother, Gordon. No one, that was, except him and Andrew Ducale of the intelligence services.

'They searched for his body, but not for long,' she said. 'It would be useless to continue anyway, the sea would . . . well, you know.'

He did.

'I haven't told anyone that you were the last person to see him alive.'

His heart stalled. 'Harriet, I didn't see him.' It was a lie. The first, he suspected, of many. But how could he tell her that his encounter with her father and Gordon had revealed the truth behind his own mother's disappearance over thirty years ago? That incident had consigned him to the mercy of social services, passing through a succession of children's homes and foster carers. He had tried hard to put the Ames family behind him since learning the truth, but now he might no longer be able to.

'We need to talk, Andy, and don't say there's nothing you can tell me, because there is. I'm a police officer and I know when someone isn't telling the truth. Whatever happened, I need to know, and you're not heartless enough to hide that from me. I can see it in your eyes.'

She was bluffing. Or perhaps she really could see his anguish. He believed he was adept at hiding his emotions. After all, he'd had years of practice in doing so as a child, where any sign of vulnerability could be seized upon and exploited by other children in the homes, and some adults. Harriet wouldn't do that, but perhaps she was concerned his guard was down.

She said, 'This is not the right place or time. Are you still living on your boat?'

'Yes.'

'Then I'll come there tonight.'

'No, not there.'

'You want somewhere public in case I make a scene.'

'You wouldn't do that, Harriet.' But he knew, as did she, that he was in greater danger of telling her something of the truth if they were alone. 'I'll buy you a drink.'

'Excuse me.'

They stepped aside to allow a uniformed officer to get to the vending machine.

'Is this yours, sir?'

Horton took his black coffee from her.

Harriet said, 'OK, where?'

'The Spice Island pub, Old Portsmouth, seven o'clock.' It was a popular venue on the harbour entrance and would be busy enough to drown out their conversation. And, as Harriet had intimated, prevent any display of emotion.

She nodded. Instead of going though, she waited. Horton eyed her enquiringly.

'I came to see Sergeant Cantelli.'

'He never mentioned it.' Horton was surprised. Had Cantelli deliberately kept silent because he knew that Harriet's family had been mixed up in his mother's disappearance? Horton had told Cantelli some of what had happened but nothing like the whole story. The same for Gaye, the forensic pathologist, who he was close to.

'That's because I didn't tell him I was coming. My intention was to discuss the Priestley case with former DCI Knight, but sadly Mr Knight has dementia, so I couldn't get anything from him. Sergeant Cantelli was the police constable on duty at the time of the investigation.'

'He's here now.'

Cantelli was heading down the corridor towards them. 'Hello, Harriet, nice to see you again.'

'And you, Barney.'

'Is this a social call or work?'

'Work, and it's you I need to talk to.'

'Ah, you've caught me, or one of my kids, coming back from Italy with a Da Vinci in our suitcase.'

She smiled. 'Not me. I'm no longer with Europol. I was just telling Inspector Horton that I'm now plain Detective Sergeant Ames of the Hampshire and Isle of Wight Police.'

'Welcome to the club, and there's nothing plain about you. Am I allowed to say that these days?' he tossed at Horton. Then to Harriet, 'We've been having our equality and diversity training, and Bliss says that's an important element of our performance reviews.'

'Instead of catching criminals,' Horton muttered. 'And Bliss doesn't think much of our performance.'

'Not much diversity in the team either,' interjected Cantelli. 'We told her we'd welcome anyone in CID, no matter who and what they are. Our performance would go up too. But all we get is another lecture on budget constraints. What do you wish to discuss? I've got some time. My recent collar, a lorry driver who's astounded that a huge wodge of cash was found stuffed in a container under his wheel arch, is awaiting the pleasure of his lawyer.'

'I'm on the Serious Case Review Team re-examining the Priestley investigation. He went missing twenty-two years ago. My intention was to interview former DCI Knight but sadly he has dementia.'

'So I heard. Good man and detective,' Cantelli said sorrowfully.

'You were first on the scene.'

'As a very young PC, wet behind the ears, on my probation period. Mr Priestley's rotting boat was moored in the Glory Hole, as us locals call it — Eastney Lake,' he explained to her puzzled look. 'Not far from Milton Locks. It was the only one left. All the others — a mixture of houseboats, old railway carriages and whatnot — had been cleared some time ago. They'd been occupied by people who were bombed out during the war, who stayed on after it. I don't know when Mr Priestley took up residence, but the council had been trying to get rid of him and his eyesore for years. The boat was a complete mess inside, but no one knew if it had been deliberately trashed or if he just liked to live like that. Most considered him an eccentric old nuisance.'

'Not so old. Fifty-one.'

'Old to me back then,' Cantelli replied good-humouredly.

Horton didn't know the case. It had been before his time.

'There was no forensic evidence to show that anyone had been inside, although, as I said, it was a tip. It was covered in mud and slime, and it stank. Talking of which, what is that horrible smell?'

'Well, it's not my perfume,' Harriet joked.

Cantelli smiled, then became more serious. 'This must be painful for you, Harriet.' His dark eyes flicked to Horton. In them he read, *a bit insensitive, giving her this case when her father is missing.* Horton silently agreed.

'Get you a tea, Cantelli?' Horton said. 'And you, Harriet?'

'Coffee, white, no sugar.'

'I'll bring them in. Take mine through, Barney, and tell DS Ames what else you can remember about the case — that is, if you can concentrate above that awful smell.'

'What is it?' Cantelli repeated.

'Walters will tell you. It's on my desk.'

Cantelli raised his dark bushy eyebrows and followed Ames into the office.

Horton was glad to have a moment to himself. His mind was racing with what Harriet's transfer meant. Yes, the force was big enough to avoid them being thrown together too often, but she was here now and could be again in the future.

He pressed the buttons, and as the machine gurgled into life, he looked towards the CID office. He had seven hours to think of what to tell her. But then he'd had three months thinking about that, and he still didn't know.

CHAPTER TWO

'You'll need your office fumigated,' Cantelli said, pinching his nose.

'And the CID room,' Walters added, stuffing his mouth with crisps.

So much for the smell putting him off his food. 'Any ideas?' Horton handed them their drinks.

'Long John Silver's treasure chest?' suggested Cantelli.

'Not big enough,' Harriet replied. 'But it does look as though it might contain something valuable. From what I can see of the exterior that isn't covered with slime, I'd say it's possibly nineteenth century. The handcuffs are not so old. Police issue too, although some time back.'

'Doesn't mean they belonged to a copper,' Cantelli said. 'You can buy them online.'

'Now you can,' Harriet answered, 'but not necessarily when the box was discarded. It might have been a long time before the World Wide Web was invented.'

'Ah, those were the days,' Cantelli sighed.

'A strange thing to fasten to it.'

'Especially with nothing, and no one, on the other end,' Cantelli again.

A loud sneeze from the outer office was followed by a thin, stooping man with a large handkerchief to his nose. The phone rang in the outer office. Horton jerked his head at Walters to answer it. He apologized to Phil Taylor about the stench.

'Can't smell a thing with my hay fever,' Taylor grumbled in his usual adenoidal way, putting his case on the floor.

'Phil, you have hay fever even when there is no hay.'

'Lucky, aren't I?'

'Do you mind if I stay?' Harriet asked.

'And me?' Cantelli added.

'Not at all. If you can stomach the pong.'

Taylor, wearing gloves and a mask, began a careful examination. He took scrapings from the outside and the inside of both ends of the handcuffs, around the lock and the two handles on either side, as well as the exterior of the box, and collected some samples of the slime.

Horton recognized Leney's voice greeting Walters before the slender, casually dressed man in his late forties entered. 'See what you can do with this, Paul.'

'Hose it down for a start,' Leney answered. 'But I'll open it instead.'

Taylor stepped back, and Leney extracted a magnifying glass from his case. 'May I?' he enquired of Taylor, who nodded. Leney, also wearing protective gloves, cleared away a little of the green slime and grit just under the side handles, to one of which the handcuffs were attached. A police siren sliced the air as it pulled out of the car park below. Horton moved to his window and closed it.

'As I thought.' Leney straightened up. 'It's a Milner's patent fire-resisting strongbox, probably made around 1836, possibly earlier or later, but not much later.'

Horton studied him amazed. Even Cantelli stopped chewing for a moment. Leney smirked. 'It's my job to know these things. Milner's were the largest safe manufacturers in the world at one time, made some of the best safes in their class. They are now known as Chatwood-Milner, been under the Chubb group brand since 1958. See, it's got the original trademark, "Milner's Liverpool".'

Horton bent down and could see the name.

'This was made as a portable book safe, books being a valuable commodity back then. It was also used for storing important paperwork — deeds, birth certificates, passports, sometimes cash and jewellery.'

'The paper would have rotted by now, I assume.'

'Not if it's still airtight. And it looks to be. These safes were resistant to water and fire, and in its day, they were also thief-resistant.' Leney extracted the tools of his trade from his briefcase. 'Not so now.' He examined the lock. 'It's an easy one. The padlock is embossed "YALE", see?' He cleared away the grit. Horton could just about make it out.

'On this side of the padlock arch, "Yale and Towne Mfg. Co." It was made most likely around late nineteenth century, slightly later than the safe — perhaps the original was lost. As we don't have the key, I'll use one of my own. Do you want the handcuffs removed?'

'No. Leave them there.'

'Right. Have this open in two ticks.' He was true to his word. Almost before he had finished speaking the padlock sprang open. He set it to one side and then lifted the lid.

Horton held his breath. Walters had joined them and froze with a crisp in his hand. Taylor sniffed and narrowed his eyes while Harriet's were fixed on the box and Cantelli was chewing a little faster. Horton knew what was running through all their minds. They'd all witnessed some gruesome contents in similar circumstances in their time.

'There are two pouches,' Leney announced.

'Bet one of them contains an ear.' Walters crunched his crisp. 'Or fingers.' He licked one of his.

'Shall I do the honours?' Leney offered.

Taylor stepped forward. 'No, I'll do that.'

Carefully he lifted them out. Horton could see by the weight there was something inside them. And there was a clinking noise as he laid them on Horton's desk.

'Why, they're beautiful!' Harriet exclaimed.

Indeed they were, thought Horton. He didn't know much about sewing, but he could see that the small pouches had been skilfully made and embroidered, one with colourful exotic birds, the other with bright summer flowers.

'Handmade,' Harriet continued. 'With a blue-ribbon drawstring. You don't see this kind of craftwork these days. They must be very old. And in such pristine condition. You were right, Mr Leney, the safe has certainly done a good job in keeping these preserved. Was it found in water?' she directed at Horton.

Walters answered. 'It was found at Sinah Lake but the area had dried out.'

Horton said, 'Did you go to the actual spot?'

'No. I saw it though. It looked dry to me.'

Then there could have been a small pool of water left, thought Horton.

Harriet voiced what they had all been thinking earlier. 'This is not the sort of thing you'd put human remains in.'

'And human remains don't clink,' said Cantelli.

'Might if it's fingers with rings on,' Walters quipped.

Taylor gently swabbed the pouches and the ribbon, carefully placed the swabs in sterilized packaging and labelled them.

'Open them for us, Phil,' Horton requested.

Taylor tenderly tipped out the contents of each, making sure to keep them separate. 'Sorry to disappoint you, Walters. No body parts.'

'There, didn't I say it was Long John Silver's treasure?' Cantelli declared, staring at the coins that lay on the desk.

'Almost, yes,' Harriet said eagerly. 'Gold and silver. I've seen similar on a rare coin-trafficking case.'

'Who's the geezer on them?' asked Walters, pointing at those from the first pouch.

Horton peered at one of the coins. 'Hand me your magnifying glass, Leney. It looks like "Carolvs II".'

'King Charles the second,' Harriet said excitedly. 'Turn it over.'

Taylor did so.

'What's the date?'

'1668.'

Cantelli whistled. 'That's a long time ago. Must be worth a lot?'

'I would think so,' Harriet said. 'The second pouch contains coins from Queen Victoria's reign.' She leaned closer to inspect them. Horton could smell her perfume even though she probably wasn't wearing any. She looked up at him. His pulse raced and quickly he steeled himself not to respond. 'You need to consult a numismatic — someone who specializes in the study of coins, medals and currency items,' she quickly explained to their blank looks.

Horton should have known she'd be knowledgeable in this area, not just because of her work with Europol but because of her expensive private education. He wondered whether her family had owned rare coins. They had certainly been in possession of some valuable jewellery, an item of which — a blue diamond brooch, surrounded by pink and white diamonds, the Portsmouth Blue — had been given to his mother, Jennifer. He didn't know where that was now and he didn't care. He wanted nothing from the Ames family. But it seemed they wanted something from him, at least the one standing next to him did.

Crisply he said, 'Walters, find a local expert, if there is one.'

'The Royal Numismatic Society will have a website and list of members,' Harriet suggested. 'Or you can try the British Numismatic Trade Association. Whoever dumped these couldn't have known the value of them.'

'What we talking about here?' Walters asked. 'A few hundred quid?'

'More in the few thousand pounds region.'

'Blimey! Who gets to claim it as treasure trove?'

'Not you,' Horton replied. 'You're just the hired transport. I suspect it will be the man who found the box at the angling club. Take photographs of them with your mobile, Walters, both front and back, and carefully — don't put your big fat fingers all over them. And use gloves.' Horton turned to Leney. 'Thanks, Paul. We needn't detain you.' To Harriet he said, 'If the contents are as valuable as you say, then we'd better get this lot over to Joliffe for forensic examination. Taylor, can you see to that? I'll let him know they're coming.' But he wouldn't tell him about the smell. Joliffe could moan for England over any small thing, and this would put him in the world-class division. 'I think the handcuffs also make this suspicious enough to warrant further examination.'

Cantelli quickly caught on. 'You think someone was being arrested for theft and managed to break out of the handcuffs.'

Harriet said, 'If so, why didn't the arresting officer take the box back to the station?'

Horton shrugged. 'No idea.' His phone rang. It was Bliss. 'My office, Inspector. Now.'

With a parting glance at Harriet, Horton made his way out, calling Joliffe as he went. He didn't tell him that he might need to wear a clothes peg on his nose.

He was detained by a uniformed officer on his short distance to Bliss's office over a burglary where the suspect had been caught and remanded in custody. There was some clerical matter to sort out, which he did swiftly before knocking and entering.

She scowled at him over his delay. 'Has that box been opened?' she fired at him almost before he had crossed the threshold.

'Yes, and its contents warrant further examination.' He didn't tell her he'd already called in SOCO.

She raised her finely plucked eyebrows.

'It's a horde of coins, some of which Detective Sergeant Ames says could be—'

'Ames? Do you mean Agent Harriet Ames? What's she doing in CID? Did you say detective sergeant?'

'Yes. She's transferred from Europol and is on the Serious Case Review Team. She—'

'Why wasn't I told?' she bristled.

Horton knew why Bliss was so put out. It wasn't solely because she wanted to know everything and took it as a personal insult if she was excluded, but also because of Harriet's wealthy and well-connected background. Bliss wasn't a social climber, but she was a highly ambitious career one.

'I only discovered it myself when she showed up a short time ago to speak to Sergeant Cantelli about a case she's reviewing, in which he was involved.'

'Is she still here?'

'I don't know.'

'Go and find out and send her in.'

So keen was Bliss for him to pass on her instructions that she asked no more about the coins and what Horton was doing about them, which suited him fine. When he returned to CID, Harriet had left.

'There wasn't anything more I could tell her that wasn't in my original report,' Cantelli said. His phone went. 'My lorry driver's lawyer has arrived.'

Walters said, 'At least the interview room will smell sweeter than in here.'

'Depends who was last in it,' was Cantelli's parting shot.

'DS Ames looked up local coin dealers and found Gareth and Judith Brindley,' Walters said. 'I called and spoke to Mr Brindley, and told him we'd come by some coins that we'd like examined. He said he'd be delighted to help, any time this afternoon would suit him. Do you want me to go?'

'No, I'll go. Give me Brindley's address and send the pictures of the coins to my phone. Print them off too.'

Brindley lived just over Portsdown Hill to the north of the city. Horton called Bliss and said DS Harriet Ames had left. He was told that the next time she came to the station he was to tell her. As he rang off, he had visions of Bliss ringing through to the officer in charge of the Serious Case Review Team and pumping her for information on Harriet. Horton had a disturbing thought that Bliss might do her utmost to try and wrangle it so that Harriet would come to work with them. She would be an asset to any team, but her proximity to him would be awkward. He wasn't sure how their meeting tonight would pan out, and for a moment he hoped he'd be too busy to make it, then scolded himself for even thinking that. He'd never been one to duck out and he wasn't going to start now.

Armed with the pictures, he was glad to escape his smelly office. The heat hit him full force. Even the breeze on his Harley was hot as he made his way north, over the moat and up the hill that bordered Portsmouth.

Soon he was turning left and then right into a residential street, at the end of which was a small parade of shops, most of which had shut down. Only a hairdresser and a pet shop survived. At the end of the road were two Edwardian houses — one had been converted to a dental clinic, the other corresponded with the address he'd been given. There was no name plate but there were CCTV cameras on the door as he pulled into the small forecourt beside two parked cars. No doubt there were cameras at the rear, he thought, alighting and removing his helmet. The coins they traded in were valuable, hence there was no address on their website, and Brindley had called the station to verify Walters was who he claimed to be, so the constable had told him.

Horton wiped a hand across his perspiring brow and removed his leather jacket, wishing that he could be transported back to the days when all you needed to wear when riding a motorcycle was whatever you wished. The roads were far too busy and dangerous for that now. He guessed he didn't look much like the copper they were expecting.

CHAPTER THREE

A woman answered the intercom. Horton introduced himself and held up his ID to the camera. The buzzer sounded and he stepped inside a pristine, cool, tiled hall to be greeted by a small, neatly dressed woman in her early to mid-thirties with chin-length neat dark hair, and heavy make-up covering slightly pitted skin. 'Mrs Judith Brindley,' she said smiling as she stretched out her hand. 'Do come through, Inspector.'

The spacious rear room was simply furnished with two modern desks placed L-shaped to the right of the window, a round conference table in the middle, a couple of cabinets around the walls and welcome air-conditioning. The man who rose from behind one of the desks with an outstretched hand was bulky with large features, straight light-brown thinning hair, and warm chocolate-coloured eyes. Horton put him about early forties. He was dressed casually and haphazardly as though clothes were of no interest to him.

'My wife is a co-director,' he said. 'Do take a seat.' Gareth Brindley gestured to the conference table. 'Would like a coffee or tea?'

'No, thank you.'

'A glass of water then? In this heat I'm sure it would be welcome.'

'I must look hot,' Horton affably replied.

'Don't we all when out in it?' Brindley rejoined in the same manner. 'Put your jacket on the back of your chair or the floor if you prefer. Or we could hang it up for you.'

'It'll be fine on the floor.' He placed his helmet on it as Judith Brindley crossed to a fridge in the corner of the room that was disguised as one of the cabinets. Horton wondered if one of the other cupboards was a safe. He opted for still water and, when they were all settled, drew out the pictures of the coins. Walters had stapled the pages together according to the pouch they had come from and had put the number of the pouch at the top of each page.

Brindley took the two sets of paper and put on his spectacles. His wife sitting beside him studied the pictures. Her eyes widened while Brindley's jaw dropped as he fumbled excitedly through the pages.

'I've got pictures of them on my phone if that helps you identify them,' Horton said, reaching into his trouser pocket, but Brindley waved an arm at him.

'No need.' He blinked and shook his head as though in wonder. He threw his wife a look. She drew in a breath and turned a dazed expression on Horton.

'Where did you get these?' she asked bewildered, rubbing her nose. 'Have they been recovered from a robbery?'

Horton wasn't going to divulge that yet. 'They were enclosed in two hand-embroidered pouches in an old tin box, which had been discarded and reported to the police.'

Her hand played nervously at her chin as she stared at him. 'But that's incredible.'

Brindley removed his spectacles, then almost immediately put them back on. He pointed to one picture. 'This is a Charles II 1661 silver coronation medal by Thomas Simon. It's worth about seven hundred pounds. And this—' he stabbed at another photograph — 'is the official Royal Mint medal issue for the Coronation of Charles II, again struck by Thomas Simon.'

'Slow down, Gareth, Inspector Horton is looking somewhat overwhelmed.' Judith smiled a little nervously.

'And who can blame him?' Brindley took a breath. 'So am I.'

'Mind if I make some notes?'

'Not at all.'

Horton leaned down and took his notebook and pen from his jacket. Judith swallowed some water with a slightly shaky hand and threw Horton a glance. From both their reactions he guessed that the coins were even more valuable than Harriet had suggested.

'I'd obviously need to examine all the items to confirm, but I'll go through them with you,' Brindley began. 'The first list, numbered one, are all Victorian. This is a Victoria gold sovereign, 1863. You can see quite clearly on the front and on the reverse the crowned quartered shield of arms within laurel wreath, die number twenty-four below. This one is an Australian Victoria gold sovereign, struck in 1872 in Melbourne, and this one, a British gold half-sovereign, struck in 1844 in London. And this beauty is a Victoria 1887 gold five-pound coin worth on its own about five thousand pounds. These very high-grade coins are now becoming scarce in the UK marketplace, so it could fetch even more, possibly up to ten thousand pounds. For this list alone you'd be looking at a value of maybe ten thousand to twenty thousand pounds.'

Horton had stopped making notes almost before he'd begun, just jotting down Victorian, gold and the value Brindley suggested.

'Now this second list of coins is the most exciting. They're from Charles I's and Charles II's reign.'

As Harriet had said.

'Aside from the one I mentioned a moment ago, this one is a Charles I 1644 Bristol mint silver half-crown worth about five thousand pounds. And this one—' he gulped, almost rendered speechless — 'if it is what it appears to be, then it's a Charles II 1668 gold five guineas, with elephant below, worth over forty thousand pounds.'

It was Horton's turn to look stunned. He was even more puzzled now about this treasure trove than he'd been before.

God, he hoped Joliffe had kept them safe, he'd need to call him to make sure.

'Can we trace the ownership?' he asked.

Judith answered. 'You have no idea, then, who they belong to? Doesn't where they were found help?'

'No.'

'And the pouches, couldn't they assist?'

'They might, but it's doubtful. We're having them and the box examined.' He didn't see any need to tell them about the handcuffs.

Brindley said, 'If they were sold and bought at auction it might be possible to discover who once owned them. You could put out a circular to the auction houses who handle the sale of rare coins. Or they could have been bought at one of the coin fairs — the World's Fair of Money, for example, which is held every year in the USA. Alternatively, they could have been in a family for a long time and passed down and got lost in a removal. Or perhaps you believe they were stolen?'

Judith studied first her husband and then Horton. 'Surely not? The thief would have sold them. They wouldn't have been thrown away or kept in a box.'

'But there must be something suspicious about them, Judith, aside from their value, for a police officer of inspector rank to be investigating.' He dashed Horton a curious glance.

Horton wondered if this had been a robbery gone wrong. Had a police officer apprehended the criminal and gone bad himself? But, as Judith had said, the coins would have gone. Maybe they were too hot to handle. But the thief, or thieves, could have waited until the heat died down. That didn't answer how they had ended up in Sinah Lake.

'Perhaps you could let us have the details of the auction houses and specialists.'

'Certainly, and we can also give you details of coin collectors, although I don't see how that will help, unless these were in their possession at one time and they sold them on, which is unlikely. If you can't trace the owner, and the Charles II coins are genuine, which on the surface I believe they are, then being over three hundred years old, they qualify as treasure under the Treasure Act. Whoever found them will be in for a nice windfall when they're sold.'

The angling club would be pleased. Horton said, 'Would you be available to come into the station to examine and officially value them, as well as make a detailed list of the coins?'

'I'd be delighted. When? Now?' He looked set to leap up and rush out in his eagerness.

'They're with our forensic expert at the moment, but as soon as he's finished with them, we'll let you know.'

Brindley looked horrified. 'Please tell him not to clean them.'

'I'm sure he won't, but I'll pass that on as soon as I leave here.' Horton rose. 'Obviously we need to keep this confidential for the time being, so I would appreciate it if you could keep this to yourselves.'

'That goes without saying.'

'Thank you.'

Judith sprang up. 'I'll email you a list of our contacts at the main auction houses and collectors' fairs.'

Horton gave her his card. Outside, true to his word, he called Joliffe.

'You might have warned me about the stench,' Joliffe grumbled.

'Have you started work on the box and cuffs?'

'I have. The sooner they're off our premises the better.'

'Don't clean the coins. Handle them as little as possible. They're very valuable. And be very careful with the pouches, they could be very old.'

Joliffe sniffed. 'Do you want me to do a thorough job, Inspector?'

'Of course, just don't put any chemicals on them. When can I expect your results?'

'Tomorrow, if there are no more interruptions.' He rang off.

Horton was used to Joliffe's grumpy ways. He checked his messages — nothing that needed his urgent attention. He donned his jacket and helmet and within three seconds was sweating. Swinging the Harley around he made for the hill that bordered the flat landscape of Portsmouth and the surrounding areas. He didn't expect Joliffe to get anything from the coins or the pouches. He wondered if the latter belonged to the reign of Charles I or II. Tracing possible ownership of the box was a possibility, but even that looked to be a long and thankless task. There might not be any crime attached to them anyway, although the handcuffs suggested it. But then again it could have been a prank that went wrong. It was pointless to waste any more time on it when he had a spate of robberies in Milton, two assaults in Southsea and one at Hilsea, not to mention a robbery at a supermarket in the city three days ago where four men, carrying knives, had robbed a man, and that was just the tip of the iceberg. So what was he doing pulling into a viewing point on Portsdown Hill?

He bought a bacon roll and Coke from the mobile catering van and took them to a patch of shade by a clump of large shrubs. The city shimmered under the afternoon heat. He could barely make out the usual landmarks of the cathedral, the tower at Oyster Quays and the port. Beyond them, the pale-grey sea shimmered in the heat haze. The Isle of Wight, across the Solent, where Harriet's family holiday home was situated, was barely visible. Even if the day had been bright and clear, he still wouldn't have seen the large house in the bay. It was completely secluded, surrounded by trees on its western and eastern sides, with a high wall around it, and it gave onto a private shore and pontoon. It had a sophisticated security system, linked to former DCI Mike Danby's security and close protection company. On that April night when he had been there, the fog would have obliterated any sightings of him and the yacht, *if* the system had been live. Horton was certain that either Richard, or his brother Gordon, would have disabled it.

Horton ate his late lunch. Harriet didn't know that Gordon was alive —and nor did any of the family, save Richard. Richard had only discovered as much shortly before that ill-fated yacht journey. However, Horton believed Richard had suspected it for some time. He'd identified a body in Nhulunbuy in Australia in 1973 as his brother's, the supposed black sheep of the family, and that had suited them both until Gordon had embarked on a course of revenge for the murders of his and Jennifer's friends from the London School of Economics.

Horton looked at the vague outlines of the boats in the Solent. He thought of Richard Ames's deserted yacht. It had taken some time to find it, from April to the end of June. Too long.

Polishing off his roll, he called Leney. 'Can you get any information on that deed box from the manufacturers — for example, who purchased it in 1836? I know it's a long shot, and it probably won't tell us who has owned it since then, but it's worth a try. And I know it could have been bought at a junk shop, but on the other hand it might have stayed in the same family.'

'Chatwood-Milner might have retained records and had them digitized. I'll also see if I can get anything on the padlock.'

There was nothing more he could do. He should shelve the mystery of that box and its contents and get back to his desk and the current serious crimes they were investigating, not to mention the older unsolved ones, and all the paperwork that went with his rank. But as he climbed on his Harley he wondered about the significance of the handcuffs. He thought of Dr Claire Needham, a psychiatrist who had assisted them when Cantelli's nephew had gone missing almost a year ago and who, thankfully, had been found safe and well. He called her. If she was available, then he'd visit her in her elegant Victorian house in Southsea and ask her views. If not, he'd put it aside and get back to his office. She answered promptly and said that she had a gap between clients if he could arrive within the next few minutes.

CHAPTER FOUR

Claire Needham crossed her long, shapely, suntanned legs. Horton resisted looking at them, keeping his eyes on her exquisitely made-up and teasing hazel eyes. She was as immaculately turned out as the last time he had met her, the previous August. Her short, brightly coloured, patterned cotton dress showed her figure off to perfection. The red nail polish on her fingers matched that on her toes. She smiled as if reading his mind. She'd be wrong though. He found her attractive, but he didn't fancy her. Maybe because she reminded him of a slightly older version of Catherine, his ex-wife.

'We've got an unusual occurrence,' he said. 'Not a crime as we know it, and this is obviously confidential.' Swiftly, he told her about the box and the handcuffs attached to it, but didn't say what the box contained, only that the contents could be valuable and that the box had been dumped in water and was very old. 'Does that mean anything to you?'

'Difficult to say without having more information.'

'Would the handcuffs symbolize anything in respect of human behaviour aside from the usual — arrest, or some kind of sadomasochist activity, which in this case I can't see being applicable.'

'The cuffs could have been put on a victim by someone who said the box contained an explosive device.'

Horton's eyes rounded. He certainly hadn't considered that. 'A form of mental torture, a threat?'

'When the handcuffed person revealed what they knew, they were released. They ran off or were killed, and the box, no longer of use, was thrown away.'

But why throw away valuable contents? And if an explosive device had been used as a bluff, surely the person would have worked out that their tormentor would have been blown up too? Unless the tormentor controlled the bomb from afar, and promised to stop it if the victim confessed or revealed where something of much greater value than the coins were kept. It was a theory worth considering.

She continued. 'Alternatively, the contents of the box were so priceless to the owner that they handcuffed the box to themselves so as not to lose it while transporting it to a safe place, or for delivery to someone. Yes, I know that doesn't answer why it was in the water, or why the contents should still be inside, but things do go wrong and people make mistakes. Could this person have fallen into the water and died, and the sea life did what it's good at?'

'There were no bones attached to the handcuffs, but I guess they could have slid out once the flesh had gone.' But he thought that would have been more likely to happen in the sea than in a lake. In the sea the currents and tides could have taken the rotting flesh anywhere, and there were many more predators than in a lake. Why hadn't the body risen to the surface after a while? Perhaps the corpse, if there had been one, had got buried in silt? Wouldn't that have preserved it though? Or perhaps it had become lodged on something, and stayed like that for years, rotting away until this drought had exposed the box, the remains having been wiped out. Surely though, something of a human being would have been left.

'I'm sorry I can't help you further,' she said, looking at her phone.

He took that as the signal their time was up. There was nothing more to be gleaned here anyway. He rose, saying, 'You've given me one new idea, the possible explosive device.' Horton felt sure Joliffe would find traces of that in some form or other in his examination, if it had existed.

He returned to the station, where the smell in CID still lingered, but the air-conditioning was a much-needed relief from the searing heat. Cantelli waltzed in shortly behind Horton with a big grin on his face. 'You got a result with your lorry driver,' Horton said.

'And how. The Big Boys have shown up and taken over.' Cantelli plonked himself down at his desk.

'The National Crime Agency?'

Cantelli nodded. 'It seems chummy is the tip of the iceberg with regards to currency smuggling. He's talking so fast that he's tripping over his words. NCA are cock-a-hoop with glee. They're hoping to get the heads-up on the rest of the gang and the brains behind it.'

'Promotion for you, Sarge,' Walters said.

'Not on your nelly, and I didn't do anything except turn up at the port when summoned. The credit goes to the customs officer and his dog. Anything exciting happen while I've been occupied?'

Horton told them both about the value of the coins, which drew a soft whistle from Cantelli and wide eyes from Walters. He then went on to tell them what Dr Needham had posited about the tin box possibly being used as a threat.

'Nasty,' Cantelli remarked. 'I'm not sure if we'd be able to find out who the threat was aimed at either. The victim would have been disposed of after he'd served his purpose. His body tossed away like that box.'

Which was what Dr Needham had said.

'You mean in that lake?' asked Walters, expressing Horton's earlier thoughts.

'I'm not so sure of that. I think his remains would have been found by now. But we'll keep it in mind.'

'But if that were the case then why ditch the box?' Walters persisted. 'Why not open it and sell the coins?'

Horton had been considering this on his way back to the station. 'They weren't of any significance. The thief got away with a far bigger booty, a bunch of old coins being peanuts compared to what he was after. He might not even have known what was in the box, it was just used as a tool for his threat.'

'You mean like handing over the keys or combination to a safe?' Walters asked.

'It's possible.'

'Must have been when we were in nappies, or not even a blink in our mother's eyes, because I don't recall any big jobs going unsolved. If you ask me, we've got about as much chance finding out what happened as me going on a diet. We've no idea when this might have happened. That box could have lain in the lake for yonks.'

Walters was right.

'And just because the box ended up on Hayling Island doesn't mean the crime, *if* there was one,' Walters stressed, 'was committed in Hampshire. Lots of holidaymakers go to Hayling, and one of them could have dumped it in the lake before the angling club got the lease on it.'

'Which was when?'

'Dunno. Mr Preston, the club secretary, didn't say. Anyone could have chucked it in there.'

'Yes, all right, we get the point. We'll wait until Joliffe is finished with it and decide what to do after Brindley catalogues the contents.'

Horton settled down to his work, shutting out all thoughts of the box and coins, and of his forthcoming interview with Harriet. Two hours later, Walters popped his head around the door to say he was off. 'Got a date with Penny.'

'That still on then?'

'Yep.'

Cantelli was next to leave. Horton stayed on until it was time to make for Old Portsmouth and his rendezvous with Harriet. On his way he tried to formulate what he'd say and how much he'd tell her, but no matter how many times he rehearsed it, it was no use.

As soon as he entered the crowded pub, he knew he'd made a mistake. She was at the bar, with a long drink in front of her and a worried expression. It was heartless of him to ask her to discuss something so sensitive and emotionally draining in this place full of laughing, chattering humanity. Harriet deserved better. It wasn't her fault her father, uncle and grandfather had been liars and accomplices to murder, and one a murderer.

He drew some curious glances, dressed as he was in his motorbike leathers and carrying his crash helmet as he walked towards her. Not because some might have thought him a Hell's Angel come to cause trouble, but because the temperature hadn't cooled very much and most people were wearing as little as possible, including Harriet in the linen trousers and short-sleeved blouse she'd worn that morning. Catching sight of him, she straightened up. Her candid gaze tore at his heart.

'I'm sorry, Harriet. We can't talk here. It's not fair on you. Let's walk.'

They made their way outside, where the cobblestoned harbour side was thronging with people drinking, eating, laughing and chatting. Children ran around squealing, and a handful of yachts and motorboats were making their way into the marinas on both sides of Portsmouth Harbour. The evening was stifling hot. Horton pulled off his jacket. They turned right and headed along the narrow street towards the ancient fortifications of the Hotwalls.

'How did you get on with your investigation today?' he asked, thinking that was a stupid thing to say. They hadn't met to talk about that.

'Dead end it seems, but I'm still reviewing it. And your coins?'

'You were correct, they're genuine and worth a great deal. It'll be interesting to see if Joliffe can find anything on them, or if the box or handcuffs can help to trace the owner.'

They side-stepped a party of four women talking as though they were four feet apart from one another and not rubbing shoulders. Coming out by the Round Tower, Horton said, 'Let's go onto the beach.'

They walked through the hole in the wall onto the small shingle beach, where only a handful of people were strolling and a couple were throwing stones into the water while their dog chased the waves. The tide was going out. The opposite shore of Gosport looked close enough to touch, and a luxury motor cruiser was heading into the harbour. It reminded him of the boat that belonged to Catherine's fiancé, Peter Jarvis, but they were somewhere off the coast of France, according to Emma, who had telephoned to tell him. In two weeks his daughter would come to stay with him on his small, modest yacht. They'd sail across to the Isle of Wight and perhaps along the coast to Chichester or Brighton.

'Why did you leave Europol?' he asked, breaking the silence. 'I thought you enjoyed the work.'

'I never went back. I didn't get on that plane.'

He glanced quickly at her. She was composed. They ambled down to the water's edge, where there was a whisper of a breeze, albeit warm. She continued. 'I'd known for some time that something was troubling my father. His insistence that I go back to the Hague and having me recalled there was his way of getting rid of me, and I don't like being manipulated or told what to do.' She threw him a look. Her voice was taut with controlled emotion. 'After you left me, I decided to follow you over to the Isle of Wight.'

Horton started with shock. No one had told him this. Andrew Ducale must have known.

'I knew you'd return to Portsmouth on your Harley and take the Wightlink ferry to the island, but as I was in Southampton, I took a taxi to the Red Funnel Fast Cat. It was cancelled so I had to wait for the car ferry. That was then delayed because of the fog. By the time I reached our house on the island, my father's yacht had gone. There was no one on the shore and the house was empty. I telephoned my brothers. Neither of them had heard from my father. Nor had my mother. I waited in the house wondering what to do. And I wondered where you were. I thought you might have gone on my father's yacht, but I couldn't see why you should have done. I was about to call you. Then I changed my mind.'

'Why?' He had returned to his own boat, where he had found Andrew Ducale waiting for him. After that he had switched off his mobile and headed out to sea, to where his mother's body had been disposed of. He had stayed away for nineteen days with the story that Ducale had put out to his bosses that he had been assigned to work with the Intelligence Directorate undercover, using his yacht to trail a known criminal in the ports, bays and marinas of Northern France. Horton wasn't sure anyone had believed it. He'd returned and been determined to put the past behind him. With each day passing, and nothing from Harriet, he thought he'd finished with the Ames family for good. Except a little nagging voice in the back of his mind always told him he hadn't, not while there was no news of Richard or Gordon, just as there had been nothing of Jennifer for over thirty years.

'Because I didn't want to know the truth,' she answered, flashing him a look that tugged at his heart. 'I knew it was bad.'

'In what way?'

'You know that he told me you were involved in criminal activity and that you'd never get promotion, let alone be able to stay on the force.'

He nodded. She'd said as much at the airport.

'I wondered what made him so afraid of you that it drove him to spite, and to warn me against you. I didn't believe that you were corrupt, and I still don't. For him to say that you had to have something on him that he didn't want to come out. You told me at the airport that my father and uncle had known your mother, and they knew why she had disappeared. You also said that my father didn't want you to discover the truth. Maybe that's why he took himself off in the yacht, because he was deeply involved in that. I know you won't tell me. But I'll tell you this, Andy: her file is no longer on the missing persons register.'

He stared at her almost open-mouthed. My God, he hadn't even checked that. What the hell had he been thinking? He hadn't expected Ducale to have it marked solved or resolved, because an explanation would have been needed. He'd thought it would simply stay there. Even when Harriet had told him earlier in the day that she'd been assigned to the Serious Case Review Team on a missing person case he hadn't thought of it. The heat must be getting to him. He'd underestimated her and he shouldn't have done. Harriet was an experienced and highly competent police officer.

Ducale had seen to it that Jennifer's file had been removed. And no doubt it would be classed as 'closed', which meant no one would have access to it, not even under the Freedom of Information Act, not for many years, and even then, it could still remain closed. Harriet wouldn't get to the truth that way.

She fixed him with a steady gaze. 'Did my father kill your mother?'

'No.'

'Are you my brother, Andy?'

'No.' Those two questions he could at least answer honestly.

'You believed he was your father though. You thought he'd had an affair with your mother in London. Then he deserted her when she was pregnant with you.'

'At one time I thought that, but it's not true.'

'Then tell me what is,' she demanded.

He left a short pause as his mind raced with what and how much to tell her. Only those things which an intelligent police officer could discover for herself. 'My mother had an affair with your uncle, Gordon Ames.'

'Then we're cousins?'

'No, Gordon is not my father.'

'But you know who is?'

His silence told her he did. He should have just lied, again.

'You're not going to say.'

'It doesn't matter. It's in the past.'

She studied him for a moment, then looked out to sea. 'It took a long time for them to find my father's yacht.'

Horton's earlier thoughts precisely.

'The investigation report says that after my father had fallen overboard, a French fishing vessel found the boat drifting and boarded her. They took it into a secluded bay along the coast and anchored it. When they read about Lord Ames's disappearance from his yacht they got scared, took the yacht out at night and cast it adrift.'

'Fingerprints?'

She looked at him before walking on. He fell into step beside her, heading towards the small fishing pier. 'None. Save those of my father.'

Convenient and strange. 'Where?'

'In the cabin, on the rail and a few sporadically throughout the boat.'

Left strategically, he thought. He knew Harriet was thinking the same. No prints of Gordon then. Had he wiped them clean, leaving just a few of his brother's lying around? Had he then taken the yacht into a secluded bay and instructed some fishermen to take it and cast it adrift in due course, after giving him enough time to get away? Or had Richard executed that plan?

'Why weren't the fishermen's prints on the boat?'

'Good question — and one I asked. Only one man went on board and he wiped off everything he touched, which was essentially the wheel and the anchor release. He didn't want to be caught.'

'But he was?' They climbed the steps onto the lower promenade and walked through another hole in the wall back into the High Street.

'Yes, and questioned. I read his statement.'

'But you don't believe it.'

'It's a logical explanation, and one the police and my family are happy to go with.'

But not her.

'It was presumed my father had gone out sailing before the fog rolled in. He'd become disorientated, slipped and fell overboard. He'd also switched off the automatic location finder. Why? Alastair and Louis, my brothers, say what does that matter? We all sail, and they say many sailors do the same, but I've never known anyone do it in fog. My brothers and the police have an explanation for that too.'

She halted by a parked car.

'They say he intended to be alone for a while, became ill when the fog came in, and before he could go to the helm to switch it back on, fell overboard. A heart attack, aneurism or massive stroke are the options. There was no suicide note and Alastair won't even contemplate the suggestion.' She flicked him a glance. 'But I did wonder, if he had been involved in killing Jennifer, and you had confronted him with it, if that would have made him take his own life.'

'Have you been on board?' he asked, deliberately avoiding her point.

'Yes. Nothing untoward, I could see.'

There wouldn't be. So, the blood from the gunshot wound had also been cleaned up, as well as Gordon's fingerprints. Not by any mythical fisherman but by someone from the intelligence services, who had found the boat, taken it somewhere, done the necessary, and then taken it out again and cast it adrift. Someone who no doubt looked every inch a fisherman even when questioned, but was no more a French fisherman than he was.

'It was what I wasn't seeing that bothered me,' she continued.

Precisely. Though she couldn't know exactly what that was. 'Perhaps there was nothing else to see.'

She cocked a sceptical eye at him.

'Perhaps it's better to leave things as they are, Harriet.'

She held his gaze for some time. 'That's what my family say.' She exhaled. 'Maybe they're right.'

'Harriet, I—' His phone rang. It was Sergeant Stride. 'I've got to take this.' She waited.

'Andy, there's been a car fire on the shore giving onto Forton Lake, Gosport. But that's not all.'

Horton's heart sank. 'There's a fatality?'

'Yes. The remains of a body have been discovered in the vehicle.'

'I'm on my way.' He rang off.

Harriet said, 'I gather you have a suspicious death.'

'Yes.'

'Where?'

He told her.

'I'll meet you there. I know it's not my case and I'm not on duty,' she hastily added. 'But neither, I suspect, are you, and it beats going home to that big empty house on the Isle of the Wight.'

'All right.' What else could he say?

CHAPTER FIVE

The burnt-out vehicle was stuck in the mud of the shore some twenty yards from the outgoing tide, facing seaward. The intense heat radiated from it along with the nauseating smell of rubber and the pork-like stench of roasted flesh. The fire had been so severe that it was impossible for him to tell what make of car it had been. All that was left was a heap of blackened twisted metal and inside it, at the rear, the chalk-white bones of what had once been a living, breathing human being.

He turned away, made to draw a deep breath, then changed his mind; the smell would only invade his senses more deeply. Harriet was yet to arrive. He gazed around, taking in the location. It was secluded. There was no public footpath along the shore, no road either, which made this a strange place to drive a vehicle. There was only an empty industrial unit with a 'To Let' board behind him in a short cul-de-sac, which culminated in a wire fence and some dense scrubland to the west, where the creek fed up before petering out. To his right, Forton Lake fed into Portsmouth Harbour. The Millennium Footbridge spanned it, joining two areas of Gosport. Across the creek from him, opposite, was more scrubland and trees, and to the right of them, closer to the bridge, were a row of houses and flats facing in the direction of the harbour. This, it seemed, was a good place for murder.

Harriet was heading towards him. He'd already called SOCO and instructed the two police officers who had first arrived on the scene to cordon off the short road. The fire-fighters were making up. He wondered how he was to explain Harriet's presence to Superintendent Uckfield, as this would be his investigation as head of the Major Crime Team. He could hardly say they were having a drink when the call came through because Uckfield would put two and two together and come up with a romantic entanglement. It was the way his mind worked and, on this occasion, Horton thought it perfectly feasible he should think that. He could say they had been discussing a case, only he hadn't been on the force when Priestley went missing.

He watched her as she viewed what was left of the body, silently and solemnly. Then she shook her head, sorrowfully. He knew she was wondering how someone could do such a terrible thing.

'I can't see any other tyre tracks,' she said, joining him, her skin a little paler as she stared about her.

Nor could Horton.

'Or tracks of any kind,' she added, scouring the ground. 'But any left by the killer will have been obscured by the firefighters.'

'I need to call Uckfield.'

'I'll see if the watch manager has anything further to add.'

The phone rang for some time and Horton was wondering if he'd need to leave a message or call DI Dennings, Uckfield's second-in-charge, when it was answered not by Uckfield but by a woman. Horton didn't recognize the voice as Uckfield's wife, Alison.

'Is Steve there?'

'He's in the shower.'

'Tell him it's Andy Horton.'

He heard voices in the background, the woman's and then Uckfield's sharp words. 'I'm on holiday!' he bellowed down the line at Horton.

'OK, sir. I'll call DI Dennings. Sorry to have disturbed you.'

'What have you got?' Uckfield snapped, before Horton could ring off.

Swiftly Horton relayed what had occurred and what he'd done so far, making no mention that Harriet was with him.

'I'll be there in twenty minutes.'

It didn't take three guesses as to what Uckfield had been doing. Horton knew the Super's history of philandering all too well and didn't approve of it. But that was Uckfield's business not his. He felt sorry for his wife. Occasionally he wondered if Alison knew of her husband's extramarital affairs. If she did, she'd never mentioned them to Catherine. They were good friends, but then Catherine might know and had never told him. Rumours sometimes abounded at the station, but nothing was openly expressed.

He walked up to the industrial unit, where the SOCO van was parked beside his Harley and Harriet's Volkswagen. Behind that the lanky photographer, Jim Clarke, was climbing out of his Ford. A police car straddled the entrance of the short road. There were no spectators or reporters. Everyone, it seemed, was down on the nearby quayside in the shops, restaurants and cafés at the Royal Clarence Waterside and Marina.

As Taylor, Tremaine and Clarke donned their scene suits, Harriet broke off talking to the watch manager, who climbed into the fire engine. As it pulled away, she returned to Horton.

'He says no one was here when they arrived. They had only the rough location given to them, the shore behind the industrial units in Dunlin Street. They knew there were no houses along this stretch, and as they approached they could see by the black smoke that it wasn't a business unit on fire, or a grass fire, so they quickly surmised it must be a car. It was well ablaze when they arrived at 7.20 p.m. They received the shout at 7.13 p.m.'

'Any idea who called it in?'

'No. I'll contact the control room and ask.'

Horton crossed to Clarke. Not that he needed to give him or SOCO instructions, they knew what to do, but he wanted Clarke to take pictures of the wider area, including the front and sides of the industrial unit, the creek, the opposite shore, the footbridge, the vehicle, and the shrubland to the west. Maitland, the fire investigation officer, would also need to be summoned, but that would be down to Uckfield.

'The caller was a Mr Jason Downs,' Harriet said returning. 'He gave his mobile number. Do you want me to phone him?'

'No. Leave that to Uckfield. There's nothing more you can do here, Harriet.' He wanted her to leave before Uckfield arrived.

She seemed to read his thoughts. 'Yes, it would be awkward to explain my presence.'

He watched her go with a troubled mind, then quickly returned to the burnt-out car, which Taylor and Beth were circling.

'It's far too hot to examine,' Taylor said. 'We'll have to do that when it's in the compound. All we can do here is scour the area around it and pick up what we can, but it won't be much, and what we do get might not be any use, because the firefighters have trampled all over the place and flooded it.'

Taylor's response wasn't unexpected.

'The vehicle is too charred to give us a registration number,' Taylor added. 'Maitland might get the vehicle identification number from the chassis later, but by the state of it, I'd say that's touch and go.'

'Do what you can, Phil.'

Horton walked down the beach, looking at the ground, until his shoes sank into the mud of the low tide. There was nothing to tell him that anyone, or anything, had been down this route. He turned and looked back towards the vehicle and the industrial unit. As Harriet had said, it was strange for a car to be on the shore. A fisherman, or anyone else wishing to access the sea, would naturally have left the vehicle in the vacant unit's car park and walked here. If it had been a lovers' meeting place, they would have been quite safe from prying eyes in the car park. He had noted that there were no CCTV cameras and nothing overlooked it. The only reason anyone would drive onto the shore was for the purpose of setting light to the car.

Uckfield, trying to zip up his scene suit over a brightly patterned summer shirt, was plodding towards the charred vehicle. He nodded a greeting to Taylor and Tremaine and viewed the remains.

'Who is it?' he tossed at Horton, stepping away from the gruesome scene.

'No idea. Too badly burnt to get anything, including gender. And the vehicle, as you can see, is a complete wreck. I haven't called Maitland.' He gave Uckfield the information Harriet had obtained about the emergency call without mentioning she had got it and, as he finished, he caught the sound of another vehicle pulling up.

'Any theories?' asked Uckfield.

'No, just questions.' Such as, who had Uckfield been with when he'd called him? But he didn't say as much. 'Sorry to interrupt your holiday.'

'I'm back at work tomorrow anyway. Been to the Isle of Wight on the boat for a long weekend, got back just after lunch.'

'With Alison and the girls?' Horton asked before he could stop himself.

'Yes,' Uckfield said firmly, glaring at him.

Uckfield hadn't wasted much time getting rid of his wife and daughters and installing someone else on his boat. Horton wondered if the woman was from the marina, or perhaps they had arranged to meet that evening on board and Uckfield had told his wife that he was staying on the boat again as he had some things to do. Things that certainly weren't connected to nautical matters.

The muscular, sixteen-stone DI Dennings was heading towards them along with the newest member of the Major Crime Team, DC Seaton, who had recently transferred from uniform and was very keen. Seaton had replaced Jake Marsden, who was now promoted and working with another unit. With them was a slender, dark-haired, dusky-skinned woman whom Horton hadn't met before.

Seeing his enquiring glance, Uckfield said, 'DS Chawla. She's a direct-entrant inspector on her sergeant's training module. Take a look.'

Horton wondered if Chawla had much experience of this. Seaton had, having been in uniform on the streets of Portsmouth for some time. Horton recalled that Seaton had been first on the scene when they'd had a badly charred victim on a boat in Horsea Marina, and he'd also been at the Hilsea Lines when a burnt body had been found in one of the tunnels. Dennings, too, had experience of this kind of grisly scene but he wasn't a very imaginative copper, which could sometimes be a blessing. As for himself, Horton often thought he had too much. Putting himself in the victim's shoes was emotionally disturbing but it could also be enlightening, allowing him to make that extra flight of fancy that helped to solve an investigation. But from what he knew of Dennings, having worked with him closely for years, nothing ever disturbed him deeply. Dennings was good at the tough stuff and the routine. He'd also kept his nose clean, unlike Horton, who'd had false rape charges heaped on him when they had worked on a surveillance operation thirty-two months ago. The episode had cost Horton his marriage and stalled his career.

It was getting dark. Uckfield would either need to get SOCO to erect the arc lights or get the car and body moved.

Dennings spoke first. 'It could be a stolen car, taken by yobs high on drugs and drink, with the owner inside. Perhaps they pushed him around, saw they'd killed him, stuffed him in the back of the car and then drove it down here and set light to it.'

And there was Horton accusing Dennings of having no imagination.

'Chawla?' asked Uckfield.

'Could have been a falling-out among drug dealers. They agreed to meet here but the victim wanted out. Or perhaps it was a love affair that went wrong, a jealous partner who came to settle a score, or someone who had been rejected and wanted revenge.'

'We'll keep that in mind. Seaton, call the undertakers and explain what we've got. Dennings, contact Maitland, ask if he wants to come over and look at it in situ — only, he'd better get a move on if he does, it'll be dark soon. Chawla, call the mechanics and arrange for what's left of the car to be taken to the secure compound.'

Horton noted Uckfield didn't ask Seaton's views. Perhaps he considered him too junior. Seaton didn't look hurt and maybe he wasn't. 'I'll leave you to it.' He'd reached his Harley before Uckfield hailed him.

'About that call earlier,' he said quietly. 'I had something to discuss with someone from the marina office.'

While in the shower?

'It isn't what you're thinking.'

'I'm not thinking anything, Steve,' Horton said flatly.

'Good, then see that you don't.'

As Horton headed back towards Portsmouth he turned his thoughts to the victim. Was he or she married, or in a relationship? Were there children? A father or mother to mourn the loss of a son or daughter? Unless someone reported the victim missing it was going to be difficult to make an identification, and no one could make a physical one from those grisly remains. Maybe Gaye would be able to get DNA, if she was to conduct the forensic autopsy. She'd been in London for a long weekend and at a summer ball last night. As far as he knew she was due back tomorrow. He sincerely hoped Uckfield would get a positive ID, not only to help with the investigation but for the family's sake. It would be a terrible shock and a harrowing ordeal for them. What had the victim done to warrant such a terrible end? Whatever it was, if they had indeed done anything, no one deserved such an awful fate. Had they just been in the wrong place at the wrong time, as Dennings suggested?

The fact it was arson reminded Horton of the Tipner Sailing Club fire last April, which was still unsolved. Thankfully they'd had no more of those since. Perhaps it had been a one-off, targeted at the club or a member, and although they'd made exhaustive enquiries, they had revealed no seething vendettas. But this couldn't be the same arsonist. It was a different MO.

On board his yacht he made a sandwich and coffee and took both on deck, where the night air was cooling. He thought of Harriet in that large house on the Isle of Wight. Was she, like him, looking out to sea, perhaps from a bedroom window, or perhaps standing on that private pontoon where her father and his brother had been a few months ago? He knew that he and Harriet hadn't finished their conversation. One day he would have to tell her, and that sent a chill through him.

That night, his dreams were of her. When she turned into a shrivelled, burnt corpse he was jolted awake. No point in trying to sleep again. Besides, the sun was up and so was he. He went for a long run along the promenade in the quiet and comparative coolness of the early morning. There was hardly a soul about. Returning, he cooked himself a breakfast of bacon, sausages, egg and toast, shaved and showered, then headed for work, keen to find out what, if anything, Uckfield and his team had got on the car fire victim.

CHAPTER SIX

Wednesday

'Nothing' seemed to be the answer, judging by the scarcity of information on the crime board and of personnel in the major incident suite. There was only Sergeant Trueman, who looked as though he'd been there all night save that his usual five o'clock shadow hadn't yet sprouted, which meant he must have gone home at some stage to shave.

'Where is everyone?' Horton asked. 'Having a lie-in?'

'What's that?'

'Not sure myself.' Horton crossed to the crime board. 'Not much to show for last night's work.'

'Don't you start. The Super was like a hippo who'd had the plug pulled out of his watering hole. I only hope he'll be in a better mood this morning.'

Horton looked doubtful. 'Agni?' He pointed to the name in the circle.

'Chawla christened him. Agni is the Hindu god of fire.'

'Very apt. We don't have an ID then?'

Trueman shook his head. 'Nope. No one's come forward to say a loved one, friend, relative or neighbour is missing, but it might be usual for the victim to stay out all night or be away from home. And it is still early. Until we can get the vehicle identification number, we can't establish who the car is registered to, and even then, as DI Dennings pointed out, they may not be the victim. Dennings thinks it could have been stolen.'

'So he said last night. A joyride gone wrong. I can see, though, you think it might have been an Audi.' That was also written on the board alongside pictures of the wreck with a big question mark beside it.

'I don't think anything. It could have been a Bentley for all that's left of it. Taylor suggested an Audi, but he won't swear to it. He and Tremaine got precious little from the site, but what they did get has been sent over to the lab. The vehicle's in the secure compound. Maitland, Taylor and Joliffe are going over it today.'

'Is Dr Clayton doing the autopsy?'

'The Super left a message for her. Don't know if she's got back to him yet. Judging by those pictures I don't think there'll be anything left to help identify the victim.'

They were certainly hideous. 'Unless she can get DNA.'

'Yeah, and then we'd need to find a match — not everyone is on the database, more's the pity.'

'It's not like you to be so grouchy, Dave.'

'Put it down to lack of sleep in this wretched heat.'

'Just think yourself lucky to have air-conditioning here.'

Trueman grunted before continuing. 'I've set up a mobile incident unit in the Royal Clarence Marina car park, and the erection of signs in the area for any sighting of a car heading in that direction, the victim's or another vehicle, between six p.m. and seven-thirty p.m.'

'I've been thinking about that. Has anyone suggested the killer could have arrived and left by boat? High water was at 5.13 p.m. and the fire call was made at 7.13 p.m., so there would have been time for someone to get to the shore on the high tide, set the fire and leave.'

'No one's mentioned that.'

'So, no one's spoken to Elkins?'

'I haven't. DI Dennings might have done.' Trueman said it in such a way that he knew Dennings wouldn't even think of contacting the marine unit. Horton thought he was probably right.

'I'll do it. They might pick up some information from boat owners and the marina staff.' As he made for CID he wondered about Jason Downs, the man who had reported the car fire. His name had been on the crime board. Who was checking him out today? Not him. He wasn't on the investigation.

He found Cantelli already at his desk. 'Can't sleep in this heat,' the sergeant said.

'Join the club.' Horton told him about the body in the car. He'd just finished when Walters slouched in. 'Don't tell me you can't sleep either,' Horton said.

'Can anyone in this blasted heat? We're not made for it.' Walters flung his jacket on the back of his chair and flopped into it. 'If I have to go anywhere today, I'll collapse.' He retrieved a handkerchief from his trouser pocket and mopped his forehead.

Horton's phone rang. It was Gaye. He made his way to his office, and before answering the call, glanced over his shoulder. 'Cantelli, update Walters about the fire last night.'

He pushed his door to. The smell from that box still lingered.

'I hear you have a burnt body,' Gaye said. 'Uckfield's asked for a forensic autopsy.'

'Are you able to do it?'

'Yes. I've booked it for tomorrow. From what I can gather from Uckfield, and the pictures he emailed over last night, it's going to be a difficult cadaver to examine.'

'Yes, there wasn't much left of it.'

'You were there?'

'First on the scene. We've got no ID on the body yet.'

'So Uckfield said. You're not on this investigation?'

'No, it's Dennings's baby.'

'Then I'll make sure to spell things out in a nice simple language.'

Gaye's private nickname for Dennings was Neanderthal Man. 'Did you have a good time last night?' Horton asked.

'Too good. Which is why the post-mortem is tomorrow. I'm not travelling back until later today anyway.'

He was glad she'd enjoyed herself with her fellow pathologists, although his mind boggled at the thought of their dinner conversation. Horton next called Elkins and told him about the car fire and his idea that the killer could have used a boat.

'I'll ask all the marina managers and club secretaries to circulate a request for anyone who saw a small boat in that area, or anything suspicious between six p.m. and eight p.m., to come forward. But it's a very long shot, Andy, at this time of year with so much activity in the harbour.'

Horton knew that. He checked his messages to see if anything urgent had happened overnight — thankfully it hadn't, and there weren't any leads on their outstanding cases. Harriet hadn't messaged or emailed him either, asking for an update on the car fire victim.

He thought of the car fire's unusual location. There were many private areas around the county for a meeting place — dense woods, deserted bays and other coastal areas — where a car could have been ignited without it being discovered for some time. So why there when, as Elkins said, there was a great deal of activity in the harbour and around the marinas? Just how busy would that creek have been at the time of the fire? He knew it wasn't his investigation, but he'd like to check out the boat idea. Chawla's theory about drug dealers could also fit with a boat being used.

He crossed to Cantelli. 'Have you got much on this morning? Yes, I know it's a daft question,' he quickly added. 'I mean in the way of meetings.'

'No.'

'Good. I'd like to take a look at last night's scene of crime. Walters, hold the fort.'

'Be nice if you could send some cavalry to help me.'

'They're all out on manoeuvres.'

47

Horton instructed Cantelli to make for Gosport. As he pulled out of the car park, Bliss drew in. Horton caught her quick, curious glance. He expected his phone to go on the way to Gosport.

'Bit of a turn-up for the books, Harriet ending up working for Hampshire?' Cantelli said, pulling into the heavy morning traffic out of the city. His tone was light, but Horton knew he was trying to gauge his reaction. 'I feel sorry for her.'

'Why, because she might have to work with us?' Horton joked.

'There is that.' Cantelli grinned before adding more soberly, 'But with her father missing . . . it can't be easy for her working on a similar case. I guess she had no choice and she needed a fresh start. Not sure she'll get it in the police though. I'd have thought Europe and maybe another career might have helped.'

'She doesn't want another career.'

Cantelli looked at him sharply before putting his eyes back on the motorway. 'You've spoken to her?'

'Yes, last night.'

Cantelli nodded thoughtfully and concentrated on changing lanes.

Horton wondered how much to tell him. He decided on half the truth, that she wished to discuss how her father's yacht had been found, and that she had accompanied him to the car fire.

'But you haven't told the Super that,' Cantelli said.

'I didn't want to explain our meeting. Uckfield would only get the wrong idea.'

'Fair enough.'

Horton knew he could confide in Cantelli with confidence, but he didn't think it right to burden him with the extent of his involvement with the Ames family and the truth about Jennifer. He also didn't think he had the right to share it. The intelligence services wouldn't like it and it would also hurt Harriet. Was that better, though, than allowing her to

48

torture herself without the full knowledge of what had happened, just as he had done for years?

'Can't you put the air-conditioning on?'

'Doesn't work. Open the window.'

'And get choked to death by petrol and diesel fumes.'

'Either that or fry.'

Horton let down the window and let in the noise and smell. He rang Walters and told him that if Bliss came nosing around, to tell her that he and Cantelli were on their way to Gosport. 'Tell her about the car fire and say that I'm visiting the location to see if it's possible the killer could have come by boat. Oh, and tell her to mention that to the Super, because I haven't told him, although I did suggest it to Trueman.' That would scupper her hopes of claiming it as her idea. She'd be at Uckfield like a shot if she thought she could get involved. But then he was a fine one to talk, trespassing on Uckfield's case.

As they turned down onto Gosport some fifteen minutes later, Horton's phone rang. It was Walters. He put it on loudspeaker.

'I've had Robin Preston on about that tin box. He wants to know if anything was in it. He got a bit tetchy when I said we were still investigating it and would be in touch.'

'Why?'

'Why what, guv?'

'Why so tetchy? Makes me wonder if he knows something valuable was inside.'

'Nah, he just doesn't trust us to tell him if there was. I told Mr Preston that the investigating officer was out, but would contact him as soon as possible. He grouched and grumbled, asked when. Next week, next year, next century? He demanded to know your name, which I gave him, and he said he expected a more rapid response from the police and to be kept fully informed. I, of course, didn't tell him he was lucky to get anyone looking at that smelly old box when we've got fires blazing and bodies all over the place.'

'Not quite.'

'I said, "Yes, sir" and repeated, "as soon as possible, sir". Bliss also wasn't very happy about not being kept fully informed. She tossed her ponytail at me and said something about dealing with you later.'

'I'll look forward to that.' Horton rang off.

'Sounds like Mr Preston isn't the only one who's grouchy,' Cantelli said. 'Where exactly do I turn off?'

'Here.'

Cantelli negotiated the streets of modern houses and apartments and followed the signs for the Royal Clarence Marina.

'Any joy with the house or flat hunting?' he asked, as they passed several properties displaying 'For Sale' and 'To Let' boards.

Moving from his boat into bricks and mortar was a condition Catherine had requested before she'd give him regular access to his daughter. She argued that a boat would be too cold for a young girl to stay on at most times of the year. Not if it was Jarvis's superyacht though. 'No. Everything I've seen is too miserable, too small or too big.'

'Have you thought of living round here? You could have a nice view of the harbour and move your boat to the marina.'

'No, I hadn't.' It would mean a longer journey to work as the ferry across the harbour from Gosport to Portsmouth only took foot passengers, but it wasn't as long a commute as Harriet had. And Cantelli was right. It was worth thinking about.

'Might be cheaper than Portsmouth too.'

Horton said he'd do an internet property search later.

The signs asking for sightings of any vehicles in the vicinity at the time of the crime hadn't been erected yet, but the mobile incident unit was being trailered into the car park as they drove past. Cantelli pulled up in front of the empty industrial unit. The remains of the police tape hung loose on the road. Uckfield had got all he needed from the scene. There were no sightseers or dog walkers. The ground around the back of the unit, and down to the shore, was well trodden, but that would have been the firefighters, him, Harriet,

Uckfield, his team and SOCO. Above the tide line, in the shingle and mud, Horton could see the indentations and scorching where the vehicle had been. Beyond it, closer to the unit, were the solid, bigger tyre tracks of the breakdown truck. The seagulls soared and called above the water. It was an hour to low tide. Horton gazed around.

'Last night's high tide was at 5.13 p.m. Two hours before the fire call. How long had the car been burning to get into the state it was? Twenty minutes? Half an hour? Which means it was set alight at approximately 6.45 p.m. By then the tide was a fair way out, but this shore would have been accessible by boat from the harbour side and possibly from further up the creek at that time or before it. I'm not sure, though, how far up a boat would have got if it had returned that way. Last night I walked down the beach as far as I could. I didn't notice any footprints or drag marks from a boat. But I only walked in a straight line from the vehicle. And there's no point in examining the shore now as this morning's high tide will have covered any tracks. Let's go for a walk.'

'In the mud and water?' Cantelli's brows shot up.

'No, we'll take the bridge.'

'And leave my car here? Might get nicked.'

'Then you can call the police. I've heard they're very efficient, despite what Mr Preston thinks. I'm sure they'll find it for you.'

'Yeah, but will it be in one piece?'

'Barney, it's not in one piece now, you'd hardly spot the difference.'

'Be careful or you'll be walking back to Portsmouth.'

They turned out of the cul-de-sac and headed along the road eastwards. On their right, giant billboards proclaimed the next phase of the development of the area that had once been the home of the Royal Navy victualling depot. To the left were some houses, and beyond them through the gaps Horton could see dense bushes, shrubs and trees, which eventually gave on to the shore.

'Why are we heading this way?' Cantelli asked.

'Maybe I just want confirmation that one small boat branching off into the mouth of Forton Lake and returning into the harbour before black smoke bellowed in the air wouldn't have been noticed. And I have it.' Horton paused as they came to the Millennium Bridge. 'Just look at the number of them in the harbour, and on the pontoons, not to mention how many might have been on the water at 7.13 p.m. when the fire call was made. And even if someone saw the boat turning under this bridge into the creek, they wouldn't have thought anything of it.'

'Not even when they saw the smoke?'

'They probably put it down to a grass fire, not knowing the different colours of smoke a fire creates depending on what's burning. And even if they did suspect a car fire or burning building, by the time the smoke was thick enough to be noticeable our killer had slipped away. He could have vanished anywhere along here, but did he also come from here? Did he meet Agni in the industrial unit's car park—?'

'Who?'

'Chawla named last night's car fire victim after the Hindu god of fire.'

'Oh. And who is Chawla?'

Horton told him. 'The killer could have brought a boat into the creek and walked up to the industrial unit, where he met Agni, killed him or knocked him out, and then drove the car down on to the shore, set it alight before jumping back in his boat and toddling off.'

They walked on in silence. The Condor ferry was heading out of the port on its way to the Channel Islands and France. Leisure craft were also making their way down from both Fareham Quay and Horsea Marina into the Solent, taking advantage of the scorching hot, calm day. There was no relief from the heat. Cantelli had his suit jacket slung over his shoulder and his tie askew. Horton didn't wear either unless he really had to, but he was still hot in his short-sleeved open-necked cotton shirt.

He halted on the bridge and looked to his left. 'This is what I wanted to verify. It's as I suspected. You can't see the car from here, it's tucked around that projection, to the west of those houses, the ones we just walked past. Nor can you see the industrial unit. It's hidden by that clump of trees. A boat heading under this bridge in either direction might have been noticed by strollers, but even if it was, I doubt anyone will be able to give a description of it, let alone the person piloting it or the name of the boat. Where could he have come from?'

'Anywhere, if you ask me.'

Cantelli was right, there were so many pontoons and harbour moorings, not to mention the marina behind them. They continued along the waterside walk heading north, with houses, flats and a pub on their left and the shimmering harbour on their right. It would have been pleasant but for the sun beating down. Horton thought this was a waste of time. He was about to suggest heading back when Cantelli said, 'He could have come from there.'

Horton looked across an area of grass peppered with wooden benches and people, to a small car park where a row of tenders were lined up. It was also a public slipway. Beyond it was a brick wall, above which he could see the masts of dinghies. The sign told them it was the Hardway Sailing Club. It was just one of many such clubs in the area. Elkins was detailed to ask around them, best to leave it to him. He said as much but added, 'Ask Gosport police to make enquiries with the occupants of those houses for anyone launching a boat at the critical time and see if the council have any CCTV footage in this area. I can't see any cameras over the car park.'

They began walking back. 'Of course, even if someone does show up on the cameras, or was seen launching a boat, or returning at the critical time, it doesn't mean to say it's our man.'

On the other side of the bridge there was the Gosport Sailing Club. Beyond it was the marina and further on from that yet another long pontoon stretching out into the harbour, at the end of which was a dredger. Elizabeth Quay was being developed as a marina to take large superyachts like Jarvis's. Horton wondered whether he could buy a bigger yacht to live on instead of a flat or house to rent. Would Catherine allow Emma to stay with him if he had a more comfortable, larger boat? Somehow, he doubted it, not unless it was the size of a small cruise ship like Jarvis's, and that would never be within his range. And even if he won the lottery or the football pools — if he decided to do one or both — he wouldn't have wanted a boat like Jarvis's.

'Let's grab a coffee, although in this heat an ice-cold drink might be more appropriate.'

'And a sausage sandwich.'

'I don't know where you put it.' Horton eyed Cantelli's lithe figure.

'My nervous energy burns it off.'

'Barney, it would take a thunderbolt to get you to generate nervous energy.'

'Oh, I don't know, you should see me on the sideline when Joe plays football.'

Horton laughed. They made their way to one of the cafés. Joe was Cantelli's youngest and the only son of five children, twin to Molly.

With coffee and a bacon roll for Horton, tea and a sausage sandwich for Cantelli, they made their way back to the car via the car park, where the mobile incident unit had been set up but wasn't yet manned. Horton had just finished his roll when Joliffe rang.

'I've got a lot of work on, Inspector, including the burnt ruins of a vehicle to examine, so I want to pass your tin box and handcuffs over to Dr Pooley. He's newly attached to the fingerprint department working as a consultant out of the university. He has all the latest equipment to test for fingerprints in this type of situation. I've already spoken to him on the phone and he's looking forward to examining them. You will have my report in due course, but to speed things up my end, I can tell you what I've got if you can come over, and you can collect those coins you're so anxious about at the same time.'

'We'll be there in half an hour.'

CHAPTER SEVEN

Joliffe greeted them with his usual dourness when they arrived in his new air-conditioned laboratory on the northern outskirts of the city. On the bench beside the deed box and handcuffs, in a plastic evidence bag, were some very small fragments of what looked like carpet and some metal. Seeing his glance, Joliffe said, 'Taylor couldn't get much from the scene of the car fire last night, and I haven't had the chance to examine them. We hope to get more from the vehicle with Maitland in twenty minutes.'

'Then we won't keep you long. What did you get from the box and handcuffs?'

'More than I expected.'

Cantelli, pencil poised, resumed chewing his gum.

'First, I made a visual examination for tissue on the handcuffs using a CrimeScope to see if any materials were present, then a presumptive test for blood, the latter of which I did not find. But I did find fatty deposits in the inner rim of one of the handcuffs, the one that wasn't attached to the box, and I was able to extract DNA from it.'

Horton exchanged a quick look with Cantelli. 'Someone *was* locked in them then.'

'It appears so.'

And was that body decomposing in the lake?

'I opened and dismantled the cuffs to expose the inner mechanism. I also swabbed the whole of the cuffs and found more DNA. As the cuffs are police issue and are most likely to have been on numerous people, I would expect to find a mixture of DNA from several people. But all is not lost, because the last person to have worn the cuffs would have deposited the most recent and therefore freshest DNA on them. It's only partial, but it's there nonetheless and something for you to work on.'

If that person was on the DNA database, Horton silently echoed Trueman's earlier comment.

'Now to the box and its contents . . .' Joliffe paused to consult his vibrating phone. 'It's your counterpart in the Major Crime Team. I'll deal with one thing at a time.' He put his phone back in his pocket. 'I didn't find any fatty deposits secreted under the handles, although there was a faint trace on the padlock. Not enough to give you a DNA match. There was nothing inside the box, but Dr Pooley might be able to get some prints or partials. As to its interior, there was dust. It doesn't look much, but looks can be deceptive. You'll need a forensic dust expert to analyse it — for example, to see if it's made up of human skin cells, human or animal hair, synthetic fibres, mineral and glass fibres, paint chips, glass, food stuffs, plant hairs, pollens, et cetera.'

'And that probably won't get us anywhere,' Horton said, although he did wonder whether there were human cells — from an ear or finger perhaps that had at one time been inside the box, as Walter had suggested. 'Are there any traces of oil or metal?'

'None.'

Then it was unlikely an explosive device had been inside, but then he'd never really considered that feasible. And if Dr Needham's idea had been correct, the explosive device would have been phoney anyway.

'I examined the pouches and ribbon. There's no blood or tissue on them, but I haven't conducted an in-depth test of the fabric, as I didn't think you wanted the material cut or damaged in any way.

'Correct.'

'The pouches are comprised of a cotton fabric with a blue silk lining and matching silk ribbon drawstring. As to its age, I can't tell you anything, people have been weaving silk into fabric for at least five thousand years — no, I don't think your fabric is that old,' he said when Cantelli almost swallowed his chewing gum.

'Could it be from Charles I's reign, like those coins?' he asked, recovering.

'The Carolean Age?' Joliffe shrugged. 'No idea. A new method for dating silk, based on its chemical composition, has recently been developed in America. But it would be expensive to carry out and would only give you a fifty to one-hundred-year window of when the silk was spun, which probably wouldn't help you find the owner of the coins. I suggest you leave that to the museum, if one purchases the coins, or to whomever finally owns them.'

Horton couldn't see their budgets stretching to that.

Joliffe added, 'The embroidery might be a better test as to the timing of the construction of the pouches. They are in remarkably good condition, no water marks, mould or insect damage. The safe did its job. You might wish to consult a textile expert, who could tell you more.'

Into Horton's mind came one they had consulted on the Chale Bay murder case, when the victim had been wearing an old-fashioned dress. Dr Louise Adams was a fashion expert at the university.

'I carefully swabbed the coins for DNA.'

Horton hoped Brindley wouldn't discover this, as he'd have a fit.

'Nothing. That's all I can tell you. I'll see that the box and handcuffs are delivered to Dr Pooley right away. Do you wish to take the coins and pouches with you or for me to engage experts?'

'We'll take them off your hands, Joliffe.'

Cantelli picked them up.

Horton said he hoped Joliffe would get some forensic information on the car fire. Outside, Horton said, 'I'll call Dr Adams, she might be able to tell us more about the pouches.'

'Is it worth it?'

'Probably not but those handcuffs bug me, and the fact that someone was in them. Can you call Mr Brindley and ask him if he's available to come and value the coins this afternoon?'

In a patch of shade outside they made their phone calls. Horton left a message on Dr Adams's voicemail asking her to call him when convenient as there was a matter he'd like her opinion on.

Cantelli came off the phone. 'Mr Brindley is very keen to examine the coins. He's coming in at three-thirty this afternoon.'

'Good, that gives us time to look at that lake. I'd like to see exactly where the box was found. I'd also like a word with who found it.' He'd only briefly read the report of one of the officers who'd attended, and Walters's subsequent one. He called Walters and asked for the contact details of those present when the box had been discovered. Walters relayed the telephone numbers of Robin Preston, the club secretary, and Peter Ashford, the pond manager, adding that they should also speak to Christopher Bosman, an environmental consultant, because Ashford had said Bosman had seen the box but had left before the police arrived because of work commitments.

Horton called Ashford, as he had been the one to discover the box, but got his voicemail and didn't leave a message. Not having Bosman's number he tried Preston, who answered promptly. Horton introduced himself and asked if he was available to show him where the box had been found.

'Why do you want to know that? Does it mean you've found something inside it?'

'I can tell you when we meet. Do have a contact number for Mr Bosman? I'd like to speak to him if he's available.'

Preston relayed it somewhat grudgingly. 'When do you want to meet?'

'In half an hour, if that's convenient?'

'It's all right with me, I work on the island, but Chris could be anywhere. I'll meet you in the car park.'

Cantelli started the engine. 'He didn't sound too pleased about it.'

'He's probably busy.' Horton rang the number Preston had given him for Bosman, who answered promptly. Horton explained who he was and that he was on his way to the lake to meet Mr Preston in connection with the finding of the box. He asked if Mr Bosman could join them.

'Of course, Inspector. I'm not far away as it happens, taking water and soil samples at Prinsted Point. I've got a gap before my next appointment. Not that I can tell you much, but I am curious, and only too glad to help if I can.'

That settled, Cantelli made for Hayling Island. 'Your half an hour was a bit over optimistic. I think the rest of the country must have decided to head for the beach,' he said as they queued interminably to get on to the one road to the island. 'If I had a blue light I'd put it on. Better ring Preston and Bosman to tell them we'll be late.'

Horton did so. Three quarters of an hour later Cantelli pulled into the car park and Horton, climbing out, apologized to the short, stout man waiting impatiently for them. He was in his early forties with steel-rimmed spectacles that had darkened from the sunlight. His thinning light-brown hair lay damp on his high forehead from the heat. His round face was flushed, as was his bull neck. His pale blue, long-sleeved cotton shirt, emblazoned with one of the local holiday park logos on the chest pocket, was also a victim of the weather, displaying large moist patches under the arms. Not that Horton held that against him. His own shirt was sticking to his back, and judging by Cantelli's dark curly hair it looked as though he had just stepped out of the shower. The sergeant had consigned his suit jacket to the boot of the car after transferring the two coin pouches to his trouser pockets, which bulged slightly. They couldn't risk leaving them in the car, and Cantelli was adamant he wasn't going to don his jacket. 'I'd keel over with a heart attack or heat exhaustion,' he'd said.

Preston briefly shook hands. Horton resisted the temptation to wipe his palm down his trousers. Cantelli wisely nodded and continued chewing his gum. 'I knew you'd be late. In this weather the world and his wife are heading for the beach. And who can blame them?' Preston said. 'It's about the only place there's a bit of a breeze and even that's not much cooler. Still, I shouldn't complain, the holiday park I work for is packed. Ah, here's Chris.' An old Suzuki with a dented passenger door and a battered rear fender under a rusting tow bar pulled in beside Cantelli's ancient Ford, making the sergeant's car look positively new and respectable.

'I tried Peter Ashford's mobile but he didn't answer,' Horton remarked.

'He's probably working.'

'Do you know where?'

'He's a road operative for the highways contractor Camplow, based in Southampton. He could be working anywhere along the coast.'

Bosman drew level. 'I'm sorry I'm so late, the traffic . . .'

'We've only just arrived ourselves,' Horton replied. Bosman looked kitted out for the tropics in a lightweight safari suit, and a wide-brimmed hat with chin strap. Having a fair complexion, and being engaged in outdoor employment, Horton could see he was obviously highly conscious of catching too much sun. His clothes obviously worked because he appeared to be the coolest of them all.

'What did you find in the box? It must be something significant to draw all this interest. Or was it the handcuffs?' Bosman asked with boyish keenness despite his thirty or so years. His long, narrow face tapered into a point which was finished off with a little fair beard streaked with auburn. 'Do you know why they were on the box? It looked very old.'

Preston keyed a code into the padlock on the steel gates that fenced off the lake.

'It's a Milner patent fire-resisting strongbox, probably made around the mid-1830s,' Horton answered, as Preston swung open the gate.

'Amazing. It couldn't have been in the lake that long because I'm sure handcuffs must have changed considerably since that time. Besides, there wasn't a lake here then,' Bosman said.

'This was part of a gravel pit,' Preston explained, shutting the gate after them. 'It was filled in by the Hayling Golf Club in 1938, who wanted to extract water for their greens. That's the clubhouse over there.'

Preston pointed to a white two-storey Art Deco building with a rounded turret on top and a balcony that looked out over the area of Sinah Common and Portsmouth to the west, the lake to the north and the Solent to the south. Horton knew of the club, although he'd never been inside.

'That side of the lake, which borders the golf club, is out of bounds to members,' Preston continued. 'And over there—' he indicated to the far right — 'is our secure compound where we keep gardening and other tools, a couple of small boats, some timber and odds and ends. This giant concrete structure in front of us is part of the Sinah heavy anti-aircraft gun site that was here during the war. It was the ammunition store. Our club was founded in 1948 and we leased the lake from the golf club in 1965. That old tin box must have got caught up on something years ago and became lodged under it until now.'

Horton knew the handcuffs didn't date from the 1930s or from the wartime period, but could they date from the 1960s?

Bosman said, 'It certainly looked to have been submerged for some time, judging by the algal growth covering it.'

'That slimy green stuff?' Cantelli asked.

'Yes.'

'What causes it?'

Preston huffed and looked at his watch.

Bosman seemed oblivious of the gesture. 'The water quality here is usually excellent and can be rich in natural food, especially when the weed is in full growth like now. But the lake is becoming more eutrophic with the silt build-up and the increased biomass.'

'What's eutrophic?' asked Cantelli.

'It's where the water becomes progressively enriched with minerals and nutrients, particularly nitrogen and phosphorus, and it can stimulate algal and aquatic plant growth. A common visible effect of eutrophication is algal blooms. That slimy green stuff, as you said, Sergeant. It can affect salt water, or fresh water like this lake.'

'You seem to know your stuff.'

'I should,' he grinned, smoothing his little beard with long slender hands. 'It's my business. I was taking water samples when Peter Ashford found the box, although I wasn't working where he was. I was looking for him to tell him I'd finished. He's the pond manager, he engaged me. I found him leaning over the box.'

'I'll show where that was.' Preston set off to their left, leaving them in no doubt that he expected them to follow. Horton was glad as the path was shaded by overhanging trees.

'Had he already called the police?' Horton asked as he walked beside Bosman. Preston was ahead of them and Cantelli behind.

'No. He said, "What do you make of this?" I said, "I haven't a clue," but I said he should call the police because of the handcuffs.'

'And he did so while you were with him?'

'Yes. He wasn't very keen to, and maybe I was wrong to insist, but it wasn't his to keep anyway. Then I had to leave as I was already late for my next appointment.'

'I was surprised the police even bothered to come out, given your shortages and the amount of crime about,' Preston grumbled over his shoulder. 'I wouldn't have troubled you, but by the time I arrived he'd already made the call and said the police were on their way.'

'What made you join Mr Ashford?' Horton asked. 'Did he call out to you or text you? Or did Mr Bosman tell you about the find?'

'I didn't,' Bosman declared.

Preston licked his fleshy lips and drew to a halt. 'I was coming along here to examine the fence, to make sure it was still intact. I had no idea Peter was here. I found him with the box. He said he'd found it over there by that clump of weeds and grass. Normally you'd get your feet wet wading out to it, but as you can see it's as dry as a bone because of this drought.'

Horton looked across the exposed shingle bed to a small knoll with some scraggly shrubbery, grass and flowers on it. 'Did you attempt to open it?'

'No. Peter said he tried the padlock but it wouldn't budge.'

That could be the faint trace of fatty deposits Joliffe had mentioned.

'I don't know how it got in the lake. It's strictly against the rules to leave litter of any kind. Although we do get our share of poor behaviour and we've had to ban some people. That hasn't happened for some time though.'

'Maybe one of them dumped it,' Cantelli suggested.

'I don't think so.' He eyed the sergeant as though he was a bit dim.

'How long has it been as dry as this?' Horton asked.

'We shut this run three weeks ago, but it was drying out two weeks before that.'

'When was the last time the area dried out?' Horton asked, trying to pinpoint if the box had been in the lake since then.

Preston scratched his head and looked at Bosman, who shrugged an answer. 'It must be a few years ago at least.'

'Do you have to be a member to fish here?' Cantelli asked.

'Yes, but members can bring a guest and we provide day tickets for prospective members to sample a selection of some of our waters. We also have an active match scene, with regular club matches and a season championship and various charity matches. This site has some of the best-looking carp in the south, with many being of the famous Leney strain.'

'I didn't know fish could be good-looking.'

Preston threw Cantelli a pitying look.

Cantelli said, 'Does every member have the combination code to the padlock for this lake?'

'Yes, although not all will fish here. We have a variety of sites, sixteen to be precise, from mixed fisheries to specimen waters. Some members will fish at all of them, others will stick to one or two. There was no one else here on Tuesday morning when that box was found — just me, Peter and Chris. As I said, the lake was closed for fishing, although that's not to stop any member from coming here to sit and have a picnic.'

Horton said, 'You'd hardly know this was here unless you were a keen golfer.'

'Or a walker. There's a footpath the other side of that fence behind us which runs eastwards, and this one takes you around the edge of the lake to our other car park, and the golf course car park and clubhouse, but you'd only know that if you looked for it or were a member of the angling club. And as you can see, this end is overgrown.'

'Have you had any break-ins recently?' asked Cantelli.

'You're wondering if someone from outside dumped the box here. Poachers break down the fence from time to time. We don't bother reporting it to the police anymore because they never do anything about it, and we've given up telling the council because they're . . . just the same.'

Horton thought Preston had been about to say 'useless' and had quickly changed his mind.

'We mend it ourselves when it happens. But it hasn't for some time and it wouldn't now because there are no fish to poach at this spot at the moment.'

'Is it all right if Sergeant Cantelli takes some photographs of where it was discovered?'

'Be my guest.'

Cantelli looked down at his shoes and then at Horton before stepping out. He crossed to the knoll and poked around in the grass, flowers and shrubs. Horton knew he was looking for anything that might have surfaced aside from the box. He saw him taking pictures with his phone.

Bosman's phone pinged and he looked at it. 'Sorry, I'll have to leave soon. Before I go, though, please tell me, have you managed to open the box? I'm bursting with curiosity to know if there was anything in it.'

'Me too,' Preston added with more reserve.

'Yes, there was a collection of rare coins.'

Bosman's eyes widened 'Really! Valuable?'

'We're awaiting an expert's opinion.'

'Will you be able to trace who they belong to?' Preston asked.

'We can try.'

'And if you don't?'

'Then depending on the value and their authenticity they will need to be declared to the coroner as treasure trove.'

Preston's expression became calculating. 'And who gets the bounty? Peter Ashford?'

Cantelli's return prevented Horton answering immediately. 'You were right, Mr Preston,' Cantelli said, sucking on a piece of grass like Farmer Giles. 'It is very dry, hardly a mark on my shiny shoes.'

Preston sniffed, while Bosman looked down at his cotton socks and sandals.

Horton continued. 'The finder, Mr Ashford, will have a claim on the treasure if the owner can't be located, and so too will the angling club and the organization with the freehold on the land.'

'The golf club. How much are we talking about?' asked Preston.

They began to walk back to the entrance, this time with Horton beside Preston, while Bosman walked ahead and Cantelli brought up the rear.

'Let's wait until our expert has examined them. I'll let you know as soon as I can. Meanwhile, it's probably best if you keep this to yourselves — aside from telling Mr Ashford, that is.'

'Do you still need to speak to him?' Preston asked. They had reached the entrance.

Ashford had been the one to find the box, and although Horton didn't think there was much more he could tell him, he nevertheless needed to update him. 'We'll contact him. Mr Bosman, you should also make a statement, certainly for the coroner, to verify that Mr Ashford found the box. Perhaps we could have your details in case we need to get in touch with you again.'

'Of course. I can type something up if it helps, sign it and email it to you.'

'Please.'

Cantelli handed over his card.

'If Peter contacts me I'll let him know that you wish to speak to him.' Bosman climbed into his car.

'I'll do the same,' Preston said more grudgingly. 'You'll be in touch?'

Horton said they would.

Cantelli made to open his car when Horton forestalled him. 'Let's find this other footpath.'

CHAPTER EIGHT

They set off across the grass heading east, skirting the lake on their right and past the gun emplacements that had been repurposed into concrete seating areas. They had the place to themselves. Anyone with any sense was either indoors in a cool, shaded room or on the beach. Horton was thankful to step onto the footpath under the trees.

'The fence looks secure enough to me, no recent breaches.'

They came out on the road leading south to the golf club. To their right before the golf club car park was a set of gates fencing off the other angling club car park that Preston had mentioned. The golf club seemed to be doing a roaring trade if the number of cars was anything to go by.

Cantelli said, 'You'd have thought it was too hot to spend the day hitting a little hard ball around.'

'Perhaps they're all in the bar.' Horton could see several people on the balcony, where there was also a pair of binoculars on a stand. He turned to the north and, across a stretch of green in the shade of the building, found the path around the lake, which opened to their left. 'This wouldn't be obvious to any casual walker. I don't think they get many of them here but there's nothing to stop someone walking into the grounds and along here.'

Cantelli chewed contemplatively on his grass. 'They wouldn't have got through the jungle of undergrowth to where the box was found.' He indicated the low hanging branches that now blocked their way. They weren't far from the angling club's second car park to their right.

'No need to when the lake is this dry. Look, we could walk around to it.'

'Bit silly then, dumping the box where it was found, it was bound to be discovered sooner or later.'

'Yes, if it was put in that location recently, and that's been bothering me.' Horton turned and they began to walk back the way they'd come. 'That box could have been there years and only just been discovered, right?'

'Right.'

'And you said it was bone dry there.'

'I did.'

'So how come, when that box was in my office, the green slime, the algae, was still damp in places? Not dripping wet but not crusty dry either, which is what it should have been if it had been where Ashford found it. Preston said that area had been dry for three weeks and drying out before then for two further weeks.'

'You think Ashford was putting it there? Hiding it, not finding it?'

'And he wasn't banking on Bosman appearing, so he had to pretend he had found it.'

'And he wouldn't have called the police but for Bosman insisting.'

'But none of that makes it a criminal offence unless the coins were stolen recently. Maybe Ashford hadn't had the chance to sell them. He could have had that box secreted elsewhere in the lake and then retrieved it to take it out along the dry bed of the lake to the other car park, but then Bosman showed up.'

They had reached the car.

Horton continued. 'He's proving hard to get hold of. I'll try him again later. Meanwhile, check for any reported robberies of coins, medals and small antiques.'

Cantelli discarded his piece of grass and substituted it for his gum. 'Nothing like that rings a bell with me.'

'Me neither.' The car felt like stepping inside an oven. 'I hope those coins are still in your trouser pockets, Barney, and didn't fall out while you were rummaging around on that exposed bank.'

Cantelli withdrew the two pouches. 'All there, but feel free to count them.'

'I trust you.'

Cantelli let down the window, a pointless exercise, as it only allowed in more hot air. 'Take a look at these while I drive.' He handed over his mobile phone. Horton flicked through the pictures of the area where the box had been found. It was as Cantelli had said: bone dry.

They made good time back to the station where Horton stopped off at the canteen to buy some sandwiches for his late lunch, while Cantelli made for CID to eat his own. Bliss wasn't in her office, but she was somewhere in the building as her car was in the car park. There was no sign of Walters, but he too had to be around because his car was also parked up. He hadn't been in his usual haunt — the canteen. He might be interviewing someone in relation to one of their cases.

Horton tried Ashford's number again. No joy. He ate his sandwiches and caught up with his messages. While doing so, Dr Adams returned his call. Horton told her about the pouches but not their contents or the background on finding them. 'Our forensic expert has told us there is a technique for dating the silk lining, but it would be expensive for us to use and probably won't help us with our investigation anyway. They're beautifully embroidered by hand and I wondered if you could examine them and see if there is anything you can tell us about it.'

'I'd be delighted, Inspector. I can do so tomorrow. I'm free at one. Would you be able to come over to the art department at the university?'

Horton said he would, barring any emergencies, and he would call her if he wasn't able to make it.

Cantelli put his head round the door. 'I've asked Gosport to instigate enquiries around the Hardway for anyone seen launching a boat around the time of the car fire and to canvas the houses directly opposite. The council say they haven't any cameras on that stretch. And there are no reported thefts of coins, medals, antiques or artworks of any kind in Hampshire. Of course, someone might not be missing them yet.'

'Any idea where Walters is?'

'None. Mr Brindley's here. Do you want to see him?'

'You deal with him, Barney. I'm going to report into Uckfield.'

The main incident suite crime board still showed Agni's name, which meant they still hadn't been able to name the victim. There was no sign of Dennings, Chawla or Seaton, but there was of Walters. 'Changed jobs and forgot to tell me?' Horton asked.

'Bliss volunteered my services to the Major Crime Team.'

'Doing what?' Horton could see her in Uckfield's office.

'Dealing with all the loonies calling in to say they saw the car fire the other side of the county in the middle of the night, and aliens departed from a spaceship after setting it ablaze.'

Horton smiled.

'I'm also monitoring feedback and enquires from social media from Bliss's statement.'

'Bliss?'

'The Super's appointed her social media supremo, so she gets her face on the telly and I get to oversee the trolls who respond.'

'Lucky you.' Bliss hadn't informed him, but then he rarely kept her informed so he shouldn't complain about not being consulted. It was a clever move on Uckfield's part, thought Horton as he knocked on Uckfield's office door. Dennings didn't translate well on camera and Bliss could take the flak should it arise, which it was bound to when they didn't solve the case within an hour like they did on the TV.

The Super waved him into a seat at the conference table. Horton told him and Bliss about his and Cantelli's visit to the scene of the crime and his theory that the killer could have travelled and left the crime scene by boat. 'That would rule out a joyrider,' he added.

'Chawla and Seaton are on a house-to-house in the immediate area. So far no one has reported screeching cars being driven at high speed typical of your joyrider high on drugs and alcohol. And no one has missed the poor soul.'

'So, it's someone with a clear intent for premeditated murder.'

'Who could be a drug dealer. They're not averse to using boats,' Bliss suggested.

'No, and the clever ones would know how to destroy a vehicle, making it very difficult to trace, as in this case,' Uckfield grumbled. 'Maitland's struggling to get the vehicle identification number because the car is severely burnt in the areas where it's usually stamped.'

'Could be pot luck?' Horton suggested, but he didn't think so. As he'd said, this murder had been carefully planned.

'There were two seats of fire,' Uckfield continued. 'One behind the front passenger seat, the other in the footwell of the front passenger seat.'

'That means the killer came with two Molotov cocktails. Unusual, that.'

'Wanted to make sure he did a proper job,' said Bliss.

'He succeeded,' Horton answered. 'It's a common enough way to start a fire, rags soaked with petrol and stuffed in a bottle.' The way the Tipner Sailing Club arson had been implemented.

'There was no evidence of glass,' Uckfield said. 'Neither Taylor, Joliffe nor Maitland could find any.'

'Interesting.'

'Perhaps he couldn't find a bottle or two to use,' suggested Bliss.

Uckfield scratched his armpit. 'The fire search dog sniffed out some further areas of possible blood staining on fragments of carpet, which Joliffe will analyse.'

Horton didn't say he'd seen the ones Taylor had managed to get at the scene.

'Maitland also believes the killer could have experienced a slight blowback from the fire, not substantial enough to have taken him to hospital with burns — no one has shown up with any, we've checked — but enough to possibly have singed him. We might also pick up traces of soil, sand and grit from that area on his shoes. But we've got to find the blighter first.'

'Could the man who reported the fire, Downs, be involved?' asked Horton.

'Dennings is interviewing him. Downs keeps his boat at the Royal Clarence Marina, says he was on his way home from it when he saw the smoke.'

'Then he knows the harbour and has a boat.'

'So do a lot of people,' Uckfield quipped. 'Including you and me. If we could get an ID, we might get somewhere. If no bugger reports him or her missing then we'll have to rely on Dr Clayton.'

Horton returned to his office. It was sad that no one had missed Agni, but then no one had missed Jennifer, except him. Her employer at the casino had said nothing of her not showing up for work, and the neighbours in their council high rise hadn't even noticed she wasn't there. If he hadn't existed, would anyone ever have reported her missing? Ducale might have done had he been in the country, but Ducale had told Horton he had been engaged elsewhere. Horton's last and loving foster mother might have too. Eileen Litchfield. She had been a close friend and colleague of Jennifer. But Eileen had also been out of the country at the time. Poor Jennifer. She had been alone in the world. She had worked hard, and he didn't mean at the casino, but for the intelligence services. She had risked a lot and sadly lost the game. She'd done her best by him too, he thought fondly, recalling the love she'd given him. But there was still that residue of anger that asked why she'd continued to work for the intelligence services after he'd been born. She knew the risks, but then he probably would have done the same in her shoes.

He called Elkins. 'Anything?'

'Nothing so far. But it's early days. You got an ID on the victim?'

'Not yet.'

He'd just rung off when Cantelli entered and sank heavily into the seat opposite Horton.

'Preston, Ashford and the golf club are going to be happy bunnies. Mr Brindley says the coins are genuine and worth more than he told you. Good job I didn't lose them.' He gave a tired grin. 'They're all safely locked away. He says they'll definitely be classed as treasure trove and the total haul should be put before the coroner. He made a list on his laptop and emailed it across to me. I've printed it off. Here.' Cantelli handed it over.

'Impressive.' Horton ran his eyes over it.

'I've told him he mustn't show anyone the list or talk about this until we can speak to the angling club, and after it's been reported to the coroner. He understands that and I believe he'll be discreet. I'll write up the reports.'

'You look all in, Barney,' Horton said with concern, noting Cantelli's high colour and his dark eyes, which seemed to have sunk deep into their sockets.

'I must admit I don't feel too good.'

'Then go home, the reports can wait until tomorrow. Are you well enough to drive? I'll get a car to drop you off.'

'No. I'll manage. It's not far.' He hauled himself up. 'This heat has caught up with me, and the air-conditioning in the interview room seems to have made me feel clammy. Hope I haven't got sunstroke or picked up some bug from that fishpond.'

'Lake. I hope not either.' Horton anxiously watched him go. It wasn't like Cantelli. He was right though, this blessed heatwave seemed to be going on for ever. The fish weren't the only creatures suffering. In this country they simply weren't used to it. But perhaps they'd better get acclimatized because the experts seemed to think they were in for more summers like this one.

He studied the list Brindley had made out. It was a considerable haul to have been dumped. And he was still very curious as to why. He thought about the slime on the box, or to give it its correct name, the algae. An idea occurred to him and he telephoned Joliffe.

'Did you take any samples of the algae on the box before sending it over to Dr Pooley?'

'Of course,' Joliffe said affronted.

'Can an analysis of it tell us where the box has been?'

'If you have samples from lakes or rivers to compare it with, yes. I'm not a forensic limnologist but I do have some knowledge of the subject. Algae comes in various sizes, colours, and morphologies, which are adapted to their habitat. They can be green, red, brown, golden-brown, or blue-green in colour. Green algae are the most abundant, as in your box. They can be found in marine, snow and freshwater environments. Yours appears to have been the latter.'

'But the box could have been in the sea?'

'As we don't get snow here, or very rarely, that is possible. Diatoms are diverse microscopic algae. Different diatom colonies present in samples, so if you have a match from a lake, pond or sea with the same diatoms that are on your box, you can say it came from the same location.'

'I'll keep that in mind.' Horton wasn't sure he would need the information, not unless it was connected to a crime, and as far as he could see, as Cantelli had said, there didn't appear to be one. Not unless the coins had been stolen and not yet reported, or there had been a human being on the end of those handcuffs who was now in a watery grave, possibly that lake. Perhaps he should get the water analysed and compare it with the algae on the box to see if it had been in a different part of the lake before being found, or even relocated, by Ashford.

He tried his number again. Still no answer, and he didn't leave a message. After another two hours' work, he rang Ashford again with the same result. Perhaps he was ignoring the call because he didn't recognize Horton's number. He could be exhausted after a hard day's manual labour in this heat and chilling out somewhere. He'd try him early in the morning.

Before going home, he checked if there was any further development on the murder investigation. There wasn't. Walters had already told him before heading home that all the leads seemed to be so far out that they had no connection whatsoever with the case. And there was nothing fresh from the mobile incident suite or from the house-to-house. Trueman said that Dennings thought Downs was on the level and he, Chawla and Seaton were staying down at the Royal Clarence waterside that evening at the same time of the incident yesterday, seeing if they could pick up any intelligence.

As Horton weaved his way through the traffic along the packed seafront to his boat, he again thought it sad that no one had missed Agni. But this time it stimulated thoughts of Harriet. He had a strong affinity for anyone whose loved ones had gone missing. There was no closure, only a yawning gap. If only her father's body could be found, or that of his brother, Gordon. Which of them had died from that gunshot he'd heard? Was Richard still alive in hiding? Did Andrew Ducale know which of the brothers was alive, or were they both dead? It was in the interest of the intelligence service, surely, to find that to be the case. Would Ducale tell him? Would Ducale tell Harriet and her family? Why had Harriet been assigned to review missing persons cases? As Cantelli had said that morning, it seemed a callous thing to do. Had she applied for the position because it was the only one available for her rank? Unlikely, given there was more than one vacancy in the force for a detective sergeant. In fact, there were many. Had someone told her it was the only way her transfer could be accommodated? Had it been arranged for her? But why? To break her?

He frowned. No, that seemed too extreme. But a conversation they'd had when they first met on an investigation and had been travelling together across to the Isle of Wight came to him. She'd told him that her family had never approved of her being a police officer. Their expectations had been that she would find a good husband and settle down, incredible in this age. He remembered one man called Rupert, an investment banker, who he'd seen with Harriet during the sailing regatta of Cowes Week. But that had been a year ago, and as far as he knew Harriet wasn't involved with anyone. Or she'd never mentioned anyone. But what did he know of her life and affairs? Nothing.

The marina was busy. He greeted a few people on the way to his boat and stopped to chat with a couple about the weather and nautical matters. On board, after swallowing what seemed like a gallon of water, he did a search for flats or houses to rent around the Royal Clarence Marina. There were a few, some too small with only one bedroom — he needed a second one for Emma — and some far too expensive. He registered with a few agents, hoping he would hear from them.

It was too hot to go for a run, so he went for a swim. That done, he took a long cold drink on deck. The sun was setting. His mind spun again to Harriet, and he cursed himself for conjuring up her fair face and those pained eyes. Before he knew it he was calling Ducale. He answered promptly, as Horton knew he would. 'Did you know that Harriet Ames has transferred to the Hampshire police?' Horton knew full well that Ducale would be aware of this, was perhaps even behind it.

'It was her wish.'

'And was it her wish to be assigned to the Serious Case Review Team and be given a missing person case?'

There was a moment's silence. 'I expect she had no choice.'

'There are plenty of vacancies.'

'*I* didn't engineer it,' Ducale said, but Horton heard the slight stress on the word 'I'. He considered asking who did but knew that Ducale wouldn't tell him.

'Any news of Richard Ames?'

'No.'

'Did you instruct this so-called fisherman to clean the boat of blood and Gordon's prints?'

There was silence.

'Whose blood was it? Gordon's or Richard's?' Horton held his breath. Would Ducale tell him? If it was Richard's then he could assume he was dead.

'It was Gordon's.'

A lie or the truth?

'Does that make any difference?' Ducale asked.

Horton's churning stomach told him it did. His racing mind quickly summarized the outcome. 'Then where is Richard? If he shot Gordon and disposed of his body overboard, are you saying he then repeated the act of his father and leaped to his death in the sea?'

'It's the obvious conclusion.'

'But not necessarily the right one. Would he really put his family through the agony of not knowing? And of giving everything up?'

'It's been done before. He wouldn't be the only peer of the realm to vanish after having committed a crime.'

Horton knew that. Richard Ames would have contacts and friends abroad. Perhaps he even had bank accounts he could access that the intelligence services didn't know about. On the other hand, perhaps Ducale and his bosses knew exactly where Ames was. He had, after all, worked for them. Maybe he did still.

Ducale said, 'I thought you'd finished with the Ames family?'

'I thought so too.' Horton rang off.

CHAPTER NINE

Thursday

The trilling of Horton's phone jolted him from sleep. He saw, with a premonition of alarm, that it was Charlotte, Cantelli's wife.

'Barney's in hospital,' she announced, clearly deeply worried. 'He's been violently sick all night and I couldn't get him to take any water. He's delirious, probably on account of being dehydrated. He's on a drip and they're pumping him full of antibiotics and sedatives but have no idea what's wrong with him. It could be food poisoning, an allergic reaction or a virus.'

'I'll come up.' Horton was already reaching for his trousers.

'No, Andy, there's nothing you can do here. He's in the best place and I'm not going anywhere. I'll make sure he's well looked after.'

Charlotte had been a nurse before having a family and had been planning to return to nursing now that the children were older.

'Barney's mother and Ellen are in charge at home,' she said. 'If it's a bug, he hasn't caught it from any of us. He might have eaten something with you yesterday. How are you?'

'Fine. Barney had a sausage sandwich. I didn't.'

'It could be that.'

'Or a virus he picked up at the lake. We were both there, although again it hasn't affected me. I'll make some enquiries and let you know what I come up with. Will you keep me posted on how he is?'

'Of course.'

Into Horton's mind flashed the thought that he couldn't get hold of Peter Ashford. He hoped he was all right, but there was no reason why he shouldn't be. Preston and Bosman were well yesterday, and if something at the lake had caused Cantelli's illness, then they would have suffered the symptoms of it directly after finding the box on Tuesday or early Wednesday morning. Perhaps Preston had spoken to Ashford by now.

He made to call Preston, when he saw that it was only just after six. He'd leave it another hour or so, although as he showered and shaved then made his way to work, the voice inside him kept saying an hour might make a difference to Barney.

At work he decided he didn't care what time it was. He tried Preston first, who, after expressing his surprise at the early morning call, said in answer to Horton's questions that he was well, and had been since Tuesday, and no he hadn't heard from Ashford. Nor had he contacted him since speaking to Horton yesterday.

'Does Mr Ashford have a landline number?'

'No. Why do you want to know that? You've got his mobile.'

'Is he married?'

'Divorced.'

'Any children?'

'Two, they live with their mother in Bournemouth. Why all the questions?'

'I was wondering if he'd been taken ill after finding the box.'

'What is this about the box? Is it contaminated or something?' he said jokingly. 'I thought you said there were rare coins inside it?'

'Did you handle it, Mr Preston?'

'I've already told you I didn't. Peter had brought it to the side of the lake when I saw it.'

'You didn't fiddle with the padlock? Or try to open the box?'

'No.'

'I'll be in touch.' He rang off before Preston could ask him anything further. Horton could have asked for the ex-wife's contact details but didn't think Preston would have them. Nor did he think he needed them, because the more he mulled it over the more he realized the cause of Cantelli's illness couldn't have been from handling the box. After all, he had never touched it. And it couldn't be anything connected with the lake because Preston and he were fine, so too was Bosman, as far as he knew. He called him anyway but got his voicemail. He left a message for Bosman to call him back.

He turned his attention to his paperwork, trying to push aside thoughts of Cantelli in hospital and of his conversation with Ducale last night. He'd spent restless hours during the night considering it. He had reasoned that even if Richard Ames were alive, it didn't affect him or his future. He wasn't sure if he believed that. No matter how he looked at it, it did affect Harriet.

He was barely concentrating. It was pointless to continue. Grabbing his helmet and jacket he decided he had to do something. He collected the pouches from the safe, leaving the coins locked away, put them in an evidence bag ready to take to Dr Adams at one o'clock and then made for Gosport. He'd pursue the possibility of food poisoning and visit the café where he had bought Cantelli the sandwich.

He left a message for Walters to say that Cantelli was in hospital, but instead of heading straight for Gosport, he detoured to Ashford's flat, having got the address off the report. It was in a 1960s four-storey council block, close to the hospital on the northern outskirts of the city. The narrow strip of grass at the front gave onto the busy dual carriageway. The traffic fumes hung in the hot sultry air and the occasional hoot of a car showed that tempers were running as high as the thermometer. There seemed no respite from it, and despite it being early morning it was still incredibly hot.

Horton made his way up to the third floor and knocked firmly on the door. Nothing. He pressed the bell but couldn't hear it sounding inside, so he hammered on the door. Only silence. He peered through the letterbox. There wasn't much to see, a narrow hall, an old carpet, a vacuum cleaner and some boots. Straightening up he found a big, bare-chested man with a huge protruding stomach, an earring and a cigarette, eyeing him cagily. 'Can I help you, mate?'

'I'm looking for Peter Ashford.'

'He ain't in. Haven't 'eard his telly and ain't seen him for a couple of days. His car ain't 'ere neither. Drives an Audi. You the bailiff?'

'No.'

The man looked as though he didn't believe him. Horton had removed his jacket and helmet but was carrying them, not trusting them to be left on his Harley for fear of them disappearing. He just hoped his Harley was still there when he returned. He didn't have the appearance of a police officer.

'Police.' He showed his ID and noted the shifting eyes, and that the man moved closer to his open doorway as though to block it. 'And you are?'

He looked about to say 'none of your business' then changed his mind and answered brusquely, 'Darren Telham'.

'Well, Mr Telham, Mr Ashford isn't in any trouble. I'm concerned about his welfare.'

'Oh yeah?'

'Do you know if any neighbours have a key?'

'Round 'ere? You must be joking! Help themselves to everything you got, soon as look at you.'

'A friend or girlfriend then, who might have a key.'

'Might have but I don't know any.'

Horton wasn't sure that was the truth but he didn't think he'd get it anyway from the big-bellied Telham. 'When Mr Ashford returns can you tell him to contact me?' Horton handed across his card. Telham took it as though it might be infected. Horton suspected it would end up in the bin.

He called Camplow, who Preston said Ashford worked for, after finding their number by searching the internet. The phone rang for some time, and just when he thought of hanging up it was answered by a disgruntled man. Horton swiftly said who he was and that he was keen to speak to one of their employees, a Mr Peter Ashford.

'You're not the only one, mate. Didn't show for work on Wednesday and no message from him.'

Worrying. 'Did he take the day off on Tuesday?' Horton knew Ashford had been at the lake but wondered if that had been official or he'd taken a sickie.

'He booked four days off: Friday, Saturday, Monday and Tuesday. A long weekend, but he should have been back on Wednesday.'

'Did he give any indication as to what he intended doing or where he might be?'

'Nothing. Left us short-staffed, and with this heat there'll be others phoning in sick. I thought you might be one of them. The roads will be bucking like Broncho on a deranged horse.'

Horton smiled at the highly colourful turn of phrase for what he could only imagine was an outbreak of raised manhole covers in the melting tarmac because of the heat.

'What's he done anyway? Scarpered with the Crown Jewels?'

'He's not in any trouble, we just need to locate him.'

'Not saying, eh? Well, if you find him tell him to phone me, or better still show up for work.'

So where was Ashford? Horton hesitated on forcing entry. There was nothing to indicate Ashford was inside and ill. In fact, he couldn't be as there was no Audi parked here. But he'd put out a call for his vehicle. He rang Sergeant Wells and asked him to get the registration number and circulate it, telling him about Cantelli being in hospital, at which news Wells expressed concern.

Horton looked up at the hill slopes, under which the gigantic hospital complex sprawled. He was sorely tempted to call in there, and yet knew there was little he could do. His time would be better spent trying to pin down what was causing the sergeant's illness. Before he set off for the Royal Clarence Marina, he called Gaye. 'Barney's in hospital,' he announced.

'My God, what's wrong with him?'

'They don't seem to know. It could be a virus, allergic reaction or food poisoning.'

'I'll find out where he is and go and see him.'

'Charlotte's there too. Let me know if you get any news.'

Thirty-five minutes later he pulled up outside the mobile incident unit in the Royal Clarence Waterside and Marina car park. Bosman hadn't returned his call. Horton would chase him up depending on what results he got here from the café. He knew it wouldn't be open yet, but he hoped that someone might be there, perhaps preparing the food. It was almost nine. He called into the unit. After showing his ID he asked how things were going.

'Nothing much, sir. A few cars seen going in the direction of the scene, and a motorbike. No registration numbers though and only vague descriptions of the vehicles — "I think it was blue", "Could have been a BMW or Mercedes", "Might have been a Renault", that type of thing, and no idea what make of motorbike. "They all look alike to me."' Horton winced at that. 'Other than that people have dropped in for a chat, to report a nuisance, complain that the police are useless and we're wasting taxpayers' money, with the occasional "I think you do a marvellous job despite the odds," but that was my mother.'

Horton laughed. 'I think you are too, and to prove it I'll get you a coffee and doughnut.'

Not from the café where he and Cantelli had grabbed some takeaway lunch though. As Horton suspected, it wasn't yet open, but he could see some movement inside. There was a small mobile café, which was open, and he bought the officer his coffee and doughnut, delivered it, stayed for another brief chat about the weather and football and then made his way to the intended café.

Rapping on the window with his warrant card at the ready, he waited until a tall, athletic-looking woman in her late thirties came to the door. She studied the card before letting him in. It wasn't the woman who had served him yesterday, but he'd seen this one behind the counter. He apologized for disturbing her and said he was there because one of his colleagues had been taken ill and the doctors had posited food poisoning. While he spoke, her horror-stricken expression turned to fury, much as he had expected.

'We've never had any incidences of food poisoning here, Inspector,' she said curtly, glowering at him. 'And I'm insulted that you could even think that. I can assure you all hygiene aspects are strictly adhered to. Look—' she pointed to a sign on the window — 'five-star rating for health and hygiene. We wouldn't have got that if we made our customers sick.'

'I felt sure it wasn't contracted here. It was just one of the avenues I had to check,' he mollified.

'Well, you can check all you like and call in the health inspector because I have nothing whatsoever to be ashamed of or to hide.'

'Perhaps you could tell me where you purchased your sausages — I was wondering if there was an ingredient that had caused an allergic reaction,' he quickly added as she looked about to explode.

'No one has ever had an allergic reaction to the sausages we serve.'

'Not that they've told you, but someone might have done.'

'There's nothing in them to have an allergy to.'

'There might be.'

She pursed her lips together and said tautly, 'I buy them from a local butcher. He makes them himself. They contain meat, salt and spices.'

'What kind of spices?'

'Thyme, fennel, sage, marjoram, black pepper.'

Horton didn't know much about spice allergies, so after he left her, he looked it up on the internet and saw that it was possible Cantelli had suffered an allergic reaction to one or more of the spices, although he hadn't remarked on the sausage sandwich being particularly spicy. Horton didn't think he'd be welcomed in this café in the future, which was a shame if he considered moving to the area. As he made his way to the marina office he called Charlotte. She said that Barney was still much the same and that Dr Clayton had visited and talked with the doctors and nurses caring for him. There had been no further episodes of nausea and diarrhoea.

'He's never had an allergy to spices before,' she said in answer to his question, 'but that doesn't mean he hasn't developed one. Spices are plant based, so they do have the potential to be allergens. I've seen allergic reactions before when nursing. Anaphylaxis, a severe allergic reaction, is rare, but could be caused by spices. I seem to recall that thyme was one of them, along with oregano. I'd have thought Barney would have had a rash though and itching in the mouth.'

The word 'plant' struck a chord. Bosman had said something about the water becoming so enriched with nitrogen and phosphorus that it could stimulate algal and aquatic plant growth. He'd been taking water samples and had been awaiting results on the levels of algae in the lake. Could Cantelli have been allergic to that? But surely not, because he had been close to that box in Horton's office and would have fallen ill before now.

Another thought occurred to him. Cantelli had also dealt with the lorry driver at the port who'd been smuggling currency. But how could that have caused an illness? Could the currency have been coated with some harmful substance as a means of putting off anyone who attempted to take it? But Cantelli would have worn gloves before handling it to preserve prints, so too would the customs officer. No, he was wrong there. It had to be a virus or something at that lake that had affected Barney but no one else. He again tried Bosman and irritatingly again got his voicemail. He left another message asking Bosman to call him, perhaps more tersely than he needed to, his anxiety making him abrupt. Immediately after Horton rang off, his phone went and with relief he saw it was Bosman. He'd probably been screening his calls.

'I'm so sorry I haven't returned your calls, Inspector,' Bosman quickly apologized. 'I had my phone on silent. I had to go to an early morning meeting, which has only just finished. I'm just on my way to another.'

Horton explained the situation regarding Sergeant Cantelli.

'I think it highly unlikely to be algal poisoning, not from Sinah Lake, although I haven't had the results of the water samples yet.'

'What would the symptoms be, if someone was taken ill?'

'If they touched the water where the algae was strong then sickness, diarrhoea and headaches would show up within a few hours. It can also lead to dehydration if the sick person can't hold down fluids.'

'This sounds very much like Sergeant Cantelli's symptoms.'

'But the area is bone dry. I don't think it can be that.'

Algae was on the box, Joliffe had corroborated that, but it couldn't be the cause of Cantelli's illness. Horton felt despondent. There was something even more seriously wrong with Barney that none of them would be able to pinpoint.

Bosman said, 'There might be something, though, in the area where the box was found. I didn't study it. I was too engrossed in the box.'

'Would you meet me there?'

'Of course, anything I can do to help. But I can't get there until midday.'

Another two hours. But it would have to do. Horton agreed.

'Will you notify Robin or Peter?' Bosman asked. 'Someone from the club should be there.'

'Have you spoken to Mr Ashford?'

'No.'

'I'll contact Mr Preston.' He called Preston and explained the situation. Preston wasn't too happy about giving up his time — the holiday park was very busy and he had urgent things to attend to — but he grudgingly agreed.

With that arranged Horton thought that while he was here, and kicking his heels until it was time to head for Hayling Island, he would explore the idea that the killer had reached the scene of crime and left it by boat. But this time he'd do it by sea. It would also keep his thoughts occupied. He called Elkins and arranged to be picked up by them in the RIB.

CHAPTER TEN

'You won't get far. The creek's dried out,' Elkins said when Horton boarded the RIB. 'You've got about three hours after high water and we're an hour too late.'

'Take me just past where the fire was.'

Ripley swung round the marina and the Gosport Sailing Club pontoon, under the bridge and into Forton Lake. Horton could see the shore where the car had been and, behind it, the top half of the industrial unit. To either side were dense shrubs and bracken, as he had noted with Cantelli. 'Go on a little further,' he instructed Ripley, who did so slowly.

They passed an old wreck. 'That's a Langstone Barge,' Elkins said. 'And beyond it is a Second World War motor minesweeper and the wreck of an old Gosport ferry, the *Vadne*. The top of the creek has become a bit of a dumping ground for old boats recently. It's quiet there and only accessible at the top of the tide.'

As he spoke Horton could see that they'd get no further. Ripley turned the RIB round.

Horton said, 'If the killer came by boat from the top of the creek, he must have done so on the high tide at 5.13 p.m., or possibly — as you said, Dai — a couple of hours after it. The call to the emergency services was at 7.13 p.m., so he obviously came earlier than that. We don't know how long the victim was dead. Our killer could have arrived early, waited for the victim, met him in the car park, killed him, then after some time drove the car down onto the shore. The car was well alight when it was called in by Jason Downs, and there was hardly anything left of it when the firefighters arrived at 7.20 p.m. So it could have been torched at, say, seven p.m., which gave chummy time to head back up the creek. What's up that end, aside from old wrecks?'

'There's a traditional boat builder, a rowing charity, some workshops, houses, the college and a pontoon with some boats moored up.'

'Who owns the pontoon?'

'Not sure but I'll find out.'

'And get the boat owners' details. One of them could be the killer.' But until they had an ID, they wouldn't be able to get a motive for the murder, and that meant they didn't have much chance of finding him. 'Is there a public slipway?'

'Not that I'm aware of, but I don't think there would be anyone to stop someone from launching a canoe or a small boat with an outboard motor from there on the high water or close to it. There's a walkway and a seating area at the top of the lake.'

'I'll find out if the council have any cameras there.' Horton consulted his watch. There was plenty of time before he was due at Sinah Lake. Too much time, he thought, but curbed his impatience with an effort. 'Let's take a look up the harbour.'

As Ripley headed north, Horton told them about Cantelli. Elkins expressed his shock and concern. 'I've just made an enemy for life at the marina café for suggesting it could have been food poisoning,' Horton added. 'I don't think it was. It could be a virus or linked to Sinah Lake, where I'm heading after this.'

Soon they were at the public slipway at Hardway where he and Cantelli had been yesterday. God, he hoped Barney was all right.

Elkins said, 'There's a public slipway by Wicor Marina. There are no CCTV cameras over it and it's too far from security in the marina office for anyone to have seen it. The same goes for Fareham Quay. No security in the marina in the evenings and the cameras are all centred on the pontoons, so he could easily have launched from there. Then there's Horsea Marina. There's easy access to the harbour from just before the marina and lock control room. Lots of boats here, Andy, and finding who the culprit is by this route will be like looking for a diamond in the sand on Wittering Beach.'

Horton glumly agreed and told Ripley to head back to the Royal Clarence Marina. He alighted and made for the marina office, where after showing his ID he asked where Jason Downs kept his boat. Locating it, he saw that it was a modest-sized motorboat with a reddish canopy stretched over the cockpit and helm. It also had a powerful outboard motor on it. He wondered if the boat had been here at the time of the fire. Perhaps Dennings had already asked around.

He checked his messages. One was from Gaye to say that she was about to start the autopsy on the car fire victim but she'd seen Cantelli, who was sedated and whose condition had stabilized. She said it looked as though he could be over the worst, but until they knew what it was, they were keeping him under observation in case he had a relapse or showed signs of any organ failure.

He felt some relief at that news and decided he had time to take a short detour to the area at the top of Forton Creek. Within ten minutes he had brought the Harley to a halt in the car park and seating area. It was a pleasant outlook but was spoiled by a jumble of rundown buildings, bits of boating paraphernalia, and abandoned and rotting boats, although the hulks made it an interesting landscape. It also confirmed his earlier suggestion to Elkins that a boat could easily have been launched along the shore here on high water.

Alternatively, he thought, swinging the Harley round, the killer hadn't gone to the scene by boat at all but by car or motorbike. For all they knew he could have walked or ridden a push-bike. If Uckfield could only get the ID. There were so many places the killer could have come from.

He made good time to Hayling Island because the morning pilgrimage to the beach hadn't yet got into full swing, and being on the Harley he could weave his way in and out of any queues. Both Bosman and Preston were waiting for him. Horton told them he wouldn't take up too much of their time. He was due to meet Dr Adams at one.

They made their way to the same location as on the previous day, Bosman carrying his sampling case, in readiness if needed.

'Have you heard from Mr Ashford?' Horton asked Preston.

'No.'

'Don't you think that strange? I'd have thought he'd be keen to know more about the box he found.'

'He's probably working away from home and too busy. Have you more news about the value of those coins?'

Preston didn't seem concerned about his pond manager. It made Horton wonder if there was some friction between them. He said, 'They've been confirmed as being worth a substantial sum of money, several thousands of pounds.'

Preston looked stunned, while Bosman gave a low whistle.

'We'll let you have a copy of the valuation report and return the coins when we've finished with the examination of the box and the handcuffs. It should be next week.' Into Horton's mind came the thought that if Ashford were no longer around to claim his share, then the angling club and the golf club would split it between them. Preston might be very happy about that. Happy enough to have killed for it? But no, he was speculating wildly. There was absolutely nothing to indicate that Ashford was dead.

'What tests can you possibly do on something that ancient that's been in water for years?' Preston asked.

'You'd be surprised.'

Preston's expression darkened.

They came to a halt. Since yesterday the area had dried out further and the ridge on which the box had been found was even more exposed.

Bosman donned a plastic overall and gloves. Horton crossed to where Cantelli had stood, Bosman beside him and Preston behind, looking anxious.

'Now, if I remember correctly, Sergeant Cantelli bent down and took some photographs on his mobile,' Bosman said.

'Yes, he returned to the footpath and said there was nothing here.'

'That's where he was wrong.'

'You've found something?' Horton asked keenly, his pulse quickening.

'I have, and now I seem to recall he had a piece of grass in his hand.'

Horton rapidly thought. 'He did. He put it in his mouth. I thought at the time he looked like Farmer Giles. He discarded it when we got to the car and replaced it with chewing gum.'

Bosman shook his head sadly. 'Then I know what's made him sick. I should have realized what it was, but I didn't really take any notice. We've all been too preoccupied with the box.'

'Tell me, please,' Horton said eagerly.

'See these plants just beyond where the box was found, and along the far edge?'

Horton noted some clumps of white cluster flowers on stalks.

'They're often confused with cowbane or greater water parsnip, when in fact they're *Oenanthe crocata*. In plain English that's hemlock water-dropwort, sometimes known as dead man's fingers. It's part of the carrot family and a plant of shallow freshwater streams, marshes, lakes like this, ponds, canals and wet woodlands.'

Horton had stopped listening at the word hemlock. He, and most police officers, knew of it. 'As in hemlock poisoning,' he said, troubled.

'Yes. All parts of the plant are extremely toxic. The tubers, stems and leaves contain oenanthotoxin, a highly unsaturated higher alcohol, which is known to be poisonous and a powerful convulsant. Poisoning by hemlock water dropwort is rare but it has caused fatalities. Animals are its usual victims, especially in the drought when cattle are driven to eat scarce vegetation.'

'Will Sergeant Cantelli get better?' Horton's gut churned.

'If he's been very sick then he'll have ejected most, if not all, of the poison. And by the sound of it he didn't ingest enough to make him seriously ill, but ill enough. Serious cases, and fatal ones, usually involve eating the roots, which can be mistaken for wild parsnips. Sergeant Cantelli didn't chew on a root, I take it?'

'Not as far as I know.'

'Then he'll be all right. The leaves and stalk are also poisonous, enough to make him very sick indeed. As well as nausea, he'd have had symptoms of lethargy, sweating and low-grade fever.'

Horton recalled Cantelli's manner before he'd gone home. 'He exhibited all those. I thought it was due to the heat, but it sounds as though the poisoning was beginning to take effect.'

'This would be followed by vomiting. And, depending on how much of the poison he'd taken, it can also cause seizures and hallucinations.'

'He had the latter, but that might have been caused by dehydration. Is there any treatment the hospital should be giving him, Mr Bosman?' Horton was already reaching for his phone.

'If he's having convulsions they need to give him an intravenous anticonvulsant and muscle relaxant like diazepam. If he isn't having any convulsions then he'll be over it soon.'

After thanking Bosman profusely and leaving him to talk to Preston, Horton returned to the footpath with his phone pressed to his ear. Charlotte answered almost immediately and Horton quickly relayed what he had learned. He heard the relief in her voice. He was also delighted to hear that Cantelli hadn't had any convulsions. She'd tell the doctors what he had discovered. She expressed her warmth and gratitude before ringing off. Horton felt a tremendous burden lift from him.

'I can't thank you enough, Mr Bosman,' Horton said when he and Preston reached him at the entrance to the car park.

'I'm only sorry I didn't recognize it at the time.'

Preston, looking perturbed, addressed Horton. 'Do you think Peter Ashford is OK? He might have eaten some of this plant.'

Now he's worried! 'He's not lying ill or worse in his flat, we've checked.' He hadn't though. All he knew was that Ashford's Audi wasn't there and he wasn't answering his door. He could have driven away from here — not to his home, but elsewhere — when, overcome with illness, he pulled off the road in an isolated spot, parked up and died. Horton was glad now that he'd put out an alert for his vehicle.

His phone rang. It was Sergeant Wells. He stepped away to answer it, wondering if he was calling with the news that Ashford had been located and the poor man was dead.

'A man's called in about finding some human remains by the breach of the sea wall at Southmoor Nature Reserve, top of Langstone Harbour.'

My God, was it Ashford? Then Horton registered Wells's words, he'd said remains, not corpse or body.

'PCs Allen and Johnson have just verified it.'

'Suspicious death?'

'They can't say, all that's showing is a skeletal hand and part of an arm.'

'I'll be there in ten minutes.'

CHAPTER ELEVEN

The early afternoon sun was beating down. There was no refuge from it or the heat. It was low tide, with no breeze to cool him. The seagulls were squealing over the mud of the harbour. There was the faintest hum of traffic from the dual carriageway to the north, and to the east, the sunlight glimmered off the vehicles crossing the Hayling Island Bridge, and onto those crossing the road to the west across the harbour into Portsmouth. The expansive harbour itself was deserted, all the activity on it would be down towards the mouth, which led into the Solent and close to Horton's marina.

To his left, the moor was scattered with dense shrubs, brambles and assorted grasses and was beginning to revert to its former state of marshland with the flora and fauna blackened, having been killed by the salt water. The ceaseless tides had swept up dark shingle, sand and mud and created lakes on the moor that the gulls, ducks and egrets seemed happy with. As the breach had widened with each tide, the sea had pushed further inland. Horton didn't think it would be long before it reached the industrial estate to the north.

He'd called Dr Adams and rearranged his appointment for early tomorrow morning. He drew level with PCs Allen and Johnson, who were with an elderly man and his dog on a lead.

'This is Mr Kirby, sir. He made the discovery,' said Allen, who then introduced Horton.

'How often do you walk this way, Mr Kirby?' Horton asked.

'I used to do it regularly. I live close by in Langstone, but with the wall gone I can only do it at low tide when you can either walk around on the shore or clamber over the debris the sea's brought in. I was in two minds whether to come today on account of the heat, but the dog was restless so I thought a short walk by the sea might not do any harm. She was off the lead and ran into the moor. I was worried about her getting stuck in the marsh. It's a disgrace this hasn't been repaired, but then no one seems to have the money or the inclination to do these things these days. I ventured further than I would normally as the fence is down.' On the muddy ground, Horton could see timber posts and wire that had served to fence off Southmoor. 'My foot slipped and I stumbled. I put out my hands to steady myself on a sort of mini cliff that the tide had gouged and had the shock of my life when I saw bones. I know enough about the human skeleton to recognize a hand and wrist when I see it.'

'If you could give your contact details to PC Allen we won't detain you any longer.'

'Already done that,' Kirby answered smartly. 'You'd better look sharpish about digging it out. Tide will be up here in a few hours.'

Horton knew that. They had until about 4.42 p.m., two hours before the high water reached here. That gave him approximately three and a half hours to work. With a glance at Allen that said keep him away, Horton climbed over the debris of porcelain and pottery fragments, stones, shingle and rubbish, into the hollow where Johnson was now standing guard over the remains. Jutting out of the soil was indeed a hand. It was almost as though the poor soul was reaching out to them.

There was a considerable amount of earth above the remains and some blackened straggly shrubs and brambles. He wondered why a dog hadn't previously sniffed it out before reaching this stage of decomposition. And what was there to say there were more bones? They might just find a hand. It was no use speculating until they could see clearly what they were dealing with.

Horton gave Johnson instructions to cordon off the path from the car park. Not that there had been anyone in it when Horton had arrived, just the police vehicle, and Horton doubted they would get any walkers. It was too hot for that, but once the news got out, they might get the ghouls and gawkers, even in the heat.

He rang Wells, reported what he had found and asked for additional officers. He also requested they bring shovels and trowels and for SOCO and Clarke to attend. Next he called Bliss and told her what was occurring, adding, 'We've got to work quickly before the tide comes up. I'll keep you posted. Did Walters tell you about Cantelli?'

'He did.'

'Well, I'm pleased to say that I found the cause of his illness, or rather Dr Bosman did. It's poisoning by hemlock water dropwort from Sinah Lake, which Cantelli encountered when examining where the tin box was found. I've told Charlotte at the hospital, and Cantelli should recover soon.'

'I gave you instructions not to follow that up. Sergeant Cantelli wouldn't have got sick if you had listened.'

He rang off shaking his head with grudging cynical admiration that she managed to twist everything round to being his fault, or someone else's, and turned his attention to the gruesome task ahead.

It wasn't long before Beth Tremaine, Clarke and the officers arrived, and along with the shovels they had brought welcome bottles of water and sunscreen. Wells's foresight, guessed Horton. After photographs and soil samples had been taken around and under the hand, and above it, Horton and the officers set to work in the sizzling heat. As they carefully cleared the earth, Clarke took more photographs and Beth more samples.

Gradually what remained of the corpse was revealed. It was lying face down, head to the east and feet to the west. He could see the back of the skull, which looked to be intact. There were some ribs on the left of the body, what looked to be the pelvis, and some bones of the left leg along with those they'd already seen of the left hand and arm. To Horton it appeared as though animals had taken away and eaten into the bones on the right-hand side of the body towards the moor, whereas the bones on the seaward side had been preserved.

Bliss rang him as they finished working and demanded an update, which he gave her. The tide had reached the base of where the original wall had been. The undertakers had arrived with a trolley and body bag.

'We've retrieved what we can. There's little more we can do because of the rising tide. Clarke's got photographs. It doesn't look on the surface to be suspicious, the skull is intact, but there's not much left of the body to tell us how he or she was killed. It appears to have been buried but not deeply, and that suggests foul play. I'm inclined to think it must have been, given that someone surely would have found it long before now if it hadn't been buried.'

'How long do you think the body's been there?'

'No idea. We'll need Dr Lauder for that. I'll let Dr Clayton know the remains are on their way, and she can liaise with him. Is there any feedback on the autopsy on Agni?'

'Not yet. I'll inform Superintendent Uckfield.'

Taking a swig of water, Horton watched as the officers and undertakers carefully lifted the bones and placed them in the body bag. He still couldn't see any visible evidence of foul play. There was also no obvious weapon under or around the corpse.

When Horton was satisfied there were no more bones, he instructed the undertakers to take them to the mortuary. He called Gaye and left her a message. Then, dismissing the other officers after thanking them warmly, he trawled the ground around where the corpse had been with Allen and Johnson. They bagged up anything and everything, including clods of mud and grit that looked, or felt, to have something encased in them. The sea washed ever closer. There was still no respite from the heat. It was a wonder they hadn't suffered sunstroke.

His phone rang three times. Seeing that the callers were the newspaper crime reporter Leanne Payne and a local BBC reporter, he ignored it. They seemed to be keeping the press busy, what with the fatality in the burnt-out car and now this.

'This looks like a T-shirt.' Allen delicately picked up a piece of filthy fabric that might have started life as blue. Horton remembered that Gaye had told him, that natural fibres such as silk, cotton and wool rotted a lot quicker and were biodegradable, so perhaps this had a nylon or acrylic composition. It could be a runner's T-shirt. Johnson called out. Horton was looking at what remained of a pair of trainers, the area around the eyelets and the laces. They found a few more fragments of clothing, a red plastic cigarette lighter, a piece of a keyring and two plastic bottles. There was no mobile phone, jewellery, or wallet to provide them with an ID.

With an aching back, Horton called it a day. He heartily thanked the police constables and they made their way back to the car park, which was surprisingly deserted, save for the police car and Horton's Harley. He'd expected some sightseers or Leanne. The weather, it seemed, had kept everyone away.

He was hot, tired, filthy and hungry. At the station, he washed his hands and cleaned himself as best he could, but the mud had stained his shirt front and trousers. After raiding the vending machine for crisps, coffee and a Kit Kat, he made for his office.

'You look as though you've been digging for more coins,' Walters greeted him.

'Bones, not coins. But I discovered what was wrong with Cantelli.'

'So I heard. He ate some poisonous grass. Just shows you how unhealthy a vegan diet is. Won't catch me eating the stuff.'

'No, Walters, your poisoning is much more likely to come from dodgy kebabs.'

'Heard you found another corpse.'

'I didn't find it, and there's not much left of the poor soul.'

'Homicide?'

'No idea, but it's possible. Bodies don't bury themselves. Any progress on any of our outstanding cases?'

'Not so you'd notice, and there's no reports of Peter Ashford's car.'

And no one had officially reported Ashford missing, just as they hadn't Agni — not unless Uckfield had an ID by now, thought Horton, entering his office to find that Allen and Johnson had deposited the findings from Southmoor on his desk.

He stared out of his window as he ate and drank. Were the remains he'd just helped excavate someone who had been reported missing? Until they had some idea of a time frame it was pointless to go through the database. He didn't even have the gender. Just as they didn't on Agni, unless Gaye had it by now. As he thought that, her Mini drew into the car park. He asked Walters to log in the evidence bags from Southmoor and made his way to the rear exit.

'You look tired,' he greeted her.

'So do you, and dirty. Your remains have safely arrived. I saw them as I was leaving and all I can say from the pelvis is it's male. I won't be able to look at them tomorrow, I've got a forensic autopsy to do in Reading. But I've fixed it for Monday, when Dr Lauder is also available.'

'The poor soul has lain at Southmoor for years by the looks of him, so another couple of days won't make any dif-ference, except to his relatives and friends.' His mind flicked to Harriet but not her missing person case, her missing father. 'I can't see how it could have been covered up so completely if it hadn't been buried.'

'Bracken grows very rapidly. It loves bodies and thrives where they're left or buried because we humans increase the nutrient load of soil and water courses.'

Horton thought of Bosman and his nutrients, or rather lack of them, in the lake. That in turn made him think of the algae on that box.

'The state of the bracken can tell us how long a person's remains have been in the soil,' Gaye was saying.

'The bracken over and around this corpse was blackened, killed off by the sea water.'

'Ah, that does pose a problem,' she said, thoughtfully. 'I looked in on Cantelli before I left. He's doing well. They're keeping him in for another twenty-four hours just to make sure. Charlotte has gone home. She's exhausted. I'm glad you found out what was causing it. Charlotte told me. You look as though you could do with a break. I've got dinghy sailing competitions this weekend at Lymington. Why don't you sail there and stay for a couple of days? I'm going as soon I finish up in Reading tomorrow.'

'I'd love to, but Cantelli was duty CID this weekend and I'm stepping in for him. Walters was duty last weekend.'

'OK. Keep me posted on Cantelli.'

'I will.'

Their conversation had taken them to the incident suite. Uckfield was waiting impatiently in front of the crime board. His face was flushed despite the air-conditioning. He raised his eyebrows with a smirk as Horton walked in with Gaye. If Gaye noticed it — which she probably did — she gave no sign. The team were all assembled, including Bliss, who looked as immaculate as ever in her crisp white shirt and black trousers. She frowned at Horton's grubby appearance. Horton fetched himself some water as Gaye began. His eyes flicked to the crime board and saw the victim still hadn't been identified, and there was still that question mark against the make of the car: *Audi?* He thought of Peter Ashford, who drove an Audi, but then lots of people did — only lots of people hadn't gone missing. How could it possibly be him? Gaye's voice pulled his attention back.

'There isn't much to tell you. The extreme heat of the fire has altered the properties of bone, both physical and chemical, making it far more difficult for forensic tests.'

Uckfield shifted. 'OK, we get that it was tough.'

Gaye ignored his jibe. 'The bones, as you can see from these pictures—' she glanced at those on the crime board — 'are chalk white, which means the temperature of the car fire was in excess of 700 degrees centigrade, and that is also borne out by the state of the almost totally destroyed vehicle.'

It was also why Maitland was still struggling to get a vehicle identification number, which according to the crime board he hadn't managed to do. Horton drank some water.

'During burning, bone weight is reduced, as is volume, making it harder to identify height, weight, age and sex. I've conducted extensive tests and used a variety of examination techniques. The bad news is that the extreme heat has destroyed organic matter, meaning I can't get any DNA from the bones. All I can tell you is that it is male, but as to height, weight and age, I can't say. One thing though is that judging by the remains of the teeth, the victim was not very young and neither was he very old.'

'Then—'

'I can tell you that from my examination of the skull there is evidence of blunt-force trauma made by a weapon that was oblong in shape. Whether or not that killed him before the fire was set is impossible to determine.'

There was a moment's silence while they all took this in.

Horton was the first to speak, thinking of his reconnaissance with Elkins that morning. 'Could it have been a paddle or an oar?'

'Possibly. There are no fragments in the wound because the fire has destroyed the evidence. But I've taken a tracing of it, and photographs, and they'll be with you later tonight, as will be my full report. I'm awaiting the results of some more tests and will let you have them as soon as they come through. I'll be examining the remains found at Southmoor on Monday.'

'Is that suspicious?' Uckfield fired at Horton.

'On the surface, no — although it appears the corpse might have been buried, which makes it so. However, Dr Clayton has explained it could have been quickly covered with bracken, and as the deceased was off the footpath, he could have fallen, or been taken ill, and lay there undiscovered until the sea breach and nature took its course.' But was that so? Horton had that itch between his shoulder blades that said it was highly unlikely.

'We'll wait until we get confirmation on Monday,' Uckfield declared, looking relieved. 'We concentrate on Agni and finding his killer.'

Horton thought the Super was glad to have three days grace in which to do so before finding himself with a second homicide investigation.

After Gaye had left, Uckfield addressed Trueman. 'Find out what the devil is holding Maitland up with that vehicle identification number.'

Horton thought Trueman was about to say, *A severe car fire that made it practically impossible to tell it was a car in the first instance, didn't you hear?* But he simply nodded.

'Seaton.'

'Yes, sir.' Seaton sat up as though he'd been given an electric shock.

'Is there anything in the reports of sightings, or people claiming to know Agni, that seem remotely possible?'

'Still going through them, sir.'

'Then do it quicker. And where's the analysis on the blood found on what was left of the carpet and other bits of metal in that car? Trueman, get onto Joliffe and find out what he's doing about it. If we can't get DNA from the body then let's hope we can get it from the blood. If the poor bugger was bludgeoned, it must be his.'

Horton addressed Dennings. 'Did Jason Downs's story check out?'

'He had a row with his wife and stormed out. He—'

'At what time?'

'Just after six. He can't remember exactly and neither could his wife, as apparently, they'd been at it for a while.'

'What was the row over?'

'Does it matter?'

Had Dennings even bothered to ask?

'Downs went to his boat and sat on it for an hour until he had calmed down. He was returning home when he saw the smoke and rang the emergency services on his mobile but didn't go to see what was alight because he thought, it being so dry, it was bound to be a grass fire.'

'Strange that he seems to be the only person who saw the smoke.'

Trueman answered. 'He's not. Other witnesses have reported into the mobile unit to say they saw it.'

But did they? wondered Horton, or was it because they wanted to feel important by saying they had seen it after the event. Maybe some were genuine. But Downs had seen it first. Horton said, 'So Downs was on his boat between six p.m., or thereabouts, and 7.13 p.m., when he made the call to the emergency services after driving round Dunlin Road on his way home. Why did he drive that way? If his car was parked in the marina car park, all he had to do was turn left and head out of it, not back towards the fire scene.'

'He saw the smoke as he was driving off. He didn't drive round that way.'

Horton thought that a bit weak. He reported that he had seen Downs's boat on the pontoon and relayed what he and the marine police had done earlier. 'Did anyone see Downs sitting on his boat?' By the ensuing silence Horton knew no one had asked.

'Check it out,' Uckfield directed at Dennings, who threw Horton a black look, but then Horton was used to them.

'Well, don't all just sit there, get back to work.'

Horton exchanged a glance with Trueman before leaving. Uckfield was more than his usual irascible self, brought on not by heat — his office was nice and cool — but probably because he was under pressure from on high to get some results. And Horton had to admit that not having an ID increased the tension. He hoped they'd get one quickly on the Southmoor remains.

The evidence bags had disappeared from his office. Walters had booked them in and gone home. Horton had two messages from the estate and letting agents, who had sent him a string of 'possible rentals' that, scrolling through, looked as bleak as those he'd already viewed online and dismissed, and those he'd viewed physically and rejected.

There was also a message from Dr Pooley to say he had some noteworthy results on the tin box and handcuffs. That at least was good news. Horton emailed him to say that he would be over tomorrow morning, hopefully about ten, unless he heard from him to say that was inconvenient. He would see Dr Pooley after his meeting with Dr Adams.

He wrote up his reports, thinking of Gaye writing hers, and of Cantelli in hospital. He'd liked to have visited him, but he was in too dishevelled a state to do so. He also thought of Peter Ashford and the possibility of his body being in that car. But how could that be? The fire wasn't connected with the tin box and coins.

Horton rubbed a hand over his face. He couldn't think straight. He was exhausted both mentally and physically and, despite the sun cream, his neck was burning from being caught in the sun. He'd tackle any ideas tomorrow.

That night, to his surprise, mercifully he slept.

CHAPTER TWELVE

Friday

Just before nine the next morning, Dr Adams greeted him with the warm smile he remembered when consulting her previously.

'You have another puzzle for me, Inspector,' she said brightly, leading him into her small office, the walls of which were covered with pictures of fashion models and drawings, and the surfaces littered with fabric and sewing implements. The windows were open, but they only let in the traffic noise and the hot sticky air. She moved some fabric off a seat and waved him into it, taking the one opposite and settling her amply proportioned frame. She was as gaily dressed as he recalled, with plenty of suntanned cleavage on display. In her mid-forties, her personality and enthusiasm were attractive and infectious.

'I have these.' He placed the evidence bag containing the two pouches on her desk.

Her dark eyes gleamed as she pushed back her long black hair. 'May I remove them?'

'Please do.'

'Oh, they are exquisite,' she cried, handling them with tenderness, stroking the exterior with her nail-varnished and bejewelled fingers. 'The property of a very talented lady. Quite beautiful. Look at the stitchwork. You have just these two?'

'Yes.'

She looked disappointed.

'What can you tell me about them?'

'They're Victorian purses — reticules, to give them their correct name. These were the precursor to a woman's handbag.'

'Then they were designed to carry coins?' Horton thought of the Victorian coins inside one of these purses, but a woman of that era wouldn't have carried coins from Charles I's and II's reign.

'Along with keys, a handkerchief, calling card and other Victorian accoutrements, possibly smelling salts or a small spring of lavender, depending on the size of the reticule. The larger ones would have carried a fan and possibly a pair of dance shoes. These being small would generally have been carried in the hand, although the drawstring silk ribbon on these shows they could also be placed around a delicate lady's wrist. How did you come by them? Oh, I don't suppose you can say,' she beamed at him.

'No, sorry, I can't at present, but there wasn't anything particularly feminine inside. I'd very much like to know who owned them.'

'That might be impossible unless we have the lady's name inside. Is it OK if I turn them inside out?'

'Please do.'

She tenderly pulled open the drawstring. 'There, as I thought, she's delicately embroidered her initials L.H. in the silk lining, but I'm not sure that gives you the answer you're seeking.'

'It doesn't, but it might eventually help. Who knows? Tell me more about them.'

'Well, the tradition of carrying these beautifully crafted reticules began in the early 1800s. There were no pockets in women's dresses of that era and Victorian women did their utmost to look their best in public, certainly those of breeding, wealth and high aspirations, which is clearly what your lady was. Each purse was skilfully crafted and embroidered like these two. This one with a beautiful exotic bird, the other, as you see, with delicate embroidered flowers. Some would boast intricate beadwork and would be trimmed with silk or lace. Others would have tassels. Many women created and decorated their purses to show off their needlework skills in public. The stitchwork on these is excellent. A very clever lady, and as I said, a wealthy one. If you'd let me photograph them, I'll do some research and see if I can come up with anything further to help you. Obviously, I'll treat it as confidential.'

He agreed and said he'd be delighted if she could assist. As he made his way to Dr Pooley's laboratory in a different part of the university campus, he considered what Dr Adams had told him. He conjectured that the two reticules had possibly been made at the same time as the safe or slightly before. Leney had said that it was dated probably around 1836, although it might not have been purchased until much later by the lady's family. Then again, it could have been bought even later in an antique shop, likewise the reticules. He didn't see how this got him much further with the case, which was not a case at all. It was time to hand the box and its contents back to the angling club. Or strictly speaking to Ashford, only he seemed to have disappeared. He'd again tried his mobile that morning without a result. He'd also called Camplow, who still hadn't heard from him.

As Horton pulled into a parking space he wondered, as he had done yesterday, if Agni could be Ashford. If Ashford had been disposed of then there would be more of the treasure to share out between Preston and the golf club. Did Preston badly need money? Had he known from the start what was in the box? Had he happened to be in the area where Ashford had found the box, or had Preston gone there to retrieve it but Ashford had beaten him to it?

And who had been in those handcuffs? Horton hadn't run the DNA through the database yet. He'd been too worried about Barney and then he'd had those remains to unearth, and they certainly weren't Ashford's.

He rang Walters and told him to check out the DNA from the handcuffs. As he made for Dr Pooley's lab he resolved that after hearing what Pooley had to say, and seeing what Walters came up with, he'd wash his hands of it. The box and contents would be returned to Preston. Yet even as he thought that he felt uneasy. If it hadn't been for those damn handcuffs and the fact that Ashford had vanished . . .

Pooley's laboratory was in sharp contrast to Dr Adams's small and littered office. This was clean, white and spacious with tidy benches and equipment, and a tall, long-bodied man of about forty with sharp eyes and a chin to match. His enthusiasm, though, equalled — no, surpassed — Dr Adams's.

'Your tin box posed quite a challenge.' Pooley's youthful face lit up. 'Metal is not the most productive surface for latent prints but it's always possible to pick up something, and I have.'

The box and handcuffs were laid out before them on the modern bench in the refreshingly air-conditioned room. The weather forecast was for another record-breaking day as far as the temperature was concerned.

'I used a variety of techniques, one being high-intensity light sources — a laser.' He beamed. 'I won't bore you with all the technical details, Inspector.'

'No, please go on, I'm very interested and it helps me to understand. I take it this will be in your report and there's no need for me to take notes?'

'Of course. I'll email it over to you shortly. To continue then, as I said, I used a form of laser treatment which is very sensitive, it can pick up marks that are old, sometimes over thirty or more years. I also used vacuum metal deposition, a favourite of mine.' He grinned as he bobbed about. He seemed so full of energy that Horton half expected him to start bouncing up and down. 'I've had a great deal of success with retrieving prints from items that have been submerged in water. However, the tin box is a bit awkward to fit into the chamber we use, which is more suitable for smaller and flatter items, so the handcuffs were fine.'

Horton returned his smile. He could get worn out just watching Pooley, whose long, thin arms seemed to be constantly on the move — a decided hazard, he thought, in a laboratory full of glass. He warmed to Pooley and admired his passion.

'We also used Recover LFT — sorry, latent fingerprint technology. It's new. First found by Loughborough University. They were able to recover marks off metals which had been wet or washed with solvents, and those that had even been wiped and scrubbed. It's very much a hope for difficult metal surfaces like stainless steel knives and fired cartridges.'

'That's good news for us.'

'Yes, and bad news for the villains. Fumigation with cyanoacrylate — that's superglue — is another method. It's generally been discounted for getting marks off items that have been wet, but this is being re-evaluated. Our own university here in Portsmouth is doing some work on this, looking at knife blades. Sea or salt water gives a better chance of superglue success, and a colleague of ours has been successful recovering marks off safes dumped in sea water. You might have heard about that.'

'No, I hadn't. It's not something I've been working on.'

Pooley went on almost breathlessly, pushing his fine, longish hair off his face. 'Well, for fresh water — what your tin box was submerged in — we use powder suspension. It's a bit low tech by comparison, but it involves painting on a mix of powder and detergent and washing it off, and it's good at finding older marks. The upshot is that from my tests I have indeed lifted prints from both the metal box and the handcuffs. Several in fact, and I've run them through the fingerprint database.'

'And?' Horton asked keenly.

'One set of prints, the most recent, belong to Peter Ashford.'

Horton did a double-take. My God, he hadn't checked criminal records for Ashford. There had been no need, as the man had reported finding the safe, but only when Bosman had insisted. 'He found the box. Why is he on the database?'

'Juvenile theft. Also receiving and selling stolen goods when he was eighteen. It made me wonder if he'd stolen this box, but I wasn't sure where the handcuffs came into it — that's your province, Inspector, not mine. And his prints are not on the handcuffs. They're on the sides of the box under the handles, which matches with what you said about him finding it. He obviously picked it up. And there are prints of his on the padlock and the lid, as though he tried to open it.'

Preston had said as much.

Pooley tapped into his laptop with such speed and energy that Horton thought he might break it. Glancing up, he said, 'There are also a more recent set of prints on the box but no match on the database.'

That could be the angling club secretary, Robin Preston, although he had insisted he hadn't handled it.

'Now, the prints I found on the inside of the handcuffs and that was not attached to the box are fascinating, because we have a match.' Pooley glowed.

'The area where Joliffe found DNA?'

'Yes. The prints are those of a Jamie Doyle. He also has a criminal record.'

Horton had his second shock of the morning. Doyle! No, it couldn't be. This was the very last thing he had expected. It might not be the same person, he told himself. It wasn't a particularly unusual name, but the Jamie Doyle he recalled went right back to his school days. A few years older than him, Doyle had been manipulative, cunning and evil. He'd bully, charm or cajole others into doing his dirty work for him — stealing, primarily. He'd been good at preying on people's weaknesses and had tried it on him, taunting him with the fact that his mother had run off with a man until Horton had used his fists, which Doyle had seen he had gotten into trouble for. Perhaps it was a different man. Or maybe he'd changed over the years, although, not according to the fingerprint database.

'What was he convicted for?' Horton asked.

Pooley called up the file onscreen. 'It's quite a record but the last offence was aggravated burglary, twenty-one years ago. Custodial sentence, ten years, served six and was released on licence.'

That sounded like the same Doyle. So, he'd been out for fifteen years and yet Horton hadn't come across him in the course of his job. Had Doyle gone straight after that last conviction? Unlikely. Had he met with an accident, died a natural death or a drug or alcohol induced one? Whatever had happened, at some stage he had been in those handcuffs. That indicated he might have been under arrest, possibly for the theft of the box, but why would the cuffs have been fastened to the box? Had Doyle got himself into something deep with villains much bigger than him? Was Dr Needham's idea right? That someone had pretended the box contained an explosive device to terrify Doyle into revealing where he'd stashed some stolen goods? Quickly, he brought his whirling thoughts back down to earth as Pooley was speaking.

'There are two further sets of prints. One on the box handles, which also matches a much fainter print on the handcuffs.'

Doyle's partner in crime perhaps? Or the person who was threatening him?

'And another on the padlock and under the handles, but not on the cuffs. There are no matches on the database.'

'What's Doyle's address on file?'

Pooley relayed it. Horton jotted it down — although he didn't need to, he'd remember it. He doubted if Doyle was still living there. After heartily thanking Pooley, Horton made for the address. He wasn't sure how he felt about meeting up with Doyle after all these years. He doubted Doyle would even remember him.

The run-down Edwardian house had been divided into bedsits. There was a tatty piece of paper stuck under the bell indicating which flat belonged to whom. Doyle's name wasn't on it. He hadn't expected it to be.

He tried three of them before he got an answer. A bleary-eyed girl opened the front door to him.

'Who are you?' she sniffed, eyeing him warily.

'I'm looking for Jamie Doyle.'

'Who's he?'

'Does he live here?'

'No idea. I don't know who lives here.' She rubbed a hand across her nose.

'But you do.'

'Yeah. What's it to you?'

'His name isn't on the paper.' He indicated the one on the door.

'That don't mean nothing. Mine's not on there neither.'

'And you are?'

'None of your bleeding business.' She slammed the door on him.

He jotted down the names but, as he returned to the station, he knew the landlord and tenants would have changed many times since Doyle's days living there. They would be able to get Doyle's most recent address from His Majesty's Revenue and Customs, or the Department for Work and Pensions if he was on benefit. They might even be able to get it from the electoral roll.

His mind went back to what Joliffe had told him and Cantelli on Wednesday, that he'd managed to get DNA from some fatty deposits inside the rim of the handcuff that wasn't attached to the deed box. That must be Doyle's. Had Walters checked it by now? He was keen to find out, but before he could ask, Walters, looking up from his computer, said, 'There's been a development on the murder investigation. Don't ask me what it is because I haven't been told, but they're all running round like excited puppies.'

'Which is more than you'll ever do.' Horton wondered if they'd got a match on the DNA from the blood found in the car. Was it Ashford? But again, Walters forestalled his question.

'I have got something though,' Walters smirked. 'A match on the DNA on those handcuffs.'

'I'll bet you a coffee and doughnut it's Jamie Doyle.'

'How did you know?' Walters's face fell.

'Dr Pooley got a fingerprint. I even went to see if Doyle was living in the same place at the time of his last conviction.'

'He won't be.' Now Walters was looking smug. 'And I bet you a coffee and two doughnuts you won't guess where he is.'

'Ah, in prison. No, that would have been on his record. He's dead. You found his death registered?'

'Wrong on both counts. I'll look forward to my doughnuts. He's on the missing persons database. Jamie Doyle went missing fifteen years ago.'

CHAPTER THIRTEEN

'Doyle's probation officer reported him missing after he failed to attend his second appointment on the ninth of October,' Walters said. 'He didn't contact us after the first missed meeting two weeks before that on Monday the twenty-fifth of September — pressure of work, stress, blah, blah, blah. He was overworked and underpaid.'

'He said that?'

'No. It's probably what he thought though.'

'And it would be true.'

'Yeah, join the club. He was probably pleased not to have to listen to another toerag spinning his lies. Anyway, Doyle had a job interview as a labourer with a local building company on the twenty-second of September. He'd been taken on but didn't show for work on the following Monday.'

'The same day he had the appointment with the probation officer.'

'Yes.'

'And the probation officer didn't know about this job or Doyle starting work?'

'He said not. Maybe it was a temporary job. And on second thoughts, Doyle thought it was going to be too much like hard work.'

'And by then he'd disappeared, which puts it sometime on Friday night or over the weekend of the twenty-third and twenty-fourth of September.'

'He was around on the Saturday, one of the tenants said they saw him, or thought they did. They heard him moving about and he had his music on loud, as usual. One also saw him go out early evening. Nothing after that. Enquiries were made among his known contacts, not many from what I've read, and not reliable. No one claimed to have seen him, but that sort wouldn't talk to us anyway.'

'Right, so you look for robberies reported around that weekend. Or to be on the safe side, any time between the twenty-second of September and the ninth of October.'

'What good will that do?'

'Doyle was a known criminal. His fingerprints and DNA are on those handcuffs and the contents are valuable. He could have been involved in a robbery that went wrong and somehow managed to get out of those cuffs or was released from them and scarpered.'

'I can't see why he should have been cuffed to the box in the first place.'

'Nor can I, unless, having got out of a set of handcuffs, he or someone else, an accomplice, snapped them on the box. They couldn't get the box open and had other stolen valuables they could easily dispose of, so they ditched the box in water.'

'Must have been a member of the angling club to have got into the grounds.'

'Not necessarily, the fence on the northern perimeter is often breached, according to Preston, and from what I saw with Cantelli it looked easy enough to cut. The lake can also be reached by a footpath along the side of the golf club car park.'

Walters reached for a packet of biscuits in his drawer. 'That means the robbery took place on Hayling Island. They wouldn't have been there otherwise, not unless there was a police chase and they were forced in that direction. It also means that there was a scuffle, or force was used on an officer, and that would have been reported.'

'Plenty for you to get your teeth into.'

Walters made to put a custard cream in his mouth. 'I suppose it's occurred to you that a police officer could have been corrupted or persuaded to release Doyle.'

'Yes, and it's also occurred to me that Doyle's hand could have been severed.'

'Didn't I say right at the beginning that it was like that previous investigation with that hand those fishermen found,' Walters triumphantly declared.

'You did. Don't I get a biscuit?'

Walters handed over the packet and Horton took one. 'But I don't think Doyle, or that box, have been in that lake for fifteen years. In fact, I don't think it was there until recently. It was somewhere where there was plenty of algae.'

'Why move it? When? And who?' Walters said with his mouth full.

'I wish I knew. There's a possibility it could have been Ashford's doing. He could have been Doyle's accomplice. He has a criminal record. He allegedly found the box, but no one saw him do so.'

'You mean he was trying to get rid of it? But why would he call the police?'

'Because Bosman insisted he did. He had no choice. Preston said he didn't know why Ashford was at the stock pond anyway. Now Ashford's running scared. He's had two days — three if you count when the box was found — to get away.'

'Why didn't they flog those coins?'

Horton reached for another biscuit. 'Too easily traced? Too scared? Perhaps they fell out or perhaps they didn't think they were very valuable. There might have been another reticule in—'

'A what?'

Horton told him what Dr Adams had said, adding, 'A third reticule could have contained precious stones or jewellery, which they did help themselves to, thinking the coins were worthless or not worth bothering with.'

'They'd hardly relock the box after stealing from it.'

'Who knows, maybe they did and tossed away the key? Or Ashford kept it all these years, only didn't get the chance to open the box before being discovered with it. Has anyone enquired about Doyle since his disappearance?'

'Nothing noted on the file. Maybe we should ask DS Ames if the Serious Case Review Team are interested in following it up.' Walters gave Horton a sly look, which he ignored.

'When was it last reviewed?'

'Dunno.'

'Start searching for those robberies or for anything suspicious that happened fifteen years ago.'

Horton entered his office, postponing his visit to the incident suite, and called up the missing person file. Doyle's hadn't been reviewed for ten years. He knew a lot about Doyle as a boy but not as a man, save what the file said about him. Horton wasn't sure if Doyle's probation officer would remember much about him, if he was still around. Doyle's prison files would also tell Horton more, but he wasn't interested in the man's character, he already knew that, he wanted to know who his associates were. And if one of them had been Peter Ashford.

He pulled up Doyle's criminal record. It was as Pooley had said, quite a record — theft, assault, receiving stolen goods, possession of Class A drugs, and his last offence, aggravated burglary. The name on file brought a smile to Horton's face. The arresting officer had been a young DC, Dave Trueman, now sergeant, and with an encyclopaedic memory that was even better than Cantelli's. He would tap into it later.

His phone rang. It was Judith Brindley. 'I'm sorry to bother you, Inspector, when you must be so very busy, but I've got the details of a couple more coin dealers you might like to contact. Only, I wasn't sure if you'd discovered who owned them.'

'Not yet we haven't. If you'd like to send over those contact details, we'd be very glad to have them.' He didn't tell her they hadn't contacted anyone yet and probably wouldn't. He didn't think it worth following up the coin dealers and auction houses because the coins hadn't been sold, and he doubted the dealers would remember who had bought them in the first place. Those coins in their Victorian reticules could have been in the same family for years.

'I will. Can you tell me where and how the coins were found?'

He'd mentioned at their first meeting about the pouches and the old tin box but not the handcuffs or that fact it had been found in Sinah Lake. Before he could answer she continued a little breathlessly.

'I only ask because I've been doing some sleuthing, online mainly, and among certain colleagues generally.' She quickly added, 'We haven't breathed a word about them being discovered and the police involvement. I've been looking into dealers who bought or sold coins from the same period as those, thinking they might also have had the ones on your list or someone might have made enquiries about them.'

'And have you found anything relevant?'

'No. The two coin dealers I'm going to email to you handled the sale of coins from Charles II's period, but that's not unusual.'

She sounded nervous, as though he might dismiss her or be angry with her. 'I appreciate your help, Mrs Brindley, but I can't tell you more than I have done already at the present.'

'Of course, I shouldn't have asked,' she replied, flummoxed.

'If we can't trace the owner then the box and coins will be handed back to the finder and we can pass your details on to that person, if appropriate.'

'But weren't there fingerprints?'

'There were.'

'From the people who found it, I expect.'

'Yes.' He saw no reason to be more specific.

'I . . . I'll send over those details.' She rang off abruptly. He got the impression he'd upset her in some way. He wondered what she'd been about to say and why she'd changed her mind.

He rose and made his way to the incident suite, wondering if he'd been too short with her. He didn't think his tone had been brusque. Perhaps it was because he wouldn't divulge more, and having steeled herself to ask him, she'd been embarrassed when he'd refused. Perhaps her husband had primed her to pump him for information and she was afraid of reporting a negative result to him. Gareth Brindley hadn't struck him as being domineering, but then what did he know? He might have been one of the less obvious type of bullies, the insidious type. Judith had struck him as being a quiet, slightly timid, gentle woman.

He put them, the coins and Doyle out of his mind as he stepped into the incident suite. The buzz of a breakthrough was obvious in the heightened activity and extra staff. Before he could ask Trueman what had occurred, or look at the crime board, Uckfield charged out of his office, pushing his short arms through the sleeves of his suit jacket.

'You're just in time.'

'For what?' Horton threw Trueman a backward glance as he fell into step beside the Super.

'A visit to the victim's address. Maitland finally pieced together the vehicle identification number and we've got a match on the DNA from the blood found in the car. It's Desmond Wenham, aged forty-one, charged for assault on his common-law wife, Claire Budleigh, five years ago.'

'No wonder he's not been reported missing; she's probably hanging out the flags. Unless she did it?'

'Might have done, but she's not living with him. Moved three years ago. Bliss and Chawla are breaking the news to her and getting what they can on him. He could have been pestering her to get back together and they arranged to meet up.'

'But why would they go to that particular shore?'

'Could have been where they first met, or first did it. She hit him, bundled his body in the back and set fire to the car.' Uckfield zapped open his car.

'She'd come prepared then with rags soaked in petrol,' said Horton cynically.

'She could have planned it. Those charges were dropped, but she's not the only one he used as a punch bag. He's got a conviction for an assault on another woman eight years ago. That's why his DNA is on record. He could have a new girlfriend who'd had enough.'

'Fire is not usually a female method of murder,' Horton said, stretching the seatbelt across him.

'No, but it has been done before. He worked for Kettering, at the port. Dennings and Seaton are there.'

Horton knew of them. He'd seen the name on work-boats, crane barges and dredgers around the harbour. 'His bosses didn't report him missing,' he said, thinking that Camplow hadn't reported Ashford's absence.

'Perhaps he's meant to be on holiday, or they thought he'd been off sick. Maybe he's a bully at work as well as in his private life, and they're glad to see the back of him. Still, that's no reason to kill the bugger.'

'No. Where does Wenham live?'

Uckfield indicated on to the motorway out of the city. 'Silas Close, north of Fareham. Just off the Wickham Road.'

Horton didn't know the close, but he knew the main road and did a quick calculation. It would be about seven miles from there south to Forton Lake.

'I told Trueman to get a unit to meet me there in twenty minutes.'

'Looks as though that was optimistic.' They slowed to a crawl on the motorway, where the overhead lights were flashing a warning of a collision further down the route.

'I've a good mind to put the blue light on. I hear the blonde bombshell is on the force.' Uckfield dashed him a crafty glance. Horton knew who he meant. Uckfield had called Harriet by that name before when she'd assisted them on a couple of cases. She'd laughed and said she'd been called a lot worse. Did Uckfield know that Harriet had been with him at the crime scene on Tuesday night? Perhaps Taylor or Tremaine had let it slip. No, Bliss had probably told Uckfield of Harriet's arrival at the station.

'Don't let the diversity and gender-neutral policy group hear you say that,' Horton replied.

'Why not? It's a compliment,' Uckfield grumbled. 'It's got so you can hardly open your mouth before someone leaps down your throat and accuses you of all sorts of things and calls you words you've never heard before, and I thought I'd heard just about all of them on the Pompey streets. You'll be pleased if Ames gets assigned to your team, or to me?' He again threw Horton that devious sidelong glance. 'Or perhaps not. Dr Clayton might get jealous.'

What was it with everyone thinking he and Harriet might be an item? They'd never given any hint of it. Nor had he and Gaye broadcast their relationship. The rumour factory seemed to be on overdrive. Horton didn't rise to the bait.

'DS Ames will be an asset to whichever team she's assigned,' Horton answered neutrally, steeling himself not to show Uckfield any emotion.

'Shame about her old man doing a Lord Lucan like that. You think he's still alive?'

'I have no idea.' He wanted to add *and what's more I don't care*, but Uckfield would see through that. The Super didn't know the story behind the Ames family and how he was involved with them, and Horton wasn't about to tell him. Fortunately, the sat nav intervened, telling Uckfield to turn left.

CHAPTER FOURTEEN

There was no answer to Uckfield's stout thudding on the door of the modern brick building in the quiet cul-de-sac.

'Break it open,' he commanded, stepping back. One of the two uniformed officers who had greeted them shoved the ramrod against the panelled door. It gave way without protest, slamming against the inside. 'Talk to the neighbours, if you can find any,' Uckfield instructed.

The select new development was eerily quiet. There was no car parked underneath the property, which was named 'The Coach House', and just silence and heat as they climbed the carpeted stairs to the living accommodation on the first and only floor. There was the lingering smell of aftershave in the lobby. Six doors gave off it, two of which were closed.

'Airing cupboard,' Horton said, opening one. There were sheets and towels stacked on the shelves and two cotton shirts on coat hangers hanging from them. He opened the second door. 'Cloakroom.' On the floor, along with four pairs of shoes, were a pair of heavy walking boots and golf shoes. There was also an ironing board and vacuum cleaner.

'I'll take the bedrooms and bathroom. You do the lounge and kitchen,' Uckfield directed.

Horton stepped into the spacious white lounge with a modern L-shaped sofa, a light-oak coffee table, standard chain store pictures and a widescreen TV on the wall. He crossed to the Juliette balcony and pulled back the slatted blinds. Below he could see one of the officers talking to an elderly man who was wearing shorts, sandals and a cotton shirt. He was tempted to throw open the patio doors to let in some air but resisted. It would barely make any difference to the heat anyway.

He turned and surveyed the room, trying to get a feel for the dead man. It was hard to contemplate that those chalk-white bones had once moved, breathed and sat here. It was best not to think of that. Instead, he thought of first impressions: Wenham had been a neat, clean man, who was not fussed about comfort, as there were no cushions or fancy frills in the room. There were no curtains at the window, just the blinds. Nothing personal in the way of photographs, books, magazines, or anything to indicate Wenham had enjoyed feminine company. But had he? He had a history of violence against women. Did that mean he hated them? It certainly meant he wanted to dominate and bully them. Did he do the same with men who he thought inferior to him? Had one of those men, or a woman, been driven so far as to kill him? This place said 'control' to Horton, but so far as he could see there was nothing to indicate any kind of sexual or sadomasochistic tendencies. That made him think of handcuffs and in turn Ashford. As he moved into the small kitchen off the lounge he wondered what Ashford's flat would say about him.

The neat pattern was repeated here, with everything put away in drawers and only the kettle and toaster on display. All was clean — Wenham's doing or a cleaning lady, he wondered. As he searched the drawers he could hear Uckfield opening and shutting cupboards in the bedroom and grunting. Horton, growing hotter by the minute, couldn't find anything revealing, and nothing to tell them who Wenham's friends and relatives might be. The telltale scraps of paper, address books, diaries, bills and notebooks that once used to be common in his early days of policing, which had often told him a great deal about the resident and provided contacts, had become extinct in some households. This was obviously one of those.

Uckfield would gain access to Wenham's bank accounts and mobile phone and Trueman might get something from Wenham's social media profile, if he had one — few people didn't, Horton being one of them. The less people knew about him the better, he thought, wondering if he would find anything on Peter Ashford on the internet. There probably wouldn't be much, if anything, on Doyle, him having disappeared fifteen years ago.

He joined Uckfield in what was clearly the spare bedroom, with a single unmade bed, an exercise bike, some weights and a set of golf clubs.

'Nothing of any note in his bedroom or here. No women's clothes, no photographs. Some expensive suits in his wardrobe. Seems golf and keeping fit were his hobbies.'

'Might not have used the equipment.'

'I'll take a look in the bathroom.'

Horton removed the clubs one by one. They looked to be expensive and brand new, as did the bag. Carefully, with his latex-covered fingers, he went through the pockets in the bag and found a bundle of score cards. They were from Cams Hall Golf Club, where Horton suspected Wenham had been a member. It was the closest to here, and situated at the very top of Portsmouth Harbour, overlooking the boats moored at Fareham Quay.

'Just the usual stuff in the bathroom — shaving gear, packet of condoms.'

Horton raised his eyebrows.

'In case he got lucky, I guess. Over-the-counter medicines. Nothing on prescription that could give us the name of his GP. What have you got there?'

'His golf score cards. I don't know how long he's played but he's not very good.'

125

'There's nothing here to throw any light on his murder unless someone didn't like his handicap.'

Horton gave a brief smile at the black humour.

'Call SOCO,' Uckfield instructed. 'I know it's not a crime scene but they can lift prints and collect hairs. We might find he had a visitor or visitors before he was killed, which could give us more on him and a motive. I'd like to know why, if he did have any callers, they haven't come forward when they heard or read DCI Bliss's appeal.'

'Because they were afraid of him?' suggested Horton. 'Or glad he's no longer around.' Horton called Taylor while Uckfield talked to one of the constables.

'Want me to stay until Taylor arrives?' Horton asked, ringing off.

'No, PC Frogmore will do that. He says the neighbours are either lacking in curiosity or have good enough manners not to come out and gawp. There's hardly a soul about. Probably all gone to the beach to get some relief from this blasted heat,' Uckfield moaned.

'Or at work,' Horton suggested.

'On Friday afternoon?'

'We are.'

'Yeah, well.' Uckfield, seeing the other officer emerge from a modest block of flats in the far corner, waved him over.

'As far as I can ascertain, sir, he was last seen on Monday morning going to work — that is, he went out in his car. I've spoken to two people — there's hardly anyone in — and both say they don't know him save to nod to and say "hello" on the occasions their paths crossed. They've seen a couple of cars outside now and again, but nothing special — people delivering, they suspect. No noisy parties, and they've never seen him clean his car. One of the neighbours says he moved in two years ago, at about the same time as she did.'

'Carry on knocking on doors, there might be more people coming home.' Uckfield addressed the other constable. 'Call the locksmith, get him to fix a stout temporary lock, no need to seal off the door. Wait for SOCO to finish, and when you've exhausted all enquires report back to me.' To Horton he said, 'We'll get officers back here tonight for those we miss questioning this afternoon.'

They headed back to the station, where Horton updated Walters on Uckfield's investigation.

Walters said he had finished looking up robberies around the time Doyle had disappeared. 'Only two, guv, both solved, and Doyle wasn't involved.'

So, dead end there. Perhaps Trueman might help with Doyle's contacts.

'The press have been on about those human remains,' Walters said. 'Want me to put out a statement and contact details asking for anyone with any information to come forward?'

'Yes, but keep it low key, in that we're not treating it as suspicious. Not until we have evidence to confirm it.'

'I'll do it now, then I'll get off home. I don't want to get pulled into the Super's investigation,' he said. 'Going to London for the weekend to meet Penny's folks.'

'Do I need to start a collection for a wedding present?' Horton teased, remembering when he had been introduced to Catherine's parents, who had been all smiles and enthusiasm, viewing him as a policeman on the rise. And he had been then. It had taken that false allegation and stalled promotion to change that.

'You never know.'

He was about to call Charlotte when she rang him to say that Barney was doing well and she hoped he could be discharged tomorrow.

'That's great news. I'm intending to get up to the hospital this evening, although Uckfield might have other ideas. We've got an ID on the man in the car. If I can't make it tonight I'll call in tomorrow morning.'

'He'll be pleased to see you, but only if you have time.'

'I'll make time.'

He searched the internet for Peter Ashford. He didn't find anyone matching his profile but there were two pictures of him on the angling club's website. Ashford was slender, very fair and with an amiable face. In one picture he was working as a volunteer on cleaning the site, in another holding a very large fish. Horton could see a tattoo on the knuckles of his right hand. He pulled up his criminal record. It was clearly the same man, only the photographs they had were of a younger Ashford with slightly longer hair, and his light-blue eyes looked wider and more fearful. Horton didn't have the court transcript, but he read how Ashford had been involved in juvenile crime, theft and vandalism, and had progressed to burglary. The last charge had been sixteen years ago when he was eighteen. He'd been lucky not to get a custodial sentence, and perhaps that had been a good thing, because it seemed he'd kept his nose clean since then. Unless he had done one last job with Doyle which had gone so badly wrong that he'd abandoned a life of crime. It was interesting that Ashford's address at that time had been just around the corner from Doyle. Doyle had been six years older than Ashford, aged twenty-five, when he had disappeared.

Horton shut down his computer and was about to leave for the hospital when Bliss summoned him to the incident suite. He would have to postpone his visit to Cantelli, which was a shame. Nothing, though, would have stopped him if Barney had still been ill. He should have taken a leaf out of Walters's book and sidled off while he'd had the chance. But then he was very curious about Wenham.

On the crime board were two photographs of the man. One a head-and-shoulders shot, the other of him posing in a golf swing. He was dark-haired, on the stout side, flabby rather than muscular, with small brown eyes, a round fleshy face and a wide mouth with thin lips that had a smirk about them.

As Horton drank some water, he wondered how the killer would react when they showed him the photographs of all that had been left of the man he'd murdered. Would he blench and throw up? Or be dismissive, unconcerned? Or perhaps he or she would try to justify what they had done.

Beside the pictures was Wenham's date of birth and height. He had been forty-three and five feet eleven inches tall.

Trueman joined him. 'I've just got this one.' He pinned up another photograph. It was of Wenham standing by his Audi Q7, looking very self-important. 'Strange thing is I know the name but not the face. As soon we got his ID I remembered hearing the name years back, but it wasn't a domestic abuse case.'

'Might not have been a case at all. Perhaps he reported a crime. It'll come to you, Dave. It always does. I'd like to ask you about . . .' But he didn't get any further with his question about him arresting Doyle, as pizzas had arrived and Uckfield called them all to order. They took up seats around the desk next to Trueman's, where the food was laid out. Tucking into a slice first, Uckfield nodded at Trueman to begin.

CHAPTER FIFTEEN

'Desmond Wenham is registered on two online dating websites and three social media apps. The latter I've only got the basic details from as we don't have his login details. The online dating sites give more information about him, and those three photographs are from his profile.'

That explained that, thought Horton.

'He describes himself as single, without dependants, a successful businessman working at managerial level in the marine industry, looking for a female who appreciates good food and wine, as he does, and who enjoys foreign travel. He's a keen golfer with a sense of humour, has his own property and is very comfortably off.'

Bliss snorted. 'No mention there of his violent temper.'

'Not the sort of thing to put on your CV,' Uckfield said with his mouth full. 'Go on, Bliss.'

'He and Cheryl Budleigh met eight years ago. He was charming, well-off and considerate. She was escaping from a previous violent relationship and thought she'd found the right man. Everything went well until he moved in with her.'

'Doesn't it always?' muttered Uckfield.

Horton had heard this story so many times that he could predict what Bliss was going to say, so too could they all.

'At first, he apologized profusely for losing his temper, shouting at her and slapping her, saying he had never done it before, et cetera, et cetera. He was under pressure at work . . . he wasn't feeling well . . . all the usual excuses. She forgave him. Then it happened again, same old story, again he was sorry. His violent tempers became more frequent and worse. He broke her wrist. At the hospital she said she'd had a fall. She told her friends the same. She had no family. When he pushed her down the stairs and she fell unconscious, he called the ambulance. But when medically examined she had old bruises that were not consistent with her injury. Finally, she admitted what he had done and that she was terrified of him. She didn't wish to see him anymore.' Bliss paused to drink. 'The hospital and social worker managed to keep him away and got her into a refuge. Thankfully there were no children. She brought charges against him, as we know, but dropped them, saying she couldn't face going to court and seeing him there. She changed her phone and her computer passwords. She deleted her social media profiles. She had her own bank account and had never had access to his. She got a new job and prayed she'd never see him again. She was fortunate to have good friends.'

'And I don't imagine she was cut up when you told her he was dead,' Uckfield said, wiping tomato from his mouth with a large striped handkerchief.

'She said he had it coming to him. She didn't say it in a vengeful way, or gleefully, or even sorrowfully, just matter-of-factly. When I asked her what she meant, she said that she wasn't the only one he bullied and threatened. He used to take delight in tormenting people. If he got something on them, some kind of weakness or secret, he'd use it to get what he wanted — promotion, money, prestige.'

Sounded a bit like Jamie Doyle, thought Horton.

Uckfield said, 'One of his victims, then, could have a motive. Did she give any names?'

Bliss shook her head. 'I pressed her on that, but she never knew who they were, she said he'd just gloat and smirk.

He'd make the occasional comment such as, "Now I'll see him squirm," and, "That will teach him a lesson he won't forget in a hurry." Cheryl learned the hard way not to ask.'

'Always a "he"?' asked Horton.

Bliss blinked. Obviously, she hadn't probed that deep.

She directed her gaze at Uckfield. 'Cheryl told us Wenham's parents were dead and he'd been an only child.'

She'd avoided answering and changed the subject. He'd come back to that in a moment. 'Wenham could have lied about that.'

Trueman said, 'His parents are dead. I checked with the Register of Births, Deaths and Marriages, and I couldn't find any siblings.'

Bliss looked triumphant at being right. 'She thought there were a couple of aunts and uncles around somewhere in the UK but has no idea where.'

Dennings piped up. 'Kettering only have Cheryl Budleigh named on Wenham's employment record as his next of kin.'

That indicated he hadn't bothered to update it when they split up. Horton addressed Bliss. 'We discovered golf clubs in his apartment. Did he play golf when they were living together?'

Chawla answered. 'She didn't say, and we didn't ask, not knowing about the golf clubs.' She threw a slightly nervous glance at Bliss before quickly continuing, 'He used to go out in the Solent with a couple of friends on a boat — not his own. As far as she's aware he didn't have one. She doesn't know who they were. He'd tell her nothing about his friends or his job. It was as though she was merely there to serve him and do what he said or wanted. Sometimes he could be quite loving, then he would change in the blink of an eye and be cruel and violent, and she never knew what she had said or done to anger him. He drank, but not excessively, and he was violent without the drink.'

Horton thought the poor woman had lived a life of hell. Had any others suffered the same torment at the hands of that smiling, confident man in the picture? Perhaps some of his dating partners had discovered it and got out quick. He hoped so.

Dennings, polishing off his pizza, said, 'Daniel Kettering didn't seem to be sorry he's gone either. Wenham was their contract manager. He'd been with them for eighteen years, started by working on the dredgers as a deckhand and worked his way up from there.'

'And probably the dirty way, from what we've learned,' said Uckfield.

'His job was to provide quotes for the hire of dredgers, work boats, barge cranes and other marine-related equipment the company hire out.'

Horton said, 'So he worked around the harbour.'

'Yes, this one and others, including Chichester, Langstone and further afield. He'd sometimes be away overnight or for a couple of days at a time.'

'When was he last at work?' asked Horton.

'Tuesday. Kettering says there was nothing different about his manner that day or before it, but he admitted he hardly saw him. One of the other members of staff might say different, but we haven't questioned them yet. They knock off at midday on Friday.'

'Go back on Monday and ask them,' Uckfield ordered.

'Wasn't Kettering concerned when Wenham didn't show for work on Wednesday morning?' asked Horton.

'He was out all day. Only discovered Wenham hadn't come into work when he returned to the office on Thursday. He didn't think much of it. He thought Wenham might be taking a couple of days off sick. There were no appointments in his diary, which is kept on his work computer, and which he has access to on his phone. One of the other members of staff could have tried contacting Wenham, I'll check on Monday. I've asked that his work computer be left untouched and said we'd send someone round to pick it up. That worried Kettering more than Wenham's death. His work email might give us something. And I told Kettering that we might need access to his office over the weekend. He said to call him any time.' Dennings wiped his mouth with the back of his hand. 'I think he's relieved not to have Wenham around. He admitted that Wenham was short-tempered, and the men hated working with him. There was nothing they could discipline him for though. There were a couple of complaints about him, but Wenham always managed to sidle out of it. "Oily" was how Kettering described him. I got Wenham's mobile number.'

Trueman said, 'I'll apply for his records. I've contacted the dating websites to ask for access to their information, waiting for replies. We'll also ask for access to his social media profiles.'

'Does Kettering employ any women?' asked Horton.

'Only one, the office manager, Amanda Rayland.'

'It will be interesting to hear what she thought of him,' said Horton. 'Has he ever bullied her or tried it on?'

'I wouldn't have thought she'd have stood for it if he had,' Dennings answered curtly.

'Kettering must have employed other women at some time, maybe Wenham tried it on with them.'

'Daniel Kettering never said,' Dennings replied sulkily.

No, and you didn't ask. 'Probably because he smoothed things over, or any woman who suffered at the hands of Wenham left and didn't wish to cause a fuss or draw attention to herself by complaining,' Horton ventured. 'The same could be said for someone he dated. If Wenham was as vengeful and vindictive as Cheryl says, then perhaps a woman told him where to get off and he didn't care for it. He got his own back on her somehow, threatened to tell her partner or husband. Maybe a woman from one of the dating websites rejected him or laughed at him. He stalked her, threatened to ruin her reputation by scuppering a new job or jeopardizing her position. She could be a professional woman — solicitor, doctor, dentist, or someone in a top position in a major company or government organization. This woman could have got her revenge. He'd pushed her so far that she killed him.' Horton paused and took a swig of his Coke. 'But I still can't see a woman setting light to his car with him in it. If she did, she must have been pushed a hell of a long way.'

His eyes flicked up to the grotesque remains. Whoever had done that hadn't stayed around long enough to see the results. He or she had taken off once the fire had started. Could a woman have arrived and left by boat? No reason why not — plenty of women sailed, rowed and paddled. Would one have enough strength to strike an oar or paddle on the back of Wenham's head to render him unconscious or kill him? Yes, was the answer.

Alternatively, a woman could have arrived with Wenham in his car. Could a woman have manoeuvred the body into the back of the car? He doubted that. It was difficult enough to move a dead body even if you were Dennings's size and had his strength. But perhaps Wenham and this woman were already on the back seat for another purpose, and it didn't take much imagination to determine what that might have been. She got out on some pretext — she needed a pee, say. She retrieved something — a small oar or paddle from a boat or something similar, a cricket bat — that she'd hidden by the industrial unit and returned to the car. Perhaps she'd told him she'd lost something in their hasty lovemaking — an earring. He'd leaned down to look for it and *wham*!

Horton voiced his theory. Uckfield's eyes narrowed as he did so, Dennings looked doubtful, while Bliss regarded him as though he'd completely lost the plot. 'But it is possible,' he insisted.

Uckfield sat back. 'OK, we keep all the women who knew Wenham in mind for it. Dennings, talk to this Amanda Rayland and see if she's a likely suspect. Find out if any other women worked there recently — when, why they left, and get their details.' He addressed Trueman. 'Do the same with the dating websites.'

'It might have been someone he met at the golf club,' Horton added.

'Seaton, get over to Cams Hall tomorrow, talk to the secretary, the professional and anyone else you can find. Who did Wenham play golf with? Did he have any regular partners? Did he play any rounds with ladies? What was he like? When was he last there?'

Seaton looked as though he'd like to go that instant.

Trueman said, 'SOCO have lifted hairs and prints from the flat. The prints match Wenham's, no others. Whoever he dated he didn't take back there, and he did his own cleaning, unless he has the most efficient cleaner in the world. Nothing more from the officers doing a house-to-house there. And no reports from the mobile incident suite.'

Chawla interjected. 'Nothing from our house-to-house either. The local officers are continuing with that now that we have a name and photograph.'

Trueman again. 'It's been issued to all officers and the mobile incident unit.'

Finishing his pizza, Horton said, 'What about Jason Downs? Have we found any witnesses to say he was sitting on his boat at the critical time?'

'Not so far,' Dennings answered.

'Might be worth going back there over the weekend when more boat owners will be down.'

Uckfield agreed. 'I'll get some officers from Gosport to assist.'

'Do we know what Downs and his wife argued about?' Horton asked. 'Just wondering if Mrs Downs was having an affair with Wenham and Jason thought he'd get even. Or Mrs Downs set out to destroy her lover, the man who was threatening or tormenting her. What's her alibi for the time of the murder?'

'Chawla, talk to her.'

'And find out where she works,' Horton added to Uckfield's instruction. 'And Jason Downs, for that matter. Wenham's killer could be a customer, either male or female.'

'Jason Downs is a surveyor,' Dennings said.

'Of boats?' posed Horton.

'I assumed a building surveyor.'

'Assuming is no good to us,' Uckfield said. 'Find out. And Dennings, get a list of Kettering's customers tomorrow and bring back his computer. DCI Bliss, you and I will draft a statement for the media and tomorrow you can release his name. That might bring out those who knew him.' Uckfield rose.

Horton said, 'What about his car? Did he buy it from the local Audi dealers? It could be worth talking to them. He might have mentioned a woman, or taken one with him to impress her when buying it. Or he could have boasted or confided something to the salesman.'

Bliss piped up. 'Or woman.'

Horton had yet to meet a car showroom saleswoman, but admittedly he hadn't much to do with buying cars. It had been a long time since he'd owned one.

Bliss continued, 'DI Horton is duty CID this weekend in place of Sergeant Cantelli. He can interview the car dealers.'

Horton wouldn't have put it past her to enlist Cantelli's help from his hospital bed if someone at the hospital admitted to knowing Wenham. He was glad to do so, although he'd have much preferred to have talked to Jason Downs or his wife. He hadn't finished yet. 'Has anyone told Sergeant Elkins about Wenham?' Going by their looks the answer was no. 'I'll tell him. He and Ripley probably know a lot of Kettering's employees and they might even know Desmond Wenham.'

'OK, you do that. Anything more on those human remains?'

'Not unless someone comes forward. Walters has put out a notice to the press and on the website. We need to wait until Monday when we have more from Dr Clayton and Dr Lauder.'

Uckfield looked relieved. Horton didn't mention his investigation into the coins, or that Ashford's prints had been on the box and Doyle's on the handcuffs. Or that both had gone missing, one fifteen years ago and the other in the last four days. The thought sparked an idea, which he kept in the back of his mind. He considered it as he made his way back to his boat. Had they both been involved in a robbery with a third party fifteen years ago? The third party had been caught with stolen goods and had gone to prison for it. Now released, he had come for the rest of the loot. Ashford had been hiding it. And now this third party had gone after Ashford and killed him when he learned he couldn't get the goods.

Several things made that unlikely. Walters had said there had been no reported thefts. Would someone have got fifteen years for robbery? Possibly, if it had entailed violence, but then it would be on record. Perhaps it wasn't solely robbery that Walters should have looked up, but convictions for manslaughter or murder, or violent assault. Because although they'd only found coins in the box, there could have been more valuable goods inside it at one point, as he'd earlier conjectured, which one of the others had taken. Not Ashford if he was living in a council flat, not unless he'd spent all the money. Doyle could have taken it, and when he wouldn't say where he'd put it, the third party could have killed him and dumped his body, probably in the sea. Unless . . . No, he was joining up the dots to fit his theory. There was nothing at all to say the human remains found at Southmoor were Doyle's. They could have been there twenty, thirty, forty years or just five. Still, it was a theory nonetheless, as was his speculation on a woman having attacked and killed Wenham. He'd visit them fresh in the morning, talk to the Audi sales staff and also to Dave Trueman, to see what he could remember about Jamie Doyle.

CHAPTER SIXTEEN

Saturday

Trueman was tucking into his breakfast. 'I'm stocking up for the day in case I don't have time to eat again.'

'Same here.' Horton took the seat opposite in the canteen and cut into his bacon. 'Cast your mind back, Dave, to when you were a young PC traipsing the mean streets of this fair city, asking the public if you could show them the way, directing traffic and helping old ladies cross the road.'

'I'm not that old, I just look it. And feel it.' He mopped up his egg with a piece of toast.

'Jamie Doyle mean anything to you?' Horton could see Trueman's mind working.

After a moment he said, 'Cocky, good-looking, charming, thought he was funny and probably was to his mates, who didn't have many brain cells between them.'

'Who needs artificial intelligence with you around? The description fits the boy I was at school with.'

'Didn't know *you* were that old.'

'I've aged well. He was three years ahead of me and a bully.'

'Like Wenham. Seems a lot of it about, sadly. I wish I could remember what it is about Desmond Wenham that's bugging me. I thought it might come to me overnight, but nothing did. Except a nightmare about Uckfield.'

Horton smiled. He had slept well.

'Not such a genius memory after all.'

'We're all fallible, Dave. Yes, even you. It'll come to you. Go on about Doyle.'

'Not much more to tell.'

'He disappeared fifteen years ago.'

'So I seem to remember. The thinking was that he took off with a woman, but no one knew who she was.'

'His prints were on the inside of a pair of handcuffs attached to an antique tin box containing valuable coins found in Sinah Lake.'

'Interesting.' Trueman's brow knitted.

Horton stabbed a sausage and took a bite. 'What's also interesting,' he continued, swallowing part of it, 'is that the man who found the box last Tuesday, Peter Ashford, is missing, and he's got a criminal record, like Doyle, albeit a long time ago.'

'Ashford doesn't ring any bells. Maybe I am losing my touch,' Trueman said mournfully.

'You were probably engaged elsewhere when he got nicked. The owner of the coins can't be traced and I'm not sure we'll ever establish who that is, so it will be a nice little treasure trove for Ashford, if and when he shows up. If he doesn't, then the angling club will be in for a windfall, which will please the secretary, Robin Preston. I thought if I could talk to anyone who knew Doyle—'

'That's it!' Trueman clicked his fingers, his eyes lighting up. 'You've done it. Thanks, Andy.'

'What?'

'Robin Preston. That's where I remember Wenham from. It was a complaint against Wenham made by Robin Preston. He claimed that Wenham had demanded money from him with menace but, when I went to investigate, he retracted it. He said he'd been mistaken, and he'd got the wrong end of the stick. It had been a joke.'

'I don't know how you do it, Dave. When was this?'

'Must be about fifteen or sixteen years ago.'

'Too long then for it to be relevant.'

'People can harbour grudges for a long time.'

Horton knew how a hurt or injustice, even a perceived injustice, could fester inside a person for years and, ultimately, destroy their reasoning and their lives. He wouldn't allow Richard Ames to do that to him, or his family, but he'd come close to it. He also knew that in extreme cases it could lead to seeking revenge, which could be in the form of murder.

'It might not be the same Robin Preston,' Horton replied. 'It's not an unusual name.'

Trueman pushed aside his plate and reached for his mug of tea. 'This guy worked for a hotel in Southsea along the Parade, a tubby man with an anxious manner probably caused by Wenham.' His phone pinged. 'It's the Super. He's missing me.' He tossed back the remainder of his tea. 'Thanks for jogging my memory.'

'Don't mention it to Uckfield yet. I'll check if my Preston is the same as yours. I'll speak to him today.'

'OK.'

'And if you can remember any of Doyle's contacts, I might get a handle on what he was doing with his paw inside a set of handcuffs.'

'Will do.'

Trueman left, and Horton sat for a moment finishing his breakfast and drinking his coffee. The angling club secretary worked in the hospitality industry, as had Trueman's Preston. Could it be the same man? What had happened for Preston to retract his complaint, if it was him? Surely, he couldn't have been paying blackmail money to Wenham all these years and had suddenly flipped? And what had Wenham threatened to expose? Cheryl Budleigh had said that Wenham liked to see people squirm and teach them a lesson. Preston had coughed up in the past. Perhaps Wenham had recently approached him, having tracked him down, and this time Preston had decided Wenham had to die.

He finished his breakfast and called Elkins. He told him about Wenham being the car fire victim and where he'd worked.

'I've met a few of Kettering's employees, including the boss, Daniel,' Elkins said. 'He's a good sort. Lives in Gosport and keeps a motor cruiser at Gosport Marina, but I don't think I've ever met Wenham. Want us to ask around about him?'

'Yes. I'll send you over a photograph. What size boat does Kettering own?'

'A Nimbus 320 Coupe, not the sort of boat to go up Forton Creek, if that's what you're thinking. Too prestigious and large.'

'Any joy with the boat owners there?'

'We managed to speak to two yesterday who weren't in the creek or harbour on Tuesday, but we'll see if we can speak to others over the weekend, although in this weather the Solent will be like the M25 with all the loonies out on it who think they can navigate the waters with Google Maps.'

'Just think of the overtime you'll be earning, Dai.'

'Huh. You can give us a hand if you've nothing better to do.'

'Much as I'd love to, I've got a sick sergeant to visit, who by the way is recovering.'

'That's good news.'

'And then I'm going to visit an Audi showroom.'

'The constabulary must be paying you too much.'

Horton rang off with a smile. Maybe Kettering had been paying Wenham too much. Audi Q7s weren't cheap. But then Wenham was single and had to spend his money on something. Cars, women and golf, it seemed. As he made for the hospital, Horton thought of Daniel Kettering. He'd know the harbour like the back of his hand. He could have used one of his company workboats to rendezvous with Wenham. Wenham could have been blackmailing him for something. An illicit affair? A tax fiddle? A crooked deal? He'd like to have talked to Kettering to get a feel for the man, but it wasn't his case.

He was delighted to see Cantelli dressed, sitting by his bed, looking pale but very much better. Beside him, to Horton's surprise, was Harriet.

She looked up at him with a smile. 'I thought I'd see how the invalid was faring. I'm delighted to see he's on the mend. Got to look after the old folk,' she joked.

'Hey, not so much of the old,' Cantelli rejoined warmly. Then to Horton, 'There's a chair going begging by the bed over there. That poor soul doesn't need it.'

Horton took it and set it down next to Harriet. She was dressed in a simple blue-cotton dress with a pale cream cardigan draped over her lap. Her arms and legs were lightly tanned. She looked so cool that anyone would have thought the small ward was air-conditioned. The windows were open, but that only served to let in hot air. The view gave out across the city, enveloped in a haze, as was the Solent. The Isle of Wight beyond was almost impossible to make out. The day felt heavier than the previous one and the sky was more leaden.

'You gave us all a fright, Barney.'

'Scared me half to death too,' Cantelli joked. 'And I'll feel a whole lot better when I get out of here, which Charlotte's arranging at the moment. The doctor's said I can go, it's just a matter of the paperwork, but that could take hours. Thanks for finding out what was wrong with me.'

'Thank Mr Bosman for that.'

'I will.'

Harriet flashed a questioning look and Horton explained.

'I promise I'll never chew grass again,' Cantelli said. 'I'll stick to my gum.'

'I'm not sure you'll ever live this down with Walters.'

'No? Well, just wait until he gets Delhi belly again.'

Horton smiled, as did Harriet. 'Are you up to hearing what we got on the box and cuffs?'

'You bet. No doubt you're keen to hear about it too, Harriet,' Cantelli said.

Horton told them about the prints Dr Pooley had found and the identity of one set of them.

Cantelli said, 'I don't know Doyle.'

'But *I* do, if it's the same man. He was at my school, a nasty piece of work.' He flashed a glance at Harriet. She knew nothing of his schooling in a failing inner-city comprehensive, so very different from her own privileged and private education. But no matter how expensive and elite, all establishments had their bullies, and he recalled her talking of one when they had been on that first investigation together, a girl on whom she had taken great delight in getting her own back on the hockey field.

He said, 'Doyle was a bully and a troublemaker, only he seemed to land everyone else in the trouble of his making.'

'It fits with what I've been thinking,' Cantelli said. 'Not much to do in here except think, and what you've just said confirms my idea. Want to hear it?'

'Yes, and I'll tell you if sucking plants has addled your brain.'

Cantelli grinned. Horton's heart lifted at the sight of it.

'It could have been some kind of scam, some years ago. There were two of them: one, the crook, Doyle, and the other posing as a police officer putting the cuffs on Doyle, saying he was nicked and he'd take him and the box to the station.'

Harriet said, 'But would someone have believed that? It's not usual to handcuff the criminal to the goods and take the goods away.'

'*Evidence, guv?*' Cantelli sniffed, in a mock cockney style. 'Doyle was caught in the act of nicking it, so . . .' Cantelli lapsed into a mock police voice. '*We need to take him and the box to the station, sir. Best way to do it is to put one end of the cuffs on the box and the other on the criminal. I've got two sets, we use them in cases like this.*'

Horton's eyebrows shot up.

Undeterred Cantelli continued. '*I'll just cuff my set, one to his other hand and the other end to me. That way where I go, he goes too. No need to worry, sir, we'll soon sort this out and get your coins back to you.* And off they merrily go.'

'Are you sure you're not still delirious?' Horton joked.

Harriet pushed her hair back with a curious thoughtful look.

Cantelli pulled a face. 'Bit weird, I admit. Perhaps those antibiotics have made me light-headed, but their victim, the owner of the coins, didn't know this wasn't usual practice. They took advantage of someone who was trusting and vulnerable.'

'I think I'd better start eating grass!' Horton said.

'As long as you don't smoke it, otherwise I might have to arrest you.'

It was good to see Cantelli back on form.

'Ashford could have been involved back then,' Cantelli continued. 'Maybe that's why he's done a runner. He's scared we'll discover that.'

Harriet said, 'But that doesn't make sense. Why didn't they open the box and sell the coins? And why dump it now?'

Cantelli looked puzzled. 'Sorry, the brain's not that bright this morning after all.'

A bed alarm began buzzing and the man in the opposite bed called for a nurse.

Horton took it up. 'Three possible reasons. One, the coins were too hot to handle, they'd be identified and traced back to the owner and therefore the thieves. Two, Doyle and Ashford didn't know where to take them to turn them into real money. Three, there was something else more valuable in another reticule in the box, so the coins looked worthless to them. It was this other treasure they were after.'

'What's a reticule?' asked Cantelli.

Horton told them what Dr Adams had said. He continued, 'They must also have got the key to the padlock from the rightful owner to have opened the box.' Horton paused in thought. 'But I can't see them unlocking it, removing what they had gone for and then carefully locking the box again. They'd have simply dumped it.'

'Perhaps they were given the wrong key and didn't realize it until they came to open the box,' Cantelli ventured.

'Are there prints on the padlock?' Harriet asked.

'Yes, Ashford's. Perhaps he hid the box at Sinah Lake years ago. I don't know how long Ashford has been a member of the club, but perhaps when he could see the lake drying out, he volunteered to clear that section because the box was there and was at risk of being found. Then Bosman came along unexpectedly and insisted he call the police. Ashford didn't have much choice and perhaps he thought it might not be a bad idea anyway, as it would divert suspicion from him. He wouldn't worry about his prints being on it because that would tally with him touching it now. He'd know that we'd be able to match them on the database and discover he had a criminal record, but by calling the police, he'd appear to be in the clear and reinforce the fact he'd turned over a new leaf.'

'But why can't you find him now?' Harriet said.

Cantelli answered. 'Perhaps he got scared that he'd be traced back to the original crime.'

'There is possibly another twist in this tale, although I don't know if and how it fits in yet — Robin Preston.' Horton updated them on what the Major Crime Team had discovered, that the car fire victim was Desmond Wenham, an abusive man with a history of violence against women and a bully who worked for Kettering, and relayed his recent exchange with Trueman, who had recalled a Robin Preston as having made and then retracted a complaint against Wenham.

'I wish I could come with you to interview Preston,' Cantelli said.

Horton was pleased to see more colour in his face, although he hoped that wasn't an increase in blood pressure or fever due to overexcitement.

Charlotte bustled in. 'Hello, Andy.'

He stood up and introduced Harriet.

'I'm pleased to meet you,' Charlotte said, beaming. 'But I'm going to break up this little work outing. Barney, pack your bags, we're ready to go.'

'I haven't got any bags, only those under my eyes.'

'Then you'd better bring them. Do you need a wheelchair?'

'Not on your life.' He stood but instantly wobbled. 'On the other hand . . .'

'We'll leave you to it,' Horton said. 'Unless you'd like me to push him?'

Cantelli eyed Horton malevolently.

'I'll think I'll be able to manage the patient, but I'll call the cops if he becomes too difficult,' Charlotte teased.

To Cantelli, Horton said, 'If you get any further inspiration while you're being waited on hand and foot, staring at four walls, give me a bell.'

Horton made his way down the corridor with Harriet. 'Any new evidence on the Priestley case?' he asked.

'No. Everything that should have been done was.'

Horton pushed open the door and they stepped into the lobby. 'You've been taken off it then?' He pressed the lift button.

'Plenty more to review, including your old school acquaintance Jamie Doyle, by the sounds of it.'

'And we've got some unidentified remains found at Southmoor, who might also have been reported missing. Harriet, did you ask to be assigned to the Serious Case Review Team?'

The lift came, interrupting her answer. They stepped back to allow some people out before entering it, then they had it to themselves. Horton was very aware of her presence.

'I was told it was that or no transfer.'

'But there are other vacancies for sergeants in the force.'

'I didn't know I would be allocated to examine missing persons files. I could have got children and adult safeguarding reviews, performance investigations or homicide case reviews.'

'Then why didn't you? Senior officers know about your father. Surely someone would have seen how painful it would be for you emotionally.'

Her eyes bored into his and it was all he could do to hold them and not look away. 'That's probably why I was given it.'

'As a test to see if you made the grade? No. I can't see the force doing that.'

'Who said it was someone inside the force?'

His heart flipped. Did she mean Ducale? Looking steadily at her, he thought not. She didn't know him, or of him. His telephone conversation with Ducale came back to Horton: *I expect she was given no choice . . . I didn't engineer it.*

The doors opened and they stepped out.

'Alastair, my elder brother, has called a family conference at our house on the island today. He's making an application to the court to have my father declared officially dead. Yes, I know it's quick, but you don't have to wait for seven years, as you probably already know, under the Presumption of Death Act.'

For a moment Horton wondered if she meant he'd know because of Jennifer. But the act had come in long after she had gone missing, and it had never occurred to him before who applied for her to be declared dead or when. Not that it mattered, then or now.

'Alastair is adamant the High Court will declare my father to be dead because of the drifting yacht. The judge doesn't need to be one-hundred-per cent satisfied that death has occurred, just that on the balance of probabilities it is more likely than not that he has died. Alastair needs to manage the family estate and businesses. I understand that. There is a great deal to do, and if we can get father officially declared dead then we can hold a funeral, but it seems too . . .' She pushed a hand through her hair. 'Well, you know.'

He did. Final. Would that draw the line under Lord Richard Ames? For the family, yes. But was he dead?

She turned to go, then turned back. 'Let me know how your investigation goes. I'm glad Barney's getting better.'

'So am I.' He watched her walk away feeling wretched for not coming clean, but how the devil could he? How could he possibly tell her that her grandfather, Viscount William Ames, had been Jennifer's lover, his father and a murderer?

He couldn't because she would have to reveal it to her family, and they wouldn't believe it. Maybe even Harriet wouldn't.

Where was his evidence? There was none, save a file possibly buried in the intelligence service's archives on Viscount Ames, who had been a Nazi sympathizer and, after the war, had continued to hold extreme right-wing views. The file might even have been destroyed. And if it did still exist it wouldn't document Ames's affair with Jennifer. Perhaps Jennifer's file had also suffered the same fate. It had been removed, and if anyone ever asked about it, it would probably be declared as being lost in transit or destroyed in a fire.

If he made his claim public — which he would never do — he'd be branded a fantasist and a troublemaker. Although it wasn't in the Ames's family interest to take him to court for slander, they could make life difficult for him in terms of his career, which Harriet had already told him had been her father's intent. He wasn't frightened of that, but he was of losing Emma and having her think the worst of her father. He knew too that Ducale wouldn't back him up. Everyone concerned with Jennifer was dead. Or were they? There might be one other man aside from Ducale and himself who knew the truth.

He put his mind back on Preston and made for the holiday village on Hayling Island.

CHAPTER SEVENTEEN

'What is it now?' Preston greeted Horton irritably in reception.

'I won't take up too much of your time.' There were several people milling about, and the coffee shop beyond was busy. Horton had also seen lots of people in the indoor pool, which overlooked the entrance. This was an adult-only destination and its average age, from what he had seen so far, had to be about seventy-eight. He'd taken a chance that Preston would be on duty, but if he hadn't been then Horton would have tried the on-site chalet where Preston lived or the nearby angling lake.

'I'm beginning to wish Ashford had never found that box,' Preston snapped, then had to change his tone and demeanour as a customer greeted him. It vanished the moment she did. 'We can't talk here.'

Horton followed him outside and they made their way through the grounds, around the outdoor swimming pool, to a seat at the far end by the trees. It looked out across Langstone Harbour. It was low tide and, aside from a few scattered seagulls, a handful of oyster catchers and crows, they had the place to themselves.

'It's not about the box,' Horton said. 'It's regarding the charges you brought and withdrew against Desmond

Wenham.' Horton watched Preston carefully. Despite Preston's eyes being hidden by his darkened lenses, Horton could see instantly this was the Preston that Trueman had remembered. His skin blanched and his body twitched. Horton wondered if he would deny it, but Preston must have realized his reactions had betrayed him.

'How do you know about that? What's it got to do with anything anyway?' he blustered.

'Was he blackmailing you?'

'Me! Of course not, why should he?'

'You tell me.'

'Well, I can't because there's nothing to tell. I haven't seen him in years and I don't want to.'

Horton studied him. Perhaps that was the truth. 'You won't, Mr Preston. He's dead. Desmond Wenham was murdered on Tuesday night. His body was found in his burnt-out car.'

Preston looked agog. His mouth opened then closed. When he spoke it was a croak. 'Murdered? My God. And you think that I . . . but that's ridiculous.' The man's voice betrayed his horror and fear. 'I resent you even thinking it. Just because I was unfortunate enough to get in his clutches years ago. Well, I'm telling you there must have been countless people since then who that evil man mentally tortured, blackmailed and threatened. I'm surprised he didn't meet a sticky end before now.'

'Why did you make the charge then retract it? What did he have over you?'

Preston pursued his lips.

'It would help us to understand why he was killed and could help us find his killer.'

Preston hesitated. Horton could see him mentally weighing up whether to keep quiet or tell the truth. After a few moments, he slumped onto the wooden bench. Horton sat beside him.

'It was sixteen years ago. I was an assistant manager at a hotel in Southsea. I got into some financial difficulties.'

'Gambling?'

'No, it was a woman. She was very demanding and I was an idiot. She wanted more and I gave her more. I could never say no. I bought her extravagant presents, took her on expensive trips and gave her money.' He cleared his throat. 'I don't need to spell it out, you've probably got the picture. I borrowed from the hotel finances. I told myself I would pay it back. Wenham found out.'

Horton was rapidly thinking as Preston spoke. 'This woman told him. She was also having an affair with Wenham?'

'Yes. She was on this dating agency website. It's how I met her. I didn't know then that she was a ruthless con artist. Or that she had other men in tow. She and Wenham were a double act. She'd get some poor sucker like me hooked. She milked me for what I had and then, idiot that I was, I started stealing from my boss. I bet she and Wenham had a good laugh at my expense. They probably split the proceeds. Then Wenham came along with his blackmail.'

Horton felt sorry for Preston. What he was telling him was providing a motive for murder for sixteen years ago, but not for now. Not unless Wenham had located Preston and had something more recent over him.

He wiped his brow and continued. 'Wenham approached me and said he knew I had been stealing from the hotel and that unless I paid up, he would go to the owner and tell him. At first, I denied it. He said he had evidence. The only evidence he could have was Marlene's word — that was her name, Marlene Arlett — only it wasn't her real name. Another lie, one of the many she spun me. By chance I saw them together on the seafront. I was filled with anger. It also made me come to my senses. I'd been planning to steal more because it was the only way I could pay Wenham, but I told him to go to the devil and do whatever he wished. I said it was no good telling my employer because *I* would, and I would also report him to the police. He laughed.' Preston's mouth hardened. The squeals of the gulls pierced the hot air and from the harbour came the drone of a boat's engine.

'It was that which made me carry out my threat. I reported him to the police and I went to my boss, the hotel owner. I told him and his wife everything. They were very understanding and extremely good to me. I said they could take every penny I had stolen from them from my wages. I'd work for nothing, or a pittance, until it was paid off. I said I had reported it to the police, and they could see by that I was genuinely sorry and very shaken up. We agreed that the money should come out of my wages gradually. I was a good manager and they didn't want to lose me. They said they would back me up, but maybe it would be better if I told the police I'd been mistaken, otherwise it might generate bad publicity and they didn't want that for me or the hotel. I wondered if Wenham would persist in blackmailing me, but Jerry Handley, the hotel owner, was a very big, strong man with some dubious contacts in London, and one word from him or one of his mates and Wenham would go running back to the hole from which he had crawled. And he did. I never heard from or saw him again. He and that witch, Marlene, moved on to their next victim.'

Horton could see why the hotel owner didn't want the police involved, or the publicity — it would draw too much close attention to his own financial affairs and his possibly dubious contacts.

'The hotel is now bedsits,' Preston said, 'like all of them along the seafront. I stayed working there for another two years then Jerry sold it and moved to Spain, where he died four years ago. We kept in touch intermittently. His wife moved back to London. He gave me very good references. I got a job here as assistant manager then was promoted to manager.'

'What happened to Marlene Arlett?'

'I don't know, and I don't care. She might have gone abroad. She might be dead. I never saw her again, thank God. I gave up online dating and took up angling. I became secretary of the club three years ago. That and my work is enough for me.'

'You live here alone?'

'Yes. I'd like to meet someone, but you know what they say — once bitten, twice shy. I was married but it didn't work out. I got divorced just before I met Marlene.'

'Where were you Tuesday night, Mr Preston?'

'Well, I wasn't killing Wenham,' he snapped, then relented. 'I was here until seven o'clock, then I went to the lake. I wanted to make sure everything was all right, and it's very peaceful there. I sat under the shade by one of the swims. That's the station where anglers fish from,' he explained. 'I was there for about an hour.'

'Alone?'

'Yes. Then I walked down to the seafront, before coming back to my chalet and watching TV.'

'And what time did you get back here?'

'About nine-thirty, nine-forty-five.'

'Did anyone see you?'

'They might have done, but I didn't speak to anyone or even nod a greeting to anyone, so no alibi. I didn't kill Wenham.'

'Do you know of anyone who would?'

'Like I said, there are probably lots of people, but I don't know of anyone in particular because I've had nothing to do with him for sixteen years. I'd better get back to work.' He rose and Horton fell into step beside him.

'Have you heard from Mr Ashford?' There still hadn't been any reports of Ashford's car. Along with his description, Horton had circulated the photograph from the angling club website.

'No, have you?'

'Is it usual for him to go off without telling his boss or neighbours?'

'No idea. Yes, I know him through the club and we talk, but that's about fishing and the lake. We don't talk about work or personal relationships. Anglers come to the lake to fish and to get away from all that.'

'Is he in a relationship?'

Preston shrugged.

'When Mr Ashford found the box, after the police had gone, did you leave the lake together?'

'Yes. When are you going to hand back the box and coins?'

'Hopefully soon. Do you own a boat, Mr Preston?'

'Only the two small ones at the angling club and they don't belong to me personally.'

Then Preston was called away by a man in overalls and looked very glad to be getting out of Horton's sight.

Horton thought his story had the ring of truth about it, but he wasn't totally convinced. He headed down to the ferry and bought some lunch from the small café. Eating it while sitting on the low wall, he surveyed the packed beach and people in the water. The currents were very strong here, and there was a sudden deep shelf that could, and had, caught out many bathers in the past. It didn't take much to be swept out to sea on this part of the beach. Opposite, the lifeboat station was at the ready in case of any incidents, of which he knew there would be many. He thought of Elkins and Ripley, who were probably being kept fully occupied, as Elkins had said. Jet skis and boats headed in and out of the narrow Langstone Harbour entrance. Across the water he could make out the masts of the yachts in his marina.

Finishing his bacon butty and Coke, he made for Portsmouth but indicated off the dual carriageway at the Broadmarsh Coastal Park, where a few minutes later he pulled into the small car park at Southmoor. It was empty, as was the road leading to it. It being the weekend, the factories and units on the adjoining industrial estates were closed. Removing his helmet, he alighted. Even the dog walkers had deserted the area. To his right he could see small boats sailing in the harbour. He wondered how Gaye was getting on with her competitions at Lymington. She was an expert sailor, like Harriet, but unlike Harriet, Gaye's speciality was in dinghies, whereas Harriet was into yacht racing. He'd raced a few times and enjoyed it. He wouldn't mind getting back to it.

His thoughts took him to the location where the remains had been found. He wasn't sure what he expected to glean from it, but he stood and examined the area recalling what Gaye had said about bracken. Yes, it was possible that the body could have been consumed by bracken very quickly and then earth had spread over it.

He felt impatient to get a clear time frame of how long the body had lain here. The soil might give them some clue as to the rate of decomposition. Beth had taken some samples. Again, he'd have to wait for the results of the analysis. Then he thought of someone who might be able to help him. He scrolled through his phone and found DC Jake Marsden's mobile number, formerly of the Major Crime Team, now promoted to detective sergeant and, since May, working with Operation Pelican, a major Hampshire police drug-busting operation. He was pleased when Marsden answered.

'Not disturbing you on your day off, am I?'

'Yes, but I don't mind. How is everyone?'

'Much the same.' Horton didn't go into the details of Cantelli's illness. 'You're not cycling, are you? I'd hate you to be charged with answering your mobile when cycling.' Horton knew Marsden cycled everywhere he possibly could. He was lean and fit.

'No. I'm in the shade in the garden with a long cold drink. We're having a barbecue.'

'Lucky you. I've got some human remains on Southmoor. I'm waiting on Dr Lauder and Dr Clayton's prognosis and the soil analysis but wondered if you could shed any light on things in the meantime, being an expert geologist, as I seem to remember.'

'A keen amateur one,' Marsden corrected. 'But I know the area very well.'

'OK then, so tell me about the geology of it.'

'The moor is made up of underlying clays, sands and chalk, overlaid with beach and tidal flat deposits with some raised marine deposits predominantly of thick, gloopy, anaerobic mud.'

Horton gazed around in the sweltering heat. 'Sounds as though I've come to the right person. Next question, how quickly would the remains have decomposed in that type of soil?'

'Difficult. I can only give you a broad idea.'

'That will do. I won't hold you to it.' He could hear laughter in the background, and a dog barking.

'Well, in humid conditions, as you know, a body can decompose quite rapidly and the tidal deposits there would have encouraged that. Sand would have slowed it down — dry sand that is, which is not what you've got at Southmoor. Decomposition would have been slower if the body had been buried in a sand dune away from the tide and animals.'

The sounds of laughter faded as Horton guessed Marsden distanced himself from the party crowd. 'We're looking at a few years then?'

'Depends on how deep it was buried.'

'Not very. Dr Clayton says the bracken would have covered him very quickly.'

'Which means he would have decayed more quickly. There is also the temperature and moisture to consider, and that area is very wet. That would have accelerated decomposition.'

Horton gazed around. 'Then it might not have been here very long at all?'

'Five years, maybe. Up to ten, possibly. I'm sorry I can't really help.'

Horton let him get back to his party. No point in searching the missing persons database then with such a wide time frame, and even then, this person might not have been reported missing. There was little he could do on that case for now. He made his way to the Audi dealers to see if he could glean more on Wenham.

CHAPTER EIGHTEEN

'Overconfident, bit of a big head, drove a hard bargain and went through the contract with a fine-tooth comb,' Horton relayed to Uckfield an hour later in the Super's office. 'He didn't have a woman on his arm and nor did he mention one. In fact, he boasted that he was single and liked it that way, but that he was never short of female company. The salesman confirmed he took the picture of Wenham standing by his brand-new Audi. He almost cried when I told him what was left of the car. He was more upset over that than Wenham. Wanted to know when the insurance would pay out as Wenham had bought it on lease.'

'We'll leave them to sort that out.'

'He had a Peugeot before, sold it privately. That might have been his deposit money.'

'We've requested access to his bank account. Dennings got the details from Daniel Kettering, but Wenham might have had more than one account, the details of which were on his now torched phone. But we'll get the information eventually. Seaton says Wenham joined Cams Hall Golf Club two years ago, wasn't very good and took lessons, but thought he knew more than the professional. He was generally tolerated but not well liked.'

'Seems to fit.'

'He last played there on the Saturday before he was killed with a fellow member, Brian Roper, who often accompanied him. Roper is on holiday in France, according to his neighbour. Seaton's been trying to contact him on his mobile phone. We've got Wenham's computer and Ben will be trawling through it before we hand it over to the Hi-Tech Unit, if we need to.'

Uckfield stretched his hands behind his head. 'Daniel Kettering said there were two instances in the past with female staff complaining about Wenham's behaviour, nothing sexual, mainly his abrasive manner towards them. When Kettering challenged him about it, Wenham said he treated women the same as he did men; they wanted equality and that was his version of it. He was given a verbal warning. Kettering, on the one hand, wanted shot of Wenham, but on the other said he was a damn good contract manager. Chawla will speak to the two women who complained, they've both left Kettering. There was another woman who left in May this year. No complaints from her. She went off sick and said the job didn't suit her. Dennings couldn't speak to the office manager, Amanda Rayland, because she's in Wales for the weekend. We'll talk to her on Monday.'

'Did Dennings get a list of customers?'

'Yes. Several around the harbour, as you'd expect: Town Camber, Fareham Marina, Elizabeth Quay and others further afield, Poole and the Isle of Wight. All contracts negotiated by Wenham. Nothing in his diary for the Monday or Tuesday before he was killed. We need to check with Amanda Rayland where he went on those days, but we might pick up something from his computer.'

'And Jason Downs and his wife?'

'Still no one to say Downs was sitting on his boat Tuesday evening, and Mrs Downs says that what she argued about with her husband is none of our business. Chawla says she pressed her, but the woman was adamant that the row has nothing to do with the victim, whom she has never heard of and neither has her husband. We'll go in heavier if and when we get more.'

'Has Bliss come up with anything from reviewing all the reports and evidence?'

'Not so far.'

And there was no sign of Bliss or her car, Horton had noted. There had also only been Trueman and Ben in the incident suite.

Uckfield sat forward. 'Dean is on my back to get a result, Andy. And he would just love for me to cock this up.'

Horton knew that the Assistant Chief Constable and Uckfield despised one another, although he wasn't certain of the cause. But then Steve was good at rubbing up a lot of people the wrong way. Maybe Dean had heard Steve's private nickname for him, the gnome, on account of him looking like one of those used to decorate a garden.

'There's something else you need to know.' Horton told him about Robin Preston. 'He has no alibi for the time of the murder. So, we need to put him in the frame for it. Maybe Wenham and Marlene Arlett had still been operating, and one of them came across Preston at the holiday park and threatened to expose his past to his bosses and get him the sack. With no Jerry Handley and his tough guys to protect him, Preston took another way out. Marlene hasn't come forward because she doesn't want to risk being arrested for fraud. But I can't see why Preston would meet Wenham at Forton Lake. It's a long way to drive from Hayling to Gosport.'

'Perhaps that was why — the further away the better, less chance of us thinking he was involved.'

'This Marlene could be the killer. She'd fit my previous scenario about it being a woman. Wenham could have been knocking her about all this time, bullying her into assisting him by finding victims, and she'd finally had enough.'

'For sixteen years?' Uckfield said disbelievingly.

'Why not? Domestic abuse can go on for years before the victim takes action. They've been intimidated and frightened into keeping quiet, and isolated from any help. Some victims suffer in silence all their lives, or until their tormentor dies either naturally or with a helping hand. Admittedly, Preston's profile of Marlene Arlett doesn't sound like she would tolerate abuse, but I've only got his word for that.'

'Ask Trueman to trace her.' Uckfield rose. 'I'm off home, got the in-laws coming for dinner, and as there's nothing else happening here, I might as well go.' He grabbed his suit jacket and briefcase. Horton followed him out. Uckfield addressed Trueman. 'I've left instructions that I'm to be called if anything new surfaces in connection with this case, but I'm not expecting it to. I'll be in tomorrow morning. I'll see you then.'

'No Sunday off for you, Dave,' Horton said, as Trueman shut down his computer. Horton gave him the gist of his day's interviews as they made their way along the corridor and down the stairs.

'I'll see what I can get on Marlene Arlett tomorrow. I've got something for you on Jamie Doyle. I've remembered who he was friendly with. Horace Baxter, commonly known as Spider Baxter.'

'Why?'

'It's the way he walks.'

'No kidding.'

'Probably. The origin is lost in the mists of time, unless he chooses to enlighten you.'

'I don't know of him.'

'Not surprising. He saw the light while serving his last sentence for assault and affray. Got religion and is now a lay preacher. You'll find Spider tomorrow at the Church of the Golden Brethren.'

'You're making this up.'

'Just look them up on the internet.'

'Oh, if they're on that oracle then it must be true.'

Trueman laughed and was delighted when Horton told him that Cantelli had been sent home.

In the quiet of his office Horton typed up his interview with Preston. Was Preston innocent of murdering Wenham? Or had he again got into financial difficulties and this time helped himself to the angling club money, which Wenham had somehow discovered?

Then there was Ashford's disappearance. Was Cantelli's theory correct and Ashford had scarpered? Or had Preston killed him? Was Preston a double murderer? It seemed unlikely to Horton as he reflected on the man's personality, manner and reaction, not just from this morning's interview but from his previous conversations. But was he right?

He sat back and thought it over. If driven hard enough, could Preston have killed two men? Taking Ashford first, had Ashford discovered Preston was embezzling the club and had threatened to expose him? Or had Preston silenced Ashford because he wanted a bigger share of the treasure from the box to pay off his debts? How would Preston have known the contents of the box were valuable? He wouldn't, not unless Ashford had told him, and he was hardly likely to do that. Perhaps Preston had caught him opening the box, despite the padlock being on it. But that meant Ashford had a key, because the padlock hadn't been forced. Had there been signs of it having recently been opened? Leney hadn't said.

Horton called up Leney's report. It wasn't mentioned. He rang Leney expecting to get his voicemail, but the forensic locksmith answered.

'I was about to call you,' Leney said, before Horton could ask his question. 'I've drawn a blank with the safe manufacturers. They have no records of the Milner safe being sold to anyone, but their details only go back to when they were taken over. They suggested there might be paper records somewhere but didn't sound hopeful.'

It was as Horton had anticipated. 'When you examined the padlock, Paul, was there any evidence it had been recently opened and relocked?'

'None.' So that answered that question, thought Horton, ringing off after briefly telling Leney about the value of the coins.

OK then, had Preston forced Ashford into confessing what was in the box? But why should Ashford have coughed up, *if* he had been Doyle's accomplice and *if* he had known the value of them? There were far too many ifs.

Horton turned his mind to the possibility of Preston killing Wenham. Motive, blackmail. Why had Wenham returned to blackmail Preston? Did he have something new over him? How had their paths crossed recently? The holiday village was not on Wenham's work or leisure radar, not unless he had attended one of their evening entertainment events, which were open to both residents and the public. Had Wenham taken a woman with him, possibly Marlene, and seen Preston on duty and threatened to expose his past corruption to his bosses unless he paid up? It sounded very much like Wenham's tactics.

Horton reached for his phone and rang the holiday village. He made up some story about an uncle having recently attended one of their shows, but he couldn't remember which one and it was bugging him. There were three in the last month, he was told, that he thought could be applicable: a 1970s night, an Abba revival, and a country and western evening.

OK, so that was one possibility. Another was that Wenham had been an angler. There was nothing in his apartment to indicate he had the slightest interest in fishing — but hold on, didn't Chawla say that Cheryl Budleigh, his former partner, mentioned he used to go fishing with someone? No, she'd only said he used to go out on a boat in the Solent. It could be fishing though. Admittedly it would have been sea fishing, but if he had been keen on that then perhaps he'd decided, or been persuaded, to try a bit of freshwater fishing. What had Preston said when Cantelli had asked him if you needed to be a member to fish there? *Yes, but members can bring a guest and we provide day tickets for prospective members to sample a selection of some of our waters.* Wenham could have had a day ticket!

Then there was the golf club the other side of the lake. In his mind's eye he saw the white Art Deco clubhouse. More of Preston's conversation came to him: *that's the clubhouse over there . . . that side of the lake, which borders the golf club, is out of bounds to members.* Had Wenham played golf there as a guest?

Or had he played in a match day? Had he seen Preston, recognized him, and thought he might again try his luck with threatening him? Getting his own back, as Cheryl had said to Bliss and Chawla. Maybe not asking for money but tormenting, goading and threatening to tell of his past to his bosses. Yes, it was possible. He'd run that past Uckfield tomorrow.

Jason Downs had a boat. Could Wenham have gone out with him? Had they been friendly, and when Downs discovered Wenham had been having an affair with his wife, he'd seen red? Why wouldn't the Downses tell them what they had argued about?

He finished his reports and decided that he couldn't wait until the next day as far as Ashford was concerned. It was time to force an entry. It might yield some further information on where he was, and possibly any past contact with Doyle, although Horton doubted the latter, it being too long ago.

CHAPTER NINETEEN

He met PCs Crampton and Gregory at the premises. Parking his Harley behind the patrol car, they drew some attention from the residents on their balconies, including the beer-bellied Darren Telham, who declared he knew Horton would be back and, no, he'd not seen Ashford or heard anything from inside the flat. Horton reiterated that they were effecting an entry because they were concerned for Mr Ashford's welfare. That stated, Gregory used the ramrod and stood outside while Crampton and Horton entered. It was immediately evident that the flat was empty.

Crampton took the small kitchen while Horton entered one of the two bedrooms. This clearly was Ashford's by the clothes lying around and in the wardrobe. There were also fishing rods stacked in the corner, nets and fishing baskets as well as some waders. On the chest of drawers were three photographs, one a collage of Ashford with his children — two boys as babies, as toddlers and when slightly older, playing in the park and on the beach. The other two pictures were of Ashford beside his sons, aged about nine and six, both in football kit, the older one in Pompey's colours. He wondered if Ashford took them to Portsmouth's home football matches. It had been some years since he had been to one and a long time since he had played for the boys' team. The younger boy's strip was unknown to Horton, probably a school or local team. Both were very much like their father — fair-skinned and haired, wiry, with angled faces and bright blue-grey eyes. They all looked happy, and Ashford appeared the doting father, but pictures could be deceptive.

He opened the drawers and rummaged around the clothes. He found Ashford's passport. Using his phone, he took a picture of it and replaced it.

The second bedroom brought him up sharp. Not only because it reminded him so much of his in the tower block where he'd lived before he'd been taken into care, but also because it brought back all too painfully what he had missed these last two years and was still missing with Emma. This was the boys' room when they came to stay with their father. There were duvets of Spiderman and posters of footballers, whereas Emma's bedroom at what had once been Horton's home had bedcovers of princesses and posters of ballet dancers and of the shows they'd all seen together. There were comics, as in Emma's room, but with different titles, as with the books, although glancing at the spines there were some the same — the Harry Potter series and the Horrible Histories books.

Seeing all this brought a lump to his throat, followed by a wave of anger, not for what had happened, or towards Catherine, but towards himself for dragging his heels on finding somewhere to live. He'd been thinking only of himself, of where he wanted to be, where he'd feel comfortable, when all that mattered was having somewhere he could make a home for his daughter. She would come and stay with him and create her own room just like her one at home, and she would once again be a part of his life. Just as these boys, despite their parents' divorce, were still part of their father's. Horton felt instinctively that Ashford would never have voluntarily left all this. Even if he had stolen those coins years ago, Horton just couldn't see him taking off for fear of being prosecuted. *Not unless he killed Wenham*, said the small voice

166

in the back of his mind. But why should he? There wasn't a single thing to put him with that.

As he heard Crampton moving around and opening drawers he also considered two more things, not to do with Ashford, but prompted by his disappearance. One was that he increasingly believed Richard Ames wouldn't have voluntarily given up his lifestyle and deserted his family. Ames would have been absolutely convinced that he, Horton, would never reveal the truth about his family's dirty history, and Horton felt certain the intelligence services would do a thorough and very good cover-up if he did decide to spill the beans. Horton was equally convinced that Richard Ames wouldn't kill himself. Ducale had to be right, Gordon had killed Richard and had then either killed himself or had disappeared again, something he was good at.

He opened drawers and found some children's drawings and a story Ashford's youngest had written. Oh, how he missed reading to Emma and making up stories at bedtime, when he had been at home which, with a pang of guilt, he knew hadn't been often. The job wasn't the kind where you could just do your contracted hours and clock off. Not even as a PC. Now as detective inspector on a case, he often had no idea when he would get home. Sometimes the work involved all-night sessions. Catherine hadn't complained at first but increasingly it had irked her, especially after Emma had been born. He'd found his in-laws babysitting more often, then Emma staying over with them frequently. Catherine didn't see why she should stay at home while he was out, and as her role as her father's marketing director in their marine equipment company expanded, so too did her overnight stays on business and abroad. He'd been in no position to complain. Now looking back, even before that false rape allegation, they had drifted apart. He'd be at home when she wasn't and vice versa.

He pushed it from his mind and studied the drawings. Obligingly, on the top of one, the youngest boy had written his name, Tye, his age, six, and his telephone number. On the inside of a book he found inscribed, *This book belongs to Cole Ashford. If you steal it you'll be exterminated.* It made Horton smile while at the same time filled him with sadness. He hoped for these children's sake that Ashford was safe and well and not a killer.

'Is there a landline?' he asked Crampton, joining her in the living room, which was basically furnished, cluttered with toys, but reasonably clean.

'No. There are some notes and bills in a drawer and I think this must be his ex-wife's address and telephone number.' She handed over a scrap of paper with an address in Bournemouth and a number that corresponded with the one Tye had written at the top of his drawing.

'There's no indication of where he might be, sir,' she continued. 'Fresh milk in the fridge, eggs and butter, some ready meals.'

There were angling magazines on the table. 'Anything with the name Doyle on it?' She shook her head. It was as Horton had predicted.

He punched in the number of Ashford's former wife. When she answered he could hear the children in the background. He introduced himself, apologized for disturbing her and said they were trying to contact Peter Ashford. 'Not in a criminal respect,' he quickly reassured. 'Mr Ashford has been helping us with regards to an investigation and we're not able to get in touch with him.'

'Have you the right number?' she asked. And relayed one.

He confirmed it was the one they had. 'When did you last speak to him, Mrs Ashford?'

'Last Sunday, when he brought the boys back.'

'Did he have them all weekend?'

'Yes. He picked them up Friday late afternoon, after school. Hasn't he been at work?'

'No, and his employer hasn't heard from him. He's also not at his flat and his car isn't there. I don't wish to worry you, but we would like to find him and make sure he's OK.

Does he have any friends he could have gone to or might be in touch with?'

'I've no idea. We've been separated for five years. You could try members of the angling club. That's where he spent most of his time.'

Horton detected a sour note there.

'What about relatives?'

'There's a brother, Kevin. He came to our wedding, but don't ask me where he is now, Pete lost touch with him years ago. His parents are divorced. His father brought them up. He died some time back. God alone knows where his mother is. She walked out when they were young.'

Horton requested that if she heard from him to get in touch and gave her his number. Before he rang off she said, 'Will you let me know when you hear from him?' but in the next breath added, 'Only, he's having the boys for the first week of their summer school holidays and I've booked to go abroad with a friend.' He rang off thinking she was more worried about missing her holiday than her ex-husband. Still, that wasn't his business. He didn't know the circumstances of their split.

He wondered what Ashford had done on the Friday before picking up his boys. Housework and shopping, perhaps. Or he could have gone to the beach or fished either at Sinah Lake or at another of the angling clubs. The same for the Monday the manager at Camplow said he had off, before showing up at Sinah Lake on Tuesday.

He looked around the flat a little longer but didn't find anything that could help. There were no contact details of any friends. Ashford's hobbies looked to be angling and following Pompey.

The locksmith had arrived by the time he'd finished inside and, while he made the front door secure, Horton thanked the officers and knocked stoutly on the open door of the flat the other side of Ashford's to that of beer-belly man, where he could hear a television blaring.

A grey-haired, unshaven man in his mid-sixties emerged in the dark, gloomy passage wearing a pair of shorts and nothing else. Horton didn't blame him, as the air was still stifling hot, despite it being early evening.

'Who is it, Nigel? If they're selling something tell 'em we don't want none.'

'It's the police,' he tossed over his shoulder.

'What's 'appened now?' she called back, resigned.

Horton said he was making enquiries about their neighbour.

'Come about next door, Maureen,' Nigel again shouted over his shoulder.

Horton wondered if the whole conversation was going to be conducted in this way. But Nigel's last words prized Maureen away from the TV and brought her waddling out in a large T-shirt and long sarong down to her grubby feet in flip flops.

'Not 'ad an accident, 'as he?' she asked worried.

'No, but we are concerned for his welfare and are trying to locate him,' Horton answered. 'When was the last time you saw him?'

Maureen answered. 'Tuesday morning. He was going to work.'

'No he weren't, he was going to that fish lake.'

'How do you know that? You were snoring your 'ead off in bed!'

''Cos he told me the night before while you 'ad your nose stuck to the TV. Said he 'ad a day off work to help clean up the lake, because it's dried out in this bleedin' awful heat. He cares for the fish, said this drought ain't good for them, ain't good for us humans neither. Says I should give fishin' a go — very peaceful, it is. I told him I got better things to do than sit on a muddy bank with a stick waiting for a bleedin' fish to come along.'

'Yeah, like sittin' in an armchair waiting for me to bring you your tea. He's very keen on the environment,' Maureen swept on.

'What the bleedin' hell 'as that got to do with anything? The police don't wanna know about that.'

'Well, they should, there's too much rubbish around 'ere.'

'Council's responsible for that, woman.'

'No, it ain't, it's the idiots who live round 'ere. Very strict is Pete with 'is boys,' she continued before Nigel could reply. 'You can hear them through these walls, laughing and shouting, and 'im telling them to pipe down, in a nice way. They got good manners, not like some.' She didn't look at her husband, but it was clear who she meant.

Horton quickly intervened. 'Have you seen anyone visit him, or does he speak of any friends?'

'Nah,' Nigel answered.

'There was that girl who came 'ere.'

'She were delivering something he ordered.'

'How would you know that? Got eyes in the back of your 'ead?'

'No, but I got ears and I 'eard 'em, and I seen her round the other flats with boxes and one of those things you 'as to sign.'

'Did you see Mr Ashford return on Tuesday or hear him in the flat?'

They shook their heads.

'You didn't see his car parked?'

'No,' they answered in unison and then looked at each other startled.

'Or see him leave for work on Wednesday?'

Nigel piped up first. 'Already said, the last time I saw him was Tuesday.'

'Yes, you did.'

'There's no need to be rude,' Maureen quipped.

'I weren't being rude. I was only sayin'.'

'There's sayin' and sayin'.'

'Wot did he ask again for then?'

Horton left them to their squabbling. The locksmith had finished. As Horton returned to his boat, he thought Nigel and Maureen's evidence bore out the fact that Ashford had gone to the lake on Tuesday and had never returned from it. From seeing the flat, Horton also thought it would take a very serious crime indeed for Ashford to take off voluntarily and abandon his sons. But perhaps Ashford hoped to get a message to them somehow and would find a way of seeing them again. Perhaps he had taken off in a panic because he knew his prints were on that box. Even so, as he, Cantelli and Harriet had discussed earlier, they could be easily explained. And how could they prove anything had been stolen? They couldn't. What could be proved though was that Doyle had been wearing those handcuffs. But that simply got him nowhere, like Doyle's whereabouts.

CHAPTER TWENTY

Sunday

It was just after midday when he stepped inside the run-down building that had once been a theatre, and still was on occasions, but was now also hired out for other purposes, the Church of the Golden Brethren being one of them. It was in Portsea, not far from the busy Hard and the Portsmouth Historic Dockyard, thronging with visitors. After another stifling hot night, it was an equally blistering day.

Horton had relayed to Uckfield his theories of the previous evening: that Wenham could have attended one of the functions at the holiday park and seen Preston there; that he might be an angler, although there was nothing in his flat to indicate that, and he might have bought a day ticket and fished with a friend; and that he might have played at Hayling Golf Club and seen Preston at the lake. He also told Uckfield of his thoughts and concerns for Peter Ashford after the search of his property.

Uckfield had ordered DC Seaton back to the Cams Hall Golf Club to find out if they had held a society day at Hayling Golf Club at any time, and if so, when? And had Wenham played? If he drew a blank, then he was to go to

Hayling Golf Club and find out if Wenham had played there as a guest of a member. On reflection, Horton considered it unlikely because there had been no score cards from Hayling in Wenham's golf bag.

'Too ashamed of his abysmal round. He threw it away,' had been Uckfield's response, which could be true.

Horton had also rung Preston, who had vehemently denied seeing Wenham at the holiday park or issuing a fishing day ticket for him. Nor did he think a member had brought Wenham to the lake as a guest, but he couldn't be certain. He was still adamant that he hadn't seen Wenham for sixteen years. Horton had requested a list of the angling club members and their contact details, which Preston had grudgingly emailed over. With Wenham's reputation for the ladies, Horton had speculated if one of the female members had brought Wenham with her. Chawla was ringing round them all, starting with the women. Trueman was trying to trace Marlene Arlett. Bliss wasn't in and neither was Dennings. Again, Horton wondered why no one had come forward claiming to have known or been with Wenham before his death, unless they were on holiday and hadn't heard or read the news.

He watched the congregation of mainly elderly women and a couple of men shuffle out, dropping their collection money onto a tin plate at the door beside the small, skinny man of about forty-five with sparkling dark eyes, sparse hair and long thin arms that waved about wildly as he spoke to each of his twenty or so flock. The wide grin took up almost all his narrow, weathered face. It had to be Spider. He vaguely resembled one. Horton hoped not the deadly poisonous kind. Was this a scam? But the money in the collection plate was hardly enough to live on. This was one of the poorer areas of the city and these people had little to spare.

A piano was being played by a large woman in a brightly coloured floral dress. Horton thought it sounded like 'Bread of Heaven' but he was probably mistaken. She was a competent musician, but the piano needed tuning and she kept adding her own musical flourishes. No reason why she shouldn't. She seemed to be enjoying herself, and he found himself smiling. It was surprisingly cool inside. The traffic noise filtered in along with a few sun rays from the small dusty windows at the top of the room.

Horton waited patiently for the congregation to leave. He could see that Spider had noted him, but his manner towards his flock never faltered as they filed out, talking and smiling. Whatever Spider had preached it seemed to have made everyone happy, and that was a good thing. Perhaps it was the Golden Brethren's philosophy.

When the last person had left, and the piano had sounded its final off-key note, Spider greeted him, his little dark eyes twinkling with curiosity and benevolence.

'Don't get many of you in here,' he said.

'Of who?'

'Hells Angels, but all sinners are welcome.'

'Even policemen?'

'You're a copper?' Spider said surprised.

Horton nodded and reached for his ID.

'No need for that. I'll take your word for it. Come to think of it, you stand like one.'

Horton didn't ask how policemen stood. 'You seem to be doing a brisk trade.'

'There are some decent folk around here, and if I can bring them a little comfort and happiness in these tough times then it's worth it. I can see you don't trust me. You think I'm on the make.'

'How do you live? That collection won't keep you in baked beans.'

'We manage.'

'But how?'

'I'm not peddling stolen goods or fleecing old ladies, if that's what you're hinting at. I saw the error of my ways in prison and converted. I also found a good woman. Ah, here she is. Freda, this is . . .'

'Detective Inspector Horton.'

The pianist in the bright floral dress held out a plump hand as she beamed at him. 'I'm pleased to meet you.' She looked as though she meant it.

'Freda was a prison visitor. She changed my life.' Spider tossed her a loving glance.

'I'm very glad to hear it.'

'I work as a street cleaner and Freda in the local supermarket. Our needs are small just so long as we have each other. We try to help others.'

'All very noble,' and perhaps true.

'How can I help you, Inspector?'

'I'm enquiring about Jamie Doyle.'

Spider's lined face creased up in thought then his expression cleared. 'I haven't seen or heard from him in years.'

'You wouldn't, he went missing fifteen years ago.'

'I was inside then, meeting Freda.' He dashed her another dazzling smile, which she returned. It really did look like true love, thought Horton. He was pleased for them — and for the general public, as it meant one less criminal on the streets.

'I'm trying to discover who he went about with before he went missing, if he had any associates. You were one of them back then, before that last stretch. I'm re-examining the file to see if we can throw any light on what happened to him.'

'He was a bad lot, but he too might have seen the light and moved away to start a new life.'

Horton very much doubted that.

'He didn't usually have anyone working with him,' Spider continued. 'I did one job with him and got caught flogging the stolen goods. As it was my fifth conviction, I got sent down. I didn't squeal on Jamie. I never squealed. Said I did the job all by myself and the coppers believed me, which they would. I often wondered if . . .'

'If what?'

'It was a setup. Not that Jamie had anything against me — leastways, I didn't think he did. But he could have done the job himself and not involved anyone. He usually liked to work alone. He was a bit of a wild card, crazy ideas, but he was also lazy and thought he was a cut above the usual. He set up this job, a house in Old Portsmouth, owners were away. It was easy getting in and there were some nice pieces — ornaments, jewellery.'

'He was with you on the job?'

'No. I did it alone. Afterwards I handed the stuff to him, and he gave me back the items he didn't want. When I came to offload mine, that's when I got caught, and my prints were in that house.' He paused and looked thoughtful. Freda reached out her plump hand and held his. 'Look, Mr Horton, I've had a lot of time to think about it and I reckon Jamie tipped off the police. I don't know why, and I wasn't bitter, just . . .'

'Resigned,' Freda furnished for him.

'And repentant when I met Freda.' He glanced fondly at her.

'But why would he set you up?'

'To see if he could, maybe? To get me into trouble? To see if I would squeal? To test me to see if I was worth working with in the future? Who knows how his mind worked? But he knew I had a string of convictions behind me ever since I was a teenager. Maybe he wanted to see if I'd get sent to prison and then have a good laugh. Jamie liked to play games.'

Horton could totally understand what Spider was saying because it fitted with the Doyle he'd known at school. He wondered how many others Doyle had played his games on. Had one of them got his revenge? Horton thought of the handcuffs, and Cantelli's theories. Was the tin box theft another of Doyle's games that had gone wrong because this time his associate wasn't as biddable as Spider? Was Sinah Lake Doyle's final resting place? Not where the box had been found but elsewhere in it. Was Ashford moving that box because it could betray where the body lay, or what was left of it?

Spider said, 'Besides, Jamie was out on probation, which was another reason why I didn't squeal on him. He'd have to go back inside.'

'Do you know of anyone Doyle used in a similar way?'

'No. Like I said, he usually worked alone.'

'What about girlfriends? Was he seeing anyone special at that time?'

'He usually loved them and left them. He was good-looking and he attracted women like flies round a dung heap, they came and went quickly. He liked the pretty, quiet ones.'

Yes, thought Horton, easier to manipulate. The same type Wenham went for, apart from Marlene Arlett, according to Preston, but that might not be true.

'We used to frequent the pubs in Guildhall Walk where all the students hung out. Jamie liked to take the piss out of them. I remember one night Jamie said there's a girl ripe for the . . . Well, let's just say he grinned and said watch the maestro in action. Janice, Julie, her name was, or something like that. Oh, he pulled her, but I didn't see anything of them together after that night because I got nicked, and although I was out on bail for a while before the case come up, I didn't associate with Jamie on account of not wanting to draw attention to him. I went to our usual haunts but he'd stopped going there.'

'Didn't you go round to his bedsit?'

'No fear, the cops might have been watching me.'

Horton didn't think they would have been, not a small-time crook like Spider, but he might have been seen by chance. Even if he had been, they probably wouldn't have thought much of it because Spider had insisted it was a one-man job — his. Horton's phone went. Quickly glancing at it, he saw it was Elkins. He'd call him back.

'But you'd been to Doyle's bedsit before,' he said.

'No. He wouldn't let anyone go there, we always met outside or in a pub.'

'Do you remember, or did you ever hear of a Peter Ashford going around with Doyle?'

Spider shook his head. He seemed convinced of that.

'Did Doyle ever mention stealing valuable coins from anyone?'

'No.'

'Did he speak about finding any coins or coming into possession of them?'

'No. I never heard anything like that.'

Spider seemed genuinely mystified. Horton pressed him a little harder on when he had last seen Doyle, and about any known contacts, but Spider stuck resolutely to what he had said. It sounded like the truth.

Spider and Freda urged him to come to one of their services, held Sunday mornings and Wednesday evenings, saying he'd always be welcome and so would his colleagues. Horton didn't think he'd get any take-up on that.

Outside, he returned Elkins's call. 'We've spoken to the managers at the Town Camber, Fareham and Wicor Marinas and Elizabeth Quay, who all have Kettering vessels on hire. The latter is the most recent one. The manager there, Nick Kerris, is the only manager I haven't met before.'

The same for Horton.

'They're shocked he's been murdered and can't think why or who could have done it. They said he was good at his job, knew his stuff and gave them a fair deal. When pushed they admitted he could be on the brusque side but didn't hold it against him. Town Camber has a crane barge on hire, Fareham Marina a workboat, Wicor Marina a dredger and Elizabeth Quay a dredger and two workboats. We've also managed to have a word with a couple of boat owners at Forton Lake and one of them says he thought he saw a motor-boat in the creek on Tuesday night at the critical time, which was reddish or had something red on it. Might not be anything in it, he's a bit vague. I've got to go, we've got hordes of people playing silly buggers on the water, keeping us and the lifeboat busy.'

Horton could well imagine. A hot sunny Sunday in the Solent brought out all the leisure sailors, fishermen and jet-skiers. Jason Downs had a motorboat with a reddish canopy. Could it have been him?

He stopped off at Oyster Quays, where he bought a pasty and coffee and took them down to the waterfront. It was a mistake. Far too busy. There was no chance of finding a quiet spot or shade. He didn't know why he had come here, probably because it was nearest — except for the Hard, and that, a stone's throw away, was also packed with tourists and local people, as well as those making their way to and from the railway station and the Isle of Wight and Gosport ferries.

He decided to walk over the small bridge to the east side of the quays, where it was slightly quieter, but he hadn't gone two paces when, looking down into the marina, he stiffened with shock. Below him on the pontoon was Lord Richard Ames's yacht and on the deck a man seeing to the sails. My God, Ames was alive! Unless this was a ghost. He clutched the rail to steady himself. His heart beat rapidly. Then the man turned and Horton let out the breath he'd been holding. This was no ghost and it wasn't Richard Ames, but the likeness was so remarkable that it had to be one of his sons. Then he recalled from the press photographs that this was the eldest son, Alastair.

Harriet emerged from the cabin and his heart stalled. He couldn't duck out of sight. He could hurry away though, but it was as if he was rooted to the spot. He watched them exchange some angry words. Harriet turned back to the cabin, and her brother grabbed her arm. She swung back. Horton had seen her upset and confused, but he'd never seen her so furious. His gut wrenched at the sight. He made to go to her aid then froze. She shook off her brother and went to alight. This time Horton managed to peel himself from the railings and hurry away. He hastened to his Harley. Maybe he should have stayed and asked her what was wrong. But it was none of his business. It was only when he arrived back at the station that he admitted to himself that he didn't much care for Alastair Ames. Was that because of the way he had looked and treated Harriet? Or was it prejudice because he reminded him so strongly of his father? Maybe both.

CHAPTER TWENTY-ONE

Monday

'I've located Marlene Arlett.'

'That was quick.' Horton ran into Trueman in the corridor outside the gents' toilets. 'Where is she?'

'In His Majesty's Prison Eastwood Park, Gloucestershire, which was why she was easy to find, although, as you said, that's not her current name.' Trueman made for the vending machine. Horton followed. 'Arlett was her maiden name. She was divorced eighteen years ago, so when she met Preston she'd reverted to it, certainly for the online dating websites. She was convicted for fraud and false invoicing, you know the sort of thing, raising invoices for goods or services not rendered and pocketing the amount. She managed to siphon off thousands of pounds from the company she was working for into her own account. A clever fraud, but one of her colleagues got curious about her luxurious lifestyle and started digging into the accounts. There was no receiving report for invoiced goods and services, they couldn't be found in the company inventory or accounted for, and there were no purchase orders for them.' He pressed the button for a Mars bar. 'She got fourteen years and she's currently served eight, she'll probably be out next year. She certainly didn't take revenge on Wenham — cast-iron alibi.'

'Anyone else involved with her?'

Trueman pressed another button for a packet of salt and vinegar crisps. 'No.'

'How many times before she got caught had she done this?'

'Twice. She put her hand up to them hoping to be given a more lenient sentence.'

'Both in this area?'

'One a marine engineering company at Hamble, the other a boat builder at Poole. The company who caught her in the act was a yacht transport business in Southampton. All the amounts were substantial, and over a long period of time.'

Horton must have looked thoughtful because Trueman said, 'Thinking of taking a ride up to Gloucestershire?'

'I've heard it's a pretty county.'

'Uckfield might like a day out, or maybe Bliss.'

'You looking to get them out of your hair?' Horton joked, refusing the offer of a crisp.

'They're not doing much except staring at the crime board, or asking if we have new leads.'

'And have you?'

'Not you as well? No! Unless you've come up with the answer.'

'I'm working on it.'

'Looks as though you have been, all night.'

Not the case. But thoughts of Harriet and Alastair Ames had occupied him. He hadn't cared for that look on Alastair's face. He'd seen it before. And he saw it again last night in his troubled dreams. 'Too hot to sleep.'

'Even on a boat!'

'Did Seaton have any joy with the golf clubs yesterday?' Horton asked.

'Cams Hall said there hadn't been any society days held at Hayling and no one he spoke to at Hayling claims to have played with Wenham. We have a list of members we're working through. Chawla hasn't found any members of the angling club yet who knew Wenham or admit to it. We've got more to contact so it's possible we'll find someone who took him there.'

And there was the office manager at Kettering and the two former female employees yet to be interviewed.

'I paid a visit to the Church of the Golden Brethren yesterday. Spider Baxter is a very happy man now he's found religion and a good woman.'

'Glad someone's happy.'

'He told me that Doyle had picked up a new girlfriend shortly before he disappeared, but all he can remember is he thinks her name was Janice or Julie or something similar.'

'Doesn't ring any bells with me.'

'Probably too vague anyway and he doesn't remember Doyle associating with Ashford. That's not to say he didn't.'

Horton left Trueman to his chocolate and crisps. A thought niggled at him as he made his way to CID. Wenham and Marlene had been an item once. They'd been involved in exploiting Preston, and Marlene had clearly continued her criminal activity alone. Wenham's position at Kettering had been negotiating contracts for the hire of crane barges, dredgers and work boats. Marlene's fraud had involved marine companies. Had Wenham picked up some tips from Marlene all those years ago and indulged in false accounting, either acting alone or in collusion with the contracting personnel at the marine companies hiring Kettering's equipment? He felt it worth checking out.

He found Walters at his desk. The constable quickly pushed his newspaper into a drawer. Horton told him about his interview with Spider Baxter.

'Sounds a right nutcase to me,' was Walters's verdict.

'He may be, but at least it's kept him clean, although that could be due to the influence of a good woman. Talking of which, how was your weekend with the prospective in-laws? By your ugly grin I take it you passed muster.'

'They thought I was the bee's knees. Lovely family. Good cooks too, both mister and missus, and Penny's brill at it.'

'They say that the way to a man's heart is through his stomach. Looks as though your heart has been well and truly captured. It's lucky then that I need your brain. I want you to see if you can trace any of Peter Ashford's relatives. Not that I think he will have gone to them, judging by what his former wife says. There's a brother, Kevin. Father dead. Mother might be too. She walked out when Peter was young, according to the former Mrs Ashford, so Peter's father raised his sons. Also call Camplow and make sure he hasn't by some miracle shown up for work today.'

'Will do. Hello, Sarge. Feeling better?' Walters interjected.

Horton spun round surprised, then scrutinizing Cantelli's dark-featured face added, 'Are you fit enough for work?'

'Feeling top of the world.'

'That won't last,' Walters smirked.

'And no cracks about plant eating,' Cantelli warned jovially. 'Have I missed much?'

'Not so you'd notice,' Walters said.

'I'll update you on the way,' Horton said, delighted to see Cantelli and glad to have him back on the case. And that's what he was going to do — work, not think of Harriet and her wretched family. Fortunately, Trueman and Elkins had given him something new to follow up.

'Where are we going? Not back to that lake, I hope,' Cantelli said as they headed out.

'No, you'll be safe from poisoning at Elizabeth Quay. We've got time to call there before we're due at the mortuary.'

'Mortuary?'

'Gaye and Dr Lauder are examining the remains. Didn't I tell you about them on Saturday?'

'If you did, that poisoning's given me amnesia.'

Horton recalled he had told Harriet as they made for the lift after seeing Cantelli. He relayed what he had discovered at Southmoor. He also updated Cantelli on his interview with Robin Preston, his search of Ashford's flat, what Trueman had told him that morning and ended with his interview with Spider Baxter, which to Cantelli's mind confirmed that Doyle had been involved in a prank or a scam with an associate, possibly Ashford, regarding the coins.

'Sounds like you had a busy weekend,' was Cantelli's verdict as he indicated off the motorway at the junction to Gosport. 'Preston could be in the frame for Wenham's murder then, and possibly Ashford too. Or Ashford was mixed up with Doyle and has scarpered. So why are we heading to Elizabeth Quay?'

'That's the most recent contract Wenham negotiated, and I think Wenham might have been on the fiddle. I know the managers at the other marinas where Kettering supply equipment and I'm certain they wouldn't have knowingly been involved in invoice fraud. The manager at Elizabeth Quay might not have been either. I'd like to meet him and form an opinion, and also get more from him about Wenham.'

'Just as long as I don't have to go on a boat. I don't think I could handle seasickness on top of what I've been through. I don't recommend it as a method of losing weight.'

'What you need is a double sausage sandwich to build you up, but not from the same café as before. I very nearly accused them of food poisoning.'

'They won't recognize me. I'll buy them.'

'Good, I could do with some breakfast.'

'And some sleep.'

Horton sighed. 'Trueman commented on my haggard looks this morning. It's worrying over you, Barney, that's aged me.'

Cantelli threw him a look before negotiating a roundabout.

Horton's phone rang. It was Walters. 'Camplow say Ashford hasn't shown again for work. Bliss also wants to know where you are. I told her you were following up enquiries on one of our cases but wasn't sure which one, seeing as I've no idea what you're doing. I also told her Sergeant Cantelli was with you. She seemed pleased about that.'

'You mean she smiled?'

'Might have done. I don't know what that looks like. With the Sarge back and CID up to full strength, she said we might manage to clear up some investigations.'

She made it sound as though they had thirty people and not three. Horton told Walters that they were interviewing the manager at Elizabeth Quay in connection with an idea he had on the Wenham murder investigation. Then they would be attending the mortuary to see what Dr Clayton and Dr Lauder could tell them about the remains.

'Want me to tell her that?'

'Only if she asks.' Bliss was bound to ring him. Cantelli turned into the road leading to the waterside and marina and pulled into the car park by the mobile incident unit.

'First let's get that breakfast,' Horton said.

That done, but from the mobile catering unit and not the café, and after a brief chat with the officer at the mobile incident unit — which yielded nothing new — they walked the short distance to Elizabeth Quay. It was still in the throes of being developed, although a couple of pontoons had been installed. At the end of one of them was a Kettering dredger. There was no one on board and it didn't seem to be doing any dredging. In front of it were two small red workboats belonging to the same company. There was considerable building work going on and Horton could see the flashing orange lights of a digger. They entered a welcoming air-conditioned office, where a woman at a low-level counter looked up from her computer and asked if she could help them. The sounds of two men arguing came from an office behind her and she flashed them an apologetic look which turned wide-eyed when Horton made the introductions and asked if they could speak to the manager.

'He's with the site foreman at the moment but I'll tell him you're here.' She hastily disappeared. Horton caught the words, 'Just damn well do what you're paid to do. What is it? Can't you see—' The angry words terminated abruptly as the speaker was made aware they had company.

A couple of minutes later two men emerged, one sturdily built with greying short-cropped hair and carrying a white

186

safety hat, wearing a high-vis jacket and a flushed, hostile expression; the other younger, about mid-thirties, tanned, fit, with a shock of dark hair, deep-set brown eyes and a strong-featured face with energy and ambition written all over it. The older man stomped out.

'Apologies for that. I'm Nick Kerris, the manager,' the younger man said. 'These workmen don't do anything unless you continually chase them. You have to be firm, otherwise they take no notice. I take it you're here about Des Wenham? Come through to my office.'

There he gestured them into seats the other side of his desk. It was littered with large technical drawings. On the wall behind him were photographs of how Elizabeth Quay had looked when it had belonged to the Royal Navy, and alongside them artist impressions of how it would be transformed by the current development company.

'I spoke to Sergeant Elkins yesterday,' Kerris said. 'It's hard to believe Wenham is dead. I can't think why anyone would want to kill him.'

'We understand you negotiated the contract for the hire of the dredger and workboats from him recently.'

'Yes. We've had the workboats for some time. They're primarily used for moving yachts and marine equipment, although mainly the latter as we don't have any yachts here at the moment. We're a deep-water berth, or will be when all the work has been finished and the channel has been dredged. The dredger's been on-site for two weeks, shifting silt out to sea.'

'It's not operating today.'

'It will be later, when the crew deem to turn up.'

'They're unreliable?' asked Cantelli with a puzzled innocence that Horton knew was feigned.

'No, not usually.' Kerris picked up a ruler. 'They haven't been so far. I guess their boss is talking to them about Wenham's, er, death. Must have been a shock for them,' he added as an afterthought.

'What made you choose Kettering?' Cantelli again.

'I've known the company for some time, having been in the marine business for years, although not always here. I only started here in March. I've moved around, working at various marinas, teaching at sailing schools, racing boats and working as crew on yachts. I got this job because of my nautical background, and the fact I'm used to dealing with all types of people.'

'No construction background then? I'd have thought that would be necessary.'

'Oh, there's a project manager with building experience and qualifications but he's not often here. If there's anything technical then he deals with that.'

'You just keep your eye on the site.'

By Kerris's expression he considered Cantelli's statement demeaning, which was probably what Cantelli had intended in order to get a reaction. He forced a smile and airily said, 'It suits me, Sergeant. It's only temporary, although the company don't know that. I don't like being pinned down to one place. Itchy-feet syndrome.' He smiled. 'Sitting behind a desk all day is not my thing. But it builds up some money so that I can take off again.'

'Sailing?'

'Yes. I knew Kettering was a sound company. And it seemed sensible to use one that is literally just across the harbour. They were also competitively priced.'

'They did you a good deal?'

'Yes. I'm not sure I follow your line of questioning, Sergeant.'

Horton answered. 'We're just trying to gather as much background as we can about Mr Wenham in order to establish who would wish to kill him.'

Kerris looked suitably sorrowful.

'Were you here last Tuesday evening between six-thirty and seven-thirty?' asked Horton.

'As a matter of fact, I was. I shouldn't have been because I usually knock off at six and the security company take over, but on Tuesday the usual officer phoned in sick, and Secure

Right, the company who provide the security, had to find another man to replace him. He didn't arrive until a quarter to eight.'

'So, you were here alone at that time?' Horton asked.

Kerris's brow knitted. 'Yes, the contractors usually finish about four.'

'Did you see the smoke from the fire?'

'No. I wasn't looking in that direction and I'm not sure I would have seen it from here anyway.'

'Then you know the fire was on the shore at Forton Lake.'

'Only because I heard about it on the morning news before I came to work. I had no idea that Wenham had been in that car.'

Horton nodded. Cantelli wrote.

'And I didn't see anything when I left,' Kerris filled the void. 'I live in the opposite direction.'

'And you went straight home from here?'

'Yes.'

'Which is where exactly?' Cantelli asked, pencil poised. 'Just for the record, sir.'

Kerris looked annoyed at the question, but he relayed his address. 'I rent the flat and live alone. Like I said, I don't want to get tied down.' He smiled uneasily.

'Who was on duty here on Tuesday night?'

'Jed Botleigh. I can give you his mobile number and the company details. But I'm not sure why you'd need them, or why you're asking me all these questions.'

'It's tiresome, I know,' Horton said at his most pleasant. 'But we're talking to all the managers who negotiated contracts with Desmond Wenham.' Did he see a slight flicker of alarm in those dark eyes?

Kerris relayed the details to Cantelli.

'Did you know Mr Wenham before you came here?' Horton asked.

'No.'

'What was he like?'

'You mean to deal with? Tough and shrewd, but fair once he got the measure of me and knew he couldn't bluff me. Not that I blamed him for trying. The construction workers are the same. You have to stand your ground.'

As they had overheard — and it hadn't been taken well, judging by the expression on the foreman's face as he was leaving. He hadn't stood his ground with Kerris. Horton thought Kerris was cocky. Not that that was a crime.

'Wenham was a strong character and I'm all for that. Came straight at you, no small talk, a "take it or leave it" type. If you're not attuned to people like that, direct individuals who want their own way, then you give in and find yourself not only with a bad deal but also not being respected. As I said, I'm used to dealing with all types, including wealthy yacht owners, some of whom think they can walk all over you. Wenham appreciated it when he met someone who knew his stuff.'

Bit of a chip on the shoulder there, thought Horton. 'What were the terms of the contract?'

'Fifty per cent up front then the remaining balance once the job's done.'

'Which will be when?'

'We've got the dredger on hire for two months. The workboats are on a month-by-month rolling basis until we get our own.'

'I'd like to have copies of the invoices and contracts, Mr Kerris.'

His eyes narrowed. 'They're confidential.'

'Not in a murder case.' Horton could play brusque too. 'But if you can't, or are unable to give them to us, we'll get permission from head office, which is . . .' Horton's eyes travelled to the large pictures on the wall where the name was displayed.

'There's no need for that. I don't see why it's relevant, but if you must I'll ask Helen to email them to you.'

'And a hard copy would be appreciated now. We can wait while it's photocopied.'

Kerris looked annoyed. He wrenched open a drawer of his desk and removed a hanging file. From it he extracted some papers.

'We can get it photocopied on the way out, sir,' Horton said as Kerris was about to rise.

Again, that hint of anger behind the eyes.

'Just a couple more questions, then we'll leave you to your work. When did you last see Mr Wenham?'

'When we met to discuss the dredger contract.'

'And that was?'

Kerris flicked through his mobile. 'A month ago, the twentieth of June. After that we liaised by phone and email. He sent the contract over as an email document, which I signed and returned by the same method.'

'Did Mr Wenham speak about his personal life?'

'He told me he played golf and asked if I did. I don't. Not the least bit interested in spending hours hitting a ball into holes. Not enough action or exhilaration in it.'

'Oh, I don't know,' Cantelli said lazily. 'I've seen some golfers get very excited.'

'I prefer to pit my wits against the weather and the sea.'

Cantelli shuddered.

Kerris eyed him pitifully. 'Racing. Now there's a challenge for you. You have to take risks. You're up against the elements, which are uncontrollable, but that's part of the fun.'

Horton thought of Harriet and her brother Alastair, and of Cowes Week. Would they enter their father's yacht? Surely not, it would be in bad taste to do so. Perhaps that was what they had been arguing over.

In the outer office Kerris asked Helen to photocopy the contracts. He seemed inclined to watch her.

Cantelli said, 'Perhaps you could email a copy to me now, sir.'

'All right,' Kerris replied with ill grace and disappeared into his office.

Horton addressed Helen. 'Did you meet Mr Wenham when he was negotiating the contract with Mr Kerris?'

'I did.'

'And that was when?'

'About a month ago.'

'Have you seen him since?'

'No.'

'What was he like?'

'OK.' Then with a quick glance at Kerris's office, she added, 'Fancied himself and his chances, like someone else I know. And I don't fancy *him*.'

Cantelli's phone pinged as Kerris emerged. 'All come through OK,' Cantelli said cheerily. Horton took the stapled photocopied contract from Helen.

'Thank you for your cooperation, sir. I'm sure everything is fine with the contracts, but we have to check and double-check everything in a murder investigation.'

Helen's mouth gaped. Kerris's eyes flashed fury but he said smoothly, 'Of course we'll do everything to help. Won't we, Helen?' It sounded more like a threat than a suggestion, thought Horton.

Cantelli obviously thought the same. Outside he said, 'Changed his tune a bit then, Mr Smooth.'

'You don't like him?'

'Not bothered either way but *I* wouldn't want to work with him. My sympathies are with that foreman. Bet he felt like telling cocksure Kerris to go to blazes. He thinks he knows it all and probably knows sweet nothing. Bet the workers love him.'

'And did he love or hate Wenham?'

'Wenham might have had something over Kerris.' Cantelli halted and did a bit of elaborate pocket searching. 'I think I left my pencil behind.' He turned then found the offending item behind his ear and enacted a drama of relief.

They walked on. 'The stage has lost a great actor to the force. Was he watching us?'

'Yep. Want me to arrest him now? It would save us a lot of time and hassle. We could beat a confession out of him, or better still take away his toys — his desk, office and computer.'

Horton laughed. 'You've been watching too many old movies while recuperating. No evidence. But we'll keep him in mind, because it appears he was alone at the time of the murder and he could have used one those workboats to meet Wenham.' Horton pointed to them on the pontoon. 'They're red, and a witness saw what he thought was a boat with something red on it heading into the creek. He could also have a motive if he was on the fiddle with Wenham. I'll tell Uckfield to look at Wenham's contracts with Kerris in particular, unless Dennings has already uncovered a fraud, although I doubt it.'

'Now who's being prejudiced?'

'When we get back, contact the security company. Find out if Jed Botleigh arrived at the time Kerris says he did, which I expect to be the case. I'll phone Uckfield.'

Horton relayed to the Super his thoughts about the fraud. 'Dennings didn't notice anything,' Uckfield said. To Horton that was no recommendation that everything was tickety-boo.

'Kerris is very sure of himself. He admits to taking the job as a stopgap until he saves up enough money to take off again, sailing or yacht racing. So, he might not have been averse to earning a bit extra. Wenham might have recognized in Kerris a fellow creature, as they're both strong characters and in love with themselves. But there was a falling out between them, maybe Kerris thought he should be paid more, or Wenham had something on Kerris and tried to blackmail him into cooperating on invoice fraud. He'd have motive, opportunity, the means and access to a possible weapon — an oar, paddle or some kind of building implement — and he knows how to handle a boat.'

'I'll get the Economic Crime Unit to look at Kettering's accounts and all the contracts. Send over the one you've got from Kerris.'

'Daniel Kettering could also be a suspect, and to my mind, Kerris and Kettering are much more likely suspects than Preston. Kettering could have discovered Wenham had fleeced him of thousands of pounds. But Wenham had found out that Daniel Kettering was also bent, that he'd been fiddling the income tax or VAT people maybe. Daniel Kettering knew Wenham would bleed him dry. He could easily have used one of his workboats to travel to meet Wenham. Does Kettering have an alibi?'

'Several, and they're all Pompey's finest. He was dining with them at a business dinner on the night in question. Kettering is not our man. Dennings and Seaton are there now interviewing the staff. And Bliss and Chawla are on their way to Gloucestershire to see what Marlene can tell us about Wenham and Preston. Preston's still very much in the frame as far as I'm concerned.'

Horton said they were due at the mortuary, where they hoped to get more on the Southmoor remains. At the traffic lights Cantelli handed him his mobile and Horton forwarded the contract details to Uckfield.

'I'm glad I'm not in an ambulance this time,' Cantelli added, turning into the hospital complex.

'So am I,' Horton replied with feeling.

CHAPTER TWENTY-TWO

'Delighted to see you up and well, Sergeant,' Gaye greeted them.

Cantelli grinned. 'And I'm glad not to be one of your patients.'

'I hope you won't be for a very, very long time, if ever, and by then I'll have retired and sailed off into the sunset.'

'How did your competitions go at the weekend?' Horton asked, trying to ignore the smell of the mortuary, although it was thankfully devoid of bodies, save the remains of the skeleton spread out on the slab before them.

'Very well. I won several events. You wouldn't believe how competitive some dinghy sailors are. They'd do any-thing to win and don't much like it when they don't — the sulks, tantrums, black looks, and that's just me.'

Lauder cleared his throat.

Horton said, 'Sorry, please go ahead, Dr Lauder.'

'What I have to tell you won't take long, and then you can get back to your sailing conversation.' Lauder viewed them over the steel rim of his spectacles.

Horton ignored the sarcasm.

'There's not much to reveal about your corpse. There is, as you can see, the skull, some ribs, the pelvis, tibia and humerus and some other bones. From my initial study — and you must bear in mind, Inspector, that I haven't examined in depth any of these bones or conducted tests on them.'

'Of course. Anything you can tell us will be helpful.'

'The size and shape of the pelvis indicates it is male, of which Dr Clayton has already advised you. As we also have the femur, tibia and humerus we can determine his height. He was five feet eight inches. I'd have to more carefully examine the fusion of the bones to tell you how old he was. I'm not in the business of guessing, but as you look about to press me, I would say, from my experience, and from the teeth, he was between twenty-five and thirty-five at the time of death. Certainly not an old man or a juvenile.' Lauder threw Gaye a look and she nodded her agreement.

'Can you give me an approximate idea of how long he's been dead?' Horton asked while his mind swam with thoughts. This was one of the critical points.

'Analysis of cortical and trabecular bone will give me a better estimate of that, Inspector, but the bones are not light and crumbling so it is not an ancient skeleton, by that I mean a century old or more. Nor is it less than five years old, there are no tags of soft tissue or ligaments and no blood pigments. The soapy texture of the surface also indicates that the remains have lain where you found them less than a few decades. What type of soil was he found in?'

Horton relayed what Marsden had told him, qualifying it with the point that they hadn't had the results of the soil analysis yet. 'I can confirm the conditions were humid and the corpse would have been exposed to tidal deposits over a period of time as well as considerable tidal activity more recently. I also believe he wasn't buried very deeply.'

'If that proves to be correct, I would conjecture that he has lain where he was discovered for at least ten years.'

Horton thought of how Doyle had been missing for fifteen years. 'From what you've told me before in similar cases, bone doesn't contain much nuclear DNA, but can you get anything from these remains?'

'Mitochondrial DNA, yes, inherited from the maternal bloodline. It lasts longer. I should be able to extract enough to give you something for a match against the missing persons database, which is what you're thinking.'

'It is.'

'There is one more significant fact,' Lauder said with a slight twinkle in his eyes which Horton could see mirrored in Gaye's.

'Dr Clayton and I have been examining the ribs you managed to recover and we've found this one has a scraping.'

Horton peered at the one Lauder was indicating. Cantelli, chewing his gum, did so too. 'Caused by an animal?' Horton asked.

Gaye answered. 'No, the pattern doesn't fit.'

Lauder picked up the conversation. 'We can send over the images we've taken of it, and I will need a much closer study before I can confirm it, but it appears that this man was stabbed with a sharp implement, which scraped his rib. Whether that was the cause of his death is another matter.'

Horton exchanged a glance with Cantelli before saying, 'How certain are you he was stabbed?'

'Ninety per cent.'

That was good enough for Horton. 'Was the killer facing the victim or was the weapon wielded from behind, when the victim's back was turned?'

'Almost impossible to say.'

Gaye said, 'There might be evidence of a knife where the bones were found.'

And Horton hadn't examined the items he and the other officers had collected and bagged up. He'd asked Walters to log them in without him looking at them. He couldn't recall picking up anything that resembled a knife blade, or seeing it among the items, but then he hadn't studied them, being more concerned about Cantelli at the time, and exhausted. And some of the items they collected had clods of earth around them. He'd rectify that immediately on his return. He asked Dr Lauder to proceed with his tests as soon as possible.

Outside the mortuary Cantelli said, 'You're not surprised that we're looking at murder, are you?'

'No. And you know who I think it is in there?'

'Jamie Doyle?'

'Yes. He went missing fifteen years ago. He was twenty-five and five feet eight inches tall.'

'It's a bit vague though, Andy. It might be someone who's never been reported missing.'

'I know.' No one seemed to be missing Ashford, except him. 'But let's assume it is Doyle for now, although I can't think what he would have been doing at Southmoor, it's a long way off his patch. There's absolutely no reason for him to have gone there, no houses to rob, no one to mug, no pubs, nothing.'

'Perhaps that's the reason he *was* there.'

Horton threw Cantelli a sharp glance. 'Drug dealing?'

'Could his supplier have come up the harbour by boat for a meet where his body was found?'

'On a high tide, yes. It would be perfect on a dark night, isolated, and at that time no walkers or runners. And a boat wouldn't have looked suspicious. Alternatively, he could have met someone in the car park at night. That would have been deserted.' His expression clouded over. 'But I'm not sure how he would have got there. He didn't have a car, or at least one isn't mentioned in the missing person report.'

'Did he drive?'

Horton shrugged.

'If he did, even if he didn't have a licence, he could have stolen a car,' Cantelli continued.

'Yes. And what about his prints and DNA being on those handcuffs? We've been discussing the possibility that he might have been killed after the robbery and his body dumped in Sinah Lake, but it could have been at Southmoor.' They stepped out into the sweltering heat. 'If so, then he voluntarily went there with his confederate, because I defy anyone to have transported a body from the car park to that spot, not unless they had a wheelbarrow. Even then they would need to have been pretty fit to push it with a dead body in it.'

Cantelli zapped open the car.

'And what was the motive? We know Doyle was hand-cuffed to that box. Why not release him from the cuffs in the car or in the car park?'

'Perhaps he was released and then he and his killer walked along the footpath.'

'But Doyle wouldn't have gone if that wretched box was back in the car, or in the possession of another person . . .' Horton paused with the seat belt in his hand. He recalled the Doyle of old. 'But hang on, he might have done. Doyle thought he could eliminate this other person. That was his intention, and why he suggested Southmoor. He could claim all the loot himself. Or . . .' He rapidly thought. 'There were three of them. Doyle played the part of the criminal, some-one else played the part of the copper — Ashford, maybe — and the third person was the source of their information, the person who knew where the coins were, and possibly other more valuable treasure in a third, or even fourth or fifth, reticule — jewellery, diamonds or whatever.'

'Doyle's girlfriend.' Cantelli started the car. 'This Janice or Julie, the one Spider told you about.'

'Yes, and she and Doyle thought they'd cut out the pho-ney copper. Only, the man who played the copper cut out Doyle. And he also cut out the woman.' Horton let down the window and rested his arm on the sill as he mulled all this over. 'She too could be buried somewhere on that moor, or perhaps he ditched her body in the sea. There might be a missing person report on her, or a body was found around that time which to date hasn't been identified.'

'Or it's never been found if she's in Sinah Lake.'

Horton sighed. 'We might be barking up completely the wrong tree, Barney, and those remains aren't Doyle's at all. We'd better wait to see if Lauder can get DNA. In the meantime, we'll look for a murder weapon in among the items collected from Southmoor.'

Cantelli went to fetch them while Horton made for CID, where Walters greeted him with the news that Peter Ashford's brother had been killed in a car accident in Manchester three years ago. 'Can't find any living relatives, and there's still no sign of him or his car.'

Horton briefed him about the Southmoor remains and that the victim could have been Jamie Doyle. 'Take a look in missing persons for a female in her twenties who went missing at the same time, or for any unidentified female found at that time. Or come to that, any suspicious deaths around then. Also, for robberies of coins, medals, jewellery or antiques around fifteen years ago, when Doyle went AWOL.'

'Will do.'

Cantelli walked in with two large black plastic bin liners and the evidence bags from the search at Southmoor. Horton cleared his desk. Cantelli spread out the bin liners and Horton, wearing latex gloves, emptied the contents of the three large bags onto them.

'It's amazing what you can find along the coast.' Cantelli picked over the stuff. 'A corkscrew, old tin cans, fragments of pottery. Might be some Roman coins or Saxon jewellery in among this lot. If there is, I bag it as treasure trove.'

'I collected them,' Horton said, turning over the various pieces of pottery and other sundry items.

'Then we'll split the vast fortune when it goes for millions of pounds at auction.'

'We should be so lucky.' Horton smiled.

'Maybe we should instigate a wider search of the area for more remains.'

'We'd sink in the boggy ground and any bones could be well scattered by now. But you've given me an idea. Speak to the council and establish when that footpath was last examined. Someone must have done so because wooden barriers have been erected either end of the broken section to stop people falling into it, and no one reported seeing bony hands or anything suspicious then.'

'This is pretty. Part of a Roman palace mosaic?'

'More like a tile from the local kitchen showroom. Find out when any work, whatever it was, has been done in that area in the last, say, twenty years. It might help us to get nearer to a time frame for when the body was buried there, especially if it isn't Doyle.'

'Bingo!' Cantelli cried, pointing at a strip of metal he'd cleared of mud, on the end of which was a red plastic handle.

Horton examined it. 'I never thought I'd say this, but thank goodness for plastic.' One of the other officers must have picked it up because Horton hadn't seen it before. And because plastic didn't rot, the knife blade in it was highly visible. The steel blade could easily have been lost in among all the debris and dirt. 'The plastic handle could still have some DNA and prints on it, and the knife blade some blood traces. Dr Pooley will love it, he'll be able to use his magic machines. Get it over to Joliffe first as priority for blood and DNA, and when he's finished with it, ask him to despatch it to Pooley promptly. I'll email both to say it's on its way.'

That he did. Then he went to report to Uckfield and bumped into him at the bottom of the stairs.

'Dean's called a briefing with the Chief at HQ,' Uckfield grumbled, marching on. 'He wants to know where we're going with the Wenham investigation. Have you got anything that will put them in a good mood?'

'The opposite. It looks as though we have another murder on our hands. Dr Lauder and Dr Clayton believe the Southmoor man could have been stabbed, there's scraping on one of the ribs to indicate it.'

Uckfield halted. 'That's all we need. Are they sure?'

'Ninety per cent until Lauder re-examines the rib.'

Uckfield pushed open the back door and they stepped into the heat. Horton swiftly told him about the knife and who the victim might be, adding, 'If it is Jamie Doyle, then he's connected with the tin box found in Sinah Lake. His DNA and prints were on the handcuffs attached to it.'

'Tell me about it later, if and when you get evidence that the knife was used and Lauder's more than ninety per cent certain the victim was stabbed. I've got enough on my plate without investigating a murder that might not be one.

You deal with it for now.' He opened the car and glanced at his watch. 'Dennings is still at Kettering. He says the staff hated Wenham, and the office manager, Amanda Rayland, couldn't stand him, said he was a male chauvinist pig of the highest order. She couldn't understand why Daniel Kettering had promoted him and often wished Wenham was back on the dredgers and as far away from the office as possible.'

'And the two women who left?'

'One emigrated to Australia two years ago, the other lives in Newcastle. We have their details but the woman who left in May, Suzanne Edley, lives locally. Amanda Rayland thinks she might have been intimidated by Wenham. No one's spoken to her yet.'

'Want me to go?'

'Why? You got nothing better to do?' Uckfield said sarcastically.

'Just keen to help,' Horton said brightly. 'And you do seem to have seconded CID to your investigation.'

'Get the details from Trueman. Oh, and Bliss says Marlene's admitted that Preston was stealing from his previous employer and that she had an affair with him and with Wenham at the same time. She claims Wenham was no big deal, although he thought he was. I'm late.'

Horton made for the canteen, picked out some sandwiches, then diverted to the incident suite and Trueman. 'Have you been able to access Wenham's bank account or mobile records yet?'

Trueman shook his head.

'I'm keen to know if he bought tickets for a gig at the holiday park on Hayling Island, which could be where he saw Preston.'

'I'll contact them, they should have a record of the transactions.'

'Thanks. Let me have Suzanne Edley's address. I'm going to interview her.'

He returned to his office, where Cantelli said the security company had confirmed Jed Botleigh took over from

Kerris on Tuesday night at 7.45 p.m. 'I haven't had time to get on to the council yet.'

'Leave that until later. We're going to interview a woman who might be able to tell us more about Desmond Wenham.'

CHAPTER TWENTY-THREE

Cantelli knocked on the door of the small terraced house in one of the narrow streets not far from the Eastney seafront. The heat blazed down on them. The emptied wheelie bin hadn't been taken in, which suggested Ms Edley was out. This was confirmed when a tall, excessively slim woman in her late thirties with an anxious expression headed towards them. She halted, looked about to bolt, then thought better of it and continued. It had to be Suzanne.

'Ms Edley?' Horton asked kindly, recognizing a nervous woman, which could be on account of seeing two men on her doorstep. She could have financial difficulties and thought they'd come to repossess a belonging or two. Perhaps she thought they were intent on selling her something. Or maybe she had some incriminating goods inside. She didn't look to have criminal tendencies, and years of experience told him she most probably didn't. 'Police.' He showed his warrant card, quickly adding at her terrified expression, 'It's all right, there's nothing to worry about. You're not in any trouble, and we haven't come with bad news. There are a few questions we'd like to ask you. I'm Detective Inspector Andy Horton and this is Detective Sergeant Barney Cantelli. We understand you worked for Kettering and we're talking to everyone who knew Desmond Wenham. You might have read he has died. We're treating his death as a homicide.'

'I only worked at Kettering for five months and for one of those I was off sick. I didn't really know him.'

It was obviously a lie. She wouldn't look at them and her skin had blanched. Horton could see there was a great deal more here. He judged Cantelli could also, and from what they had learned of Wenham, he suspected what that might be.

'Can we have a brief talk? Shall we go inside?'

'No. I mean, not in the house. The girl I share with is on nights.'

Again, a lie. He was certain no one was in, unless the occupant was a very sound sleeper and hadn't heard them knocking. But Horton could see Suzanne was very nervous about being alone with them in her house.

'Then how about we buy you a cup of tea?' Cantelli said, judging the situation correctly as Horton knew he would. 'There's a café on the seafront and this hot weather makes me thirsty.'

'All right. Just let me put the shopping away.'

He got a small smile. Yes, Horton thought, safety in a public place. She disappeared inside, shutting the door behind her.

Cantelli said, 'I don't think there's anyone in there. Perhaps she won't come out.' But she did a few minutes later, looking more composed. It was, Horton thought, as though she'd given herself a talking to and had decided on what course of action to take with them.

They walked up the road. Cantelli chatted pleasantly about the weather and his sister's café at the other end of the promenade. Horton could see him weaving his magic, and Suzanne began to relax. She smiled a few times and told Cantelli she had often been in Isabella's café and enjoyed the food there.

On the packed seafront Horton went inside the coffee shop to buy the drinks while Cantelli, continuing to put

Suzanne at ease, found a vacant seat under the shade of a parasol on the veranda, overlooking the stony beach.

The sea glistened and children squealed with delight in the water as Horton made for the seat with their drinks. The Solent was awash with yachts, motorboats and jet skis, punctuated by a cargo ship heading out of Portsmouth and a giant container ship heading towards Southampton. The Isle of Wight was shrouded in a heat haze, but he could make out the ferries trundling back and forth across the water.

When they were settled with their drinks, Cantelli gradually brought the conversation round to Wenham. Horton let him lead the interview. Putting vulnerable and nervous witnesses at ease was one of the things Cantelli was particularly good at.

'When did you start working for Kettering?'

'The beginning of January. New Year, new job and all that. I was their customer account clerk, which meant I answered the telephone, processed enquiries, liaised with the marina managers. I enjoyed the job. I work for Hovertravel now. It's my day off, you're lucky you caught me at home.'

'We are, and we're grateful for your time and help. So you came into contact with Mr Wenham a great deal?' Cantelli asked almost casually.

She looked down at her cup of tea and then her eyes flicked between them. 'I did.' Her jaw tightened.

'You didn't like him?'

She remained silent. Cantelli threw Horton a sidelong glance.

'It's all right, Suzanne, we know what he was like,' Cantelli said gently.

Her head came up. The nervous expression was back in place.

'He's the reason you left, isn't he?'

'Amanda told you, I suppose. The office manager.' She took a sip of tea.

Horton answered. 'Amanda hasn't said much, just that she believes Wenham is the reason you went off sick and left the company. That's true, isn't it?' Horton wondered if Amanda had spoken to Dennings about this. Maybe she had and Dennings hadn't thought much of it.

'Amanda warned me what he was like and I didn't take any notice.'

Cantelli wasn't taking notes, as she would have clammed up if he had got out his notebook.

'I blamed myself for falling for all the bullshit, but he was so convincing and so charming.'

I bet! Wenham could see that Suzanne was naïve, vulnerable, innocent — just the type he went for. Horton's conversation with Spider came to him about Doyle and his type of victim — the same, this Julie or Janice.

'Amanda hated him. I thought she was bitter because of her own failed relationships. Eventually I agreed to go out with him. We had a meal and then went on to the casino. I drank quite a bit, but I wasn't drunk, just a bit light-headed. I was having fun.' She paused to bite her nails, frowning as she recalled the evening. 'It was after one o'clock when we left. I thought he was taking me home then I realized he was driving in the opposite direction, past the office and down towards the harbour. I told him I was tired and that I wanted to go home. He said we'd take look at the view across the harbour, it was a nice night. I felt uncomfortable and said I could see the harbour any time. He joked and said we'd only be a few moments and what was the hurry?'

She shifted and her eyes darted warily between them. It was an expression Horton had seen many times before — and recently, he thought, but couldn't remember where.

'I told him I had to get back, but he wouldn't listen. He drove down to Tipner Sailing Club and parked the car to the left of the clubhouse. There was no one about at that time in the morning and there's only the old derelict boatyard next to it.'

'We know the place,' Horton said, thinking of the arson attack at the sailing club in April.

'I could see this meant trouble, but I thought surely he would listen to me. I asked him to take me home. He started in on me. I pushed him away and demanded that he open the car. He said he'd do no such thing. He joked and said something about there being no such thing as a free meal and surely I knew that. He didn't believe I was *that* naïve. He said I had led him on. I hadn't, I swear it. Or if I did, I didn't realize it. He said I had to pay my dues for the meal and the gambling.'

A child squealed with laughter. It seemed so out of place, but Suzanne didn't notice.

'I tried to get away, but he was very strong and . . .'

'He became violent,' Cantelli said.

Again, that terrified expression, followed by one that Horton could only think of as shame. He was despising Wenham even more.

'I struggled. He said it was what girls like me wanted. I tried to pull away but couldn't. I didn't see how I could get out of it.'

She took a deep breath and exhaled. Horton could see Cantelli's sympathetic expression and under it he sensed his anger. Horton felt it too. Wenham was a nasty bastard.

She said, 'If it hadn't been for that fire, I dread to think what would have happened.'

'Fire?' Horton asked, his pulse skipping a beat. My God, had they been there the very night of the arson attack on the sailing club?

'There was this whoosh and huge flames. He let go of me and got out of the car, swearing. I did too and I ran like the devil, praying he wouldn't come after me. I knew that if he did, he'd grab me and get me back inside that car.' Her face was flushed and her eyes were fearful as she relived the memory. She again bit into her nails.

'Go on,' Cantelli said gently.

'I looked round and could see him in the light of the fire going to the waterside. I ducked behind a shrub by the roadside. Then came the sound of the fire engines in the distance. I saw him running back to his car and he drove away at speed.'

I bet he did, thought Horton. Wenham wouldn't have wanted to get caught there.

'I waited until he'd gone and the fire engine had arrived, then I ran to the main road. I walked home. I didn't want a taxi driver yapping away to me. I held it together until I got home then I went to pieces. My lodger was at work. I pretended to be ill the next day. I *was* ill. I couldn't tell her. I couldn't tell anyone. I felt so ashamed.'

Horton said, 'You have nothing to be ashamed about, Suzanne. It wasn't your fault. You didn't do anything wrong.'

She gave a sad smile and drank some tea. 'I couldn't go into work. I couldn't face him ever again. My doctor signed me off. I've had some mental health issues in the past and she could see I was struggling. I handed in my notice by letter along with the sick note. Amanda came to see me and asked if I was OK. I didn't tell her about him. I said I was sorry, but the job wasn't for me. I was struggling mentally. I think she guessed that something had happened with him because she said she'd see he got the sack this time. I told her nothing happened, that she was wrong. If she or I complained then it would have to go to tribunal, and I knew he would twist everything to make it sound as though I had led him on. I couldn't face that, or people knowing.'

Horton wondered if the same had happened to others over the years — people who, rather than complaining, had ducked out, quickly and quietly. And Daniel Kettering had said and done nothing. Why? Because Wenham had something on the boss, just as he'd speculated to Uckfield earlier.

'I was afraid he would be vindictive and come after me.'

Horton could well imagine her hiding behind the door of her house, scared stiff he would show up.

'I have to ask you, Suzanne, where were you last Tuesday between six and eight in the evening?' He didn't think she had decided to get revenge on Wenham.

'At home.'

'With anyone?'

209

She shook her head. 'My lodger was at work. I didn't kill him. Will I have to give a statement?'

'It might be best if you would.' Although Horton wasn't thinking solely in respect of Wenham's murder. There was that unsolved sailing club arson. 'You can come to the station and Sergeant Cantelli here will take it. Would that be all right? There's no hurry, sometime in the next couple of days.' He handed over his card and Cantelli did the same.

'Just call me when you're ready,' Cantelli said.

'I will, thank you. In fact, it's helped to talk about it.'

'Shall we walk back with you?' Cantelli asked.

'No, I'll stay here a few minutes. Thank you for the tea.'

'I don't care for that devil at all,' Cantelli said with feeling as they walked back to the car. 'I'm not surprised someone killed him.'

'Wenham made a lot of enemies. I'm not sure she told us the whole truth, but only because it was too painful for her. The timing is interesting.'

'The sailing club arson.'

'Yes, and Wenham got out of the car and ran to the harbour side. Let's call at Tipner before we go back to the station.'

The Tipner Sailing Club was the other side of the motorway from the police station. It was a stone's throw from the international ferry port. The old boatyard close to it had been sold for redevelopment, which hadn't yet begun. A year ago a salvage operation had uncovered the body of a woman on one of the sunken sailing boats. It was during that investigation he had met Harriet, who had assisted them as the case was believed to have European connections.

Cantelli parked up where Suzanne said Wenham had. There were several vehicles here now, the club being open and busy.

Climbing out, Horton said, 'He ran down there.'

They made their way the short distance down an alleyway to the harbour side. There to the right was the club compound that had been struck by fire.

Horton said. 'The fire was reported by a passing yachtsman heading into Horsea Marina at 1.34 a.m. The night was clear and still, and the Molotov cocktail thrown from the sea, over those steel gates. Wenham had a perfect view of the arsonist.'

'And he took off because he didn't wish to explain why he was here, and we know Suzanne was too terrified to tell.'

'Wenham, true to form from what we've discovered, started blackmailing the arsonist, which is why there haven't been any more sailing club arsons.' They had been wondering for a while why only this club had been targeted, and one reason was that the arsonist had a personal grudge against one of the three people whose dinghies had been torched: the chief constable, Councillor Levy or Venda Atkinson, and a retired dentist. 'Wenham demands more money and our arsonist has had enough. Instead of a sailing club, he torched that car with Wenham in it.'

'That rules out Preston and Kerris.'

'But does it?'

'I can't see Robin Preston as the sailing club arsonist.'

Horton couldn't either. 'No, he's not fit or agile enough to have thrown that Molotov cocktail, and I don't think he would know his way around the harbour in the dark. He told me he doesn't sail or own a boat. He uses the angling club one on the lake and that's about it.'

'And Nick Kerris hasn't got a motive for the fires.'

'That we've yet to find. But he knows the harbour and he knows how to handle a boat. I'd like to know what he was doing at the time of this arson, although I'm sure he'll claim not to remember. He could have been forced into invoice fraud with Wenham in return for his silence.'

'His name didn't come up on the Tipner membership list or for being blackballed. It might be someone who works at Kettering or who works around the harbour, and that's a lot of people.'

'Get the Kettering staff and customer list from Trueman and ask Walters to start cross-checking it with the Tipner Sailing Club lists. See if anyone appears on both.'

They returned to the station where a heavily perspiring Walters flapped his hand in front of his reddened face. 'Is it getting warm in here or I am having a hot flush?'

'It's getting hotter.' Horton looked up at the air-conditioning system. 'Now you come to mention it, I can't hear the air-conditioning.'

'Typical for it to go on the blink just when you need it. I can't find any reports of missing women that fit the time you requested, guv, and no reports of unidentified females or suspicious deaths yet unresolved.'

'Maybe a woman wasn't involved with Doyle and that tin box, or her accomplice didn't dispense with her.'

'And I can't find anything reported on stolen coins or antiques or jewellery around that time.'

Horton left Cantelli to update Walters, then in his office read through the reports from the Gosport police that they had instigated in connection with the car fire homicide. A couple of the residents opposite the Hardway Sailing Club had seen dinghies being launched from the public slipway on that Tuesday but they couldn't remember the time. It would have been at high water though. Nor could they recall the people launching them or the cars in the car park. The officers hadn't noted the colour of the dinghies because they hadn't been tasked to ask that question. Had any of them been red, as Elkins had discovered? He wondered though if that now mattered given that the Elizabeth Quay workboats were that colour and Kerris was in the frame for Wenham's murder.

He tapped into the Police National Computer. Nick Kerris didn't have a criminal record, but Horton wondered if he had left his previous employment under a cloud or there had been suspicions about him. It wouldn't be anything that would show up on his employment record because the development company wouldn't have hired him at Elizabeth Quay.

He rose and crossed to Cantelli. 'You look shattered. I don't want you having a relapse. It's been a long hot day, get off home.'

'I'll tackle the council about Southmoor tomorrow.'

'And we might have something from Joliffe and Dr Pooley on that knife.'

Uckfield's car was back. Horton made for the incident suite, stopping off at Bliss's office on the way, where he updated her on the Tipner Sailing Club arson in relation to Wenham. Before he'd even finished, she'd risen, and they made their way up the stairs. The Super was in a worse mood than when he'd left. His meeting with Dean obviously hadn't gone well. He brightened up a little when he heard Horton's report. Getting the killer and the sailing club arsonist in one hit would certainly please ACC Dean, not to mention the Chief Constable.

Trueman said there had been no record of Wenham having bought tickets for any gigs at the Hayling Island holiday park and there was nothing so far on Wenham having recently dated anyone he'd met online. Seaton reported that no one claimed to have played golf with him at the Hayling Golf Club, and Chawla had drawn a blank with the angling club members. Dennings said the Economic Crime Unit were going into Kettering tomorrow. 'If they pick up something on the Elizabeth Quay contracts, that could give us enough to bring Kerris in.'

Horton updated them on the Southmoor remains, relaying what he and Cantelli had discussed earlier about a possible scam being executed by Ashford and Doyle some fifteen years ago, and that the remains could be those of Doyle, and that Ashford had gone missing.

Uckfield scratched his nose. 'It's all ifs and buts. Wait until we get confirmation on DNA and that it is murder. Meanwhile, officially post Ashford as missing and instigate basic enquiries.'

Horton would also get Cantelli delving into Ashford's background and employment history to see if they could prove a past link with Doyle.

CHAPTER TWENTY-FOUR

Tuesday

Horton filed the missing person report the next morning after verifying with Camplow's manager that Ashford hadn't been in contact, that his ex-wife hadn't heard from him and after Sergeant Wells had sent a unit around to Ashford's flat to make sure he hadn't returned home. Horton had also tried Ashford's mobile again and it went straight to voicemail. Ashford had either ditched the phone and was on the run because he was fearful of being charged with theft and the murder of Doyle, or he was dead inside his car in a secluded spot after chewing on hemlock water dropwort.

He drew back his office blinds, opened the window and closed the blinds again. There wasn't a breath of wind, and the air-conditioning hadn't been fixed. Last night on his run he had mentally revisited their interview with Suzanne Edley. Again, he experienced that odd feeling that he'd seen her before. It was the look she had given them, half-terrified and guilty. But he couldn't think why it bugged him and where he'd seen it.

Joliffe rang to say there had been no traces of blood on the knife. And no residual DNA. He'd sent the knife over to

Dr Pooley. Horton messaged Pooley and asked him to fast-track it. As he came off his phone, he saw that he had a message from Spider Baxter. Spider had remembered something about Jamie's last girlfriend and he was cleaning the streets round Southsea Common, if Mr Horton was around that way. If not, he'd be happy to see him at the Church of the Golden Brethren tomorrow evening. Horton decided now was the lesser of two evils. Besides, he was curious to hear what Spider had to say.

He found him sitting on the grass under a patch of trees close to the Holiday Inn just off the seafront from the funfair, his cleaning barrow in the road by a group of parked cars. Spider had discarded his orange high-vis jacket and his cap and was biting into a large sausage roll. Horton parked the Harley, removed his helmet and walked across to him. He sat beside him on the straw-like grass.

'Hot work.'

'It is when wearing this stuff.' Spider pointed to the bright orange trousers. 'Still, these days you coppers have to wear enough body armour to fight the Battle of Hastings.'

'You get to discard some of it when you become a detective. You've remembered something about Doyle's girlfriend?'

'I should have thought about it before, but it was something Freda said to me this morning about her boy that jogged my memory. I say boy, he's a man now and works for the railways. He's from her first marriage, her husband died years ago. That's when she decided to take up prison visiting — she'd done it enough times for him when they were married, she thought she might just as well continue it voluntarily, like. He died in Wandsworth, you know.'

'No, I didn't. About this girl, you've remembered her name?'

'No.'

'That's a pity, although I doubt it makes much difference. Doyle could have had a string of girls after her or at the same time.'

'He could, but you know how I told you he said this one was ripe?'

Horton nodded.

'Well, she was quiet, like. Shy, seemed a bit of a loner, innocent, naive.'

Suzanne Edley popped into Horton's mind.

'But there was another reason he chose her, and Freda saying about her Carl's acne — that's her boy, when he was a teenager — brought it all back. I remember now that this poor girl wasn't pretty like Jamie's usual sort, she had terrible acne.'

Horton wasn't sure how that helped him. It must have cleared up by now.

'Jamie joked something cruel about it.'

Horton despised Doyle even further, but what Spider said rang true with the boy he'd known. 'Why did he pick her up then?'

'Why do you think?' Spider said somewhat scornfully. 'A girl like that with very few fellows after her, and there's good-looking Jamie swanning in and flattering her, she'd be putty in his hands. Doyle said, no need to look at her when you're shagging her, is there? They all look alike in the dark. I'm sure you can guess some of the other cruel things he said, Mr Horton.'

He could and his heart wrenched for the woman. She must have been terribly hurt by Doyle. Once he'd got what he wanted, he'd have got rid of her in the most callous way possible. He wondered what had happened to her. Then thoughts tumbled through his mind. Among them was the dawning of where he'd seen Suzanne's expression before. And not only that, but one of her gestures too. Suzanne's hand had gone to her mouth. She'd bitten her nails. He recalled recently another woman whose hand had gone to her mouth and gently touched her nose. But no, it couldn't be.

Spider had nothing more to tell and Horton made his way back to the station, his mind buzzing with ideas. The air-conditioning still hadn't been fixed. The weather had grown heavier and the heat even more intense and humid.

After downing a beaker of water and pouring another from the water cooler, he entered CID and took the seat next to Cantelli. Walters was with Seaton in the incident suite, working on the sailing club and Kettering lists.

'I've got Ashford's employment history,' Cantelli said. 'But I can't see any connection with Doyle, although that doesn't mean to say there isn't one. Ashford worked on and off, labouring on building sites before working for Mowlem's, the firm that maintain the roads and pavements on behalf of Portsmouth Council. He then moved to Jacobs, the road contractors for Havant Council, before leaving to work for Camplow five years ago. Doyle could have been taken on as a casual labourer at any of those companies.'

'I doubt it, too much like hard work for him.'

'I've also spoken to someone at the council about Southmoor. The footpath has been inspected twice. Once after the initial breach two years ago. Then six months ago, after which they sent out contractors to erect the wooden barriers for safety reasons. They're wrangling with the environment agency and the landowner over who should pay to repair it, which means nothing will be done. A local reporter was there six weeks ago. She wrote a feature on it and there are some photographs. Can't see any bones sticking out.'

Horton smiled at the dark humour.

'I found her article on the internet. The usual sort of thing, risk of flooding, danger to the businesses to the north of it and houses to the east, sea reclaiming the marshland, protected historic area, et cetera.'

'Send me the link, I'd like to read it.' His phone rang. It was Lauder.

'It's as I told you, Inspector, the examination of the rib bears out a knife wound. From my tests your victim has been dead fifteen years, and I know that for a fact because I've extracted DNA from the remains. You have a match.'

Horton knew what he was going to say. He'd been right. And the idea that had been planted in his mind after his conversation with Spider returned full force.

'We've found Doyle,' he said to Cantelli after coming off the line. 'It's as we thought, the remains are his. Joliffe's just confirmed it. Doyle and Ashford teamed up on the theft of that box years ago. With the sea wall breached, which Ashford read about in the newspaper — the article you found, Barney — he knew it might only be a matter of time before the remains were found and identified, and Sinah Lake was too close to home for him. He was moving that box away from it where he dumped it years ago, when Bosman surprised him. If he'd left it where it was it would never have been found, and even if it had been, we couldn't prove it was connected to him.'

'We still can't, unless we find him and he confesses.'

'Get the full details on Doyle's and Ashford's criminal records. See if there's anything there to link them, a previous job maybe, or perhaps they had the same probation officer. Ashford's never served a custodial sentence, so he can't have met Doyle in prison.'

'He might have if he'd been held on remand.'

'True. It has to be him. And they got their information from this third party, as you and I discussed — a woman, Doyle's girlfriend. Spider told me the girl was shy, vulnerable, naïve, much like Suzanne. And he's just told me that she had very bad acne. I think I know who it might be. Judith Brindley.'

Cantelli looked stunned then sceptical.

Excitedly, Horton continued. 'She wears very heavy make-up and under it her skin is pitted. Her age matches, and her name begins with a J. Her expression when I showed her the coins and the reticules was one of horror, fear and guilt.' His mind spun back to that first meeting, that first look, that first conversation, and the subsequent one on the telephone.

Cantelli still looked doubtful.

'You didn't meet her,' Horton said, rising. 'I did.'

'It's too much of a coincidence, Andy.'

'I've already told myself that, but I have to find out.'

He hurried as fast as the traffic and speed limits would allow to the house just over the hill. There was only one car parked in front of the house — Judith's or Gareth's, he wondered as he pressed the intercom. He was pleased when Judith opened the door to him.

'My husband's on a valuation,' she said, letting him in.

'It's you I wanted to speak to.' Under his intense gaze, she flushed and put her hand to her mouth, as was her habit. A nervous gesture, yes, but one he thought she had developed years ago as a mechanism to try and hide the bad skin around her chin and mouth. She wasn't wearing the heavy make-up she had sported on his first visit, and he could see more clearly now how the devastating acne had left its marks. She hadn't expected anyone to call.

She turned and led him through to the air-conditioned conference room. He decided to launch straight in. It was a gamble, but he was certain it would yield results. 'You recognized the coins when I first came here a week ago, didn't you?'

She answered quickly but wouldn't look at him. 'I've become an expert over the years, having worked in museums and with numismatics. We both recognized what you had.'

'It was more than that. They struck a chord with you, especially when I mentioned they'd been in embroidered pouches in a tin box. You looked startled and that wasn't just ordinary surprise. You asked how I had come by them.'

'A straightforward and reasonable question.' She turned towards the fridge.

'But you knew already.'

She retrieved a bottle of water. He watched her straighten up with it in her hand. Slowly she turned towards him. Since their first and only meeting she had become drawn and her bloodshot eyes belied the fact she'd been sleeping badly.

'Why don't you tell me about it, Mrs Brindley?' Fear showed in every aspect of her face. 'You knew who once owned them,' he gently pressed. She studied him, a tremble in her hand. Only the gentle whir of the air-conditioning broke the silence. 'Who did they belong to, Mrs Brindley?' he persisted.

She sank onto the chair. 'A very nice elderly man called Norman Howe.'

Horton suppressed his triumph. He took the seat next to her, eager to hear her story. Whatever her part in the robbery, it appalled and half terrified her. 'Go on,' he encouraged kindly.

'I was living in a bedsit in Southsea. Norman owned the large house on the corner next door and was my landlord.' She looked at him, seeking reassurance or forgiveness, he wasn't certain. 'One day Mr Howe locked himself out and I helped him. Then his central heating broke down and I called the plumber. He also had a large garden, so I arranged for some gardeners to come and cut back his trees and shrubs and generally keep on top of things. We became good friends. He had some lovely things in his house, beautiful paintings and rugs.'

'And valuable coins that he showed you.'

She nodded. 'He was very trusting. Too trusting.'

'So, you stole from him,' he said in a casual manner, knowing instinctively and from years of experience that she couldn't have done, but wanting to see her reaction, which was as he had expected — appalled and shocked.

'I would never do that.'

'But you knew someone all those years ago who did.'

'I was stunned when you turned up with them.'

'And worried that your part in their theft would come out.'

'No, please, I didn't steal them, you must believe me,' she pleaded. 'I had no idea they had been taken.'

'But you must have done, otherwise you'd have told me when I came here who had owned them. You'd have admitted to knowing that person. You'd have had nothing to hide and would've been happy to cooperate, as would your husband.'

'He knows nothing about it,' she flashed, her eyes moist with tears. 'Please, Inspector, you must believe me when I tell you I am not a thief.'

No, Horton didn't think she was. 'But you told someone about them.'

She slumped dejected, as though trying to coil in on herself. If what Spider had said was true, this woman had been deeply hurt by Doyle and the painful memories had come flooding back, but he couldn't show his sympathy yet. He needed more from her.

'That person subsequently robbed the owner. Or perhaps it was your idea to rob Mr Howe, and you and Jamie Doyle thought it would be a laugh, a student prank.'

Her face blanched. 'You know about Jamie? But how could you? You've arrested him? I don't want to see him. I couldn't bear that. Please don't make me see him. Don't tell him about me.' Tears sprang to her eyes. Horton could see her distress was genuine.

'You won't see him, Judith,' he said softly. 'He's dead. His remains have been found at Southmoor.'

'Dead? But I don't understand.' She searched his face looking for the trick and saw none. 'He really is dead,' she repeated, and took a long draught of water. The air-conditioning whirred and outside came the bleeping of a lorry reversing.

'Tell me what happened, Judith,' Horton said, knowing it would be painful for her.

After a moment she drew herself up and began. 'I was a student at Portsmouth University. I met Jamie in a pub in Guildhall Walk. I rarely went into pubs or out with the other students, as it wasn't really my thing, but I was lonely and desperately trying to fit in. I was very conscious of my skin. I had terrible acne and people can be very cruel. Most of the time I just wanted to hide away, but I was persuaded by a fellow student to go out. Jamie was talking to some people up at the bar. I don't know who they were. I went up to buy a drink and he said he'd buy it. I could hardly believe he was speaking to me. I refused because I thought he was going to take the mickey, but he insisted. He talked to me looking right into my eyes. He didn't stare at my mouth and chin, which people usually did. I wore a fringe to hide it on my forehead. He was very kind. He bought me another drink and then another and he walked me home. It developed from there.'

'He told you he was on probation and about his past?'

'Yes. I didn't care about that. I believed him when he said he'd turned over a new leaf. For the first time in my life I had a boyfriend, and a very good-looking one too. There were so many beautiful girls around me, so confident with their perfect skins, and he'd chatted me up. I couldn't believe that he'd chosen me.'

But Horton could. Judith was vulnerable, even now that came through. It must have been awful for her years ago. Just as Spider had said, Doyle had capitalized on her vulnerability, not then for any criminal purposes, but he'd have had fun seducing her and using her in whatever way he thought fit, testing her to see how far she would go to please him. Horton didn't need much imagination to guess what Doyle was up to with the young, innocent Judith, who wasn't quite so innocent when he had finished with her, but had been traumatized by her relationship with him. Doyle hadn't been a bully boy like Wenham and exerted physical violence — no, his tactics were more subtle. But then, Horton corrected his thinking, if what Cheryl Budleigh had said about Wenham was true, he too began in a charming manner until he could physically and mentally torture and intimidate his victims. Horton despised men like that.

'You told Jamie about Mr Howe and the coins.'

She nodded miserably. 'It was one afternoon. We were in my bedsit. Mr Howe knocked on the door in a terrible state. He'd locked himself out again. By then I had a key because he used to do it often, and I liked to make sure he was OK. I took him home, settled him down and made him a cup of tea.'

'While Doyle poked around.'

'No. He didn't come in with me. He stayed in bed.' Her eyes dropped.

'And when you returned, Doyle asked you about him.'

'I told him about the paintings and ornaments that Mr Howe had collected over the years and the tin box with some coins in it. Mr Howe had shown them to me a couple of times. His grandmother had embroidered the purses. They were beautiful. I said the coins were valuable. But Jamie couldn't have stolen them because you said they were inside the box. Did you find the box with Jamie's body?'

'No, but we have evidence that he was involved with stealing that box. We believe he was killed by an accomplice. Do you know who that was?'

'No. I never met any of his friends. Oh, except for one and I'd rather forget that encounter.'

'When was this?'

'It was in September, not long before the term started.'

Doyle had gone missing on Saturday night on 23 September. So, the timing fitted.

'I hadn't gone home for the holidays because I couldn't bear to be away from Jamie. I was working at the Portsmouth Museum. I'd always been interested in small finds and my degree subject was history. I hadn't seen Jamie for some days, and he wouldn't answer my calls and texts. I was desperate to see him, so I went to his bedsit. I had never been there. He said his landlord wouldn't like it if he knew he had a woman there. He was very strict about those things and Jamie might get thrown out.'

I bet. Jamie didn't want her to see how he lived and what stolen goods he might have inside.

'A man answered the door. He told me I was nothing to Jamie. He had only wanted to use me. Jamie had talked and laughed about me with him. This man said some hurtful things about me and my appearance, and intimate things that only . . . only Jamie could have told him.' Her hand flew to her mouth, tears welled in her eyes. 'It was disgusting and awful. This man said Jamie had finished with me — did I really think that I was the love of Jamie's life? I was a fool. I turned away upset and bumped right into Jamie. He was furious. I thought he was going to hit me. He grabbed my arm and marched me down the road. He told me it was over between us. He said some terribly cruel personal things about me. It was as though he had hit me — worse, if you can understand that.' She swallowed hard. 'I felt so ashamed. I ran off crying, wanting to end it all. I looked at the sea at the end of South Parade Pier and thought, if I jumped, would I drown?' She paused. Horton let her compose herself.

'I don't know how long I stayed there, getting wet and cold, but eventually I went back to my bedsit, packed my suitcase and caught the night train home to my parents in Suffolk. I felt a total failure. My parents called it a nervous breakdown and thought I'd been studying too hard.' She gave a weak smile, obviously recalling their kindness. 'They told me to take some time off, that I could return and finish the course in another year. They were sure the university would have me back. But the last thing I wanted was to return to Portsmouth and continue studying for a history degree.' She drank some water. 'I was ill for a time but gradually got better, and my skin, although still bad, also seemed to settle down. I took various jobs — in a museum and an antique shop, where I learned more about small finds including coins and medals. I attended auctions and coin fairs — that was where I met Gareth, at a coin fair in London. He was an archaeologist with a keen interest in small British finds and coins.' She fiddled with her wedding ring. 'At first, I put him off. He was from Portsmouth of all places — I thought, why did it have to be here? And he wanted to set up in business here. I thought, I can't come back. I might run into Jamie. What would I do? How would I feel? But then I told myself he probably wouldn't even have recognized me. I was nothing to him, just a laugh, a sick joke. But it would be painful for me to recognize him and remember.'

'But you did return.'

'Yes. It meant so much to Gareth, and therefore to me. I never said a word to him about Jamie and haven't to this day. At first, I was terrified of running into him, but as the months became years, and we grew busier, it got easier. And Gareth is so kind and a wonderful husband. I relaxed.'

Until, Horton thought, he had shown up with the coins. 'On your return, did you visit Mr Howe, the elderly gentleman?'

'No.' She glanced down. 'I expect he died some years ago.'

Horton suspected it too.

'My parents and Gareth know nothing about Jamie. Does this have to come out?' She eyed him beseechingly.

'I don't think so, but you might be advised to talk to your husband. I'm sure he'll understand. Did Mr Howe have any relatives?'

'He had a son who never came to see him even though he lived in London, which isn't very far from here.'

'Did you and Jamie ever go to Southmoor, or the Broadmarsh Coastal Park?'

'We never went anywhere except my bedsit.'

'Did you or Jamie have a car?'

'No. I didn't drive then. He might have done, but I never saw him driving a car. He'd arrive by bus or on foot.'

'This man who answered the door to you. Do you know his name?'

She shook her head.

'Can you describe him?'

'I was too upset and shocked at being verbally attacked like that. All I can recall is that he was about my age, slim and fair.'

That would make him late thirties or early forties now. Ashford's age and description, but that was a far cry from it having been Ashford. 'If you can remember anything more about him, Mrs Brindley, it could help us. Did he have an accent?'

'I don't think so. At least, I don't remember registering one. But I had seen him once before — he'd been working with the gardeners in Mr Howe's grounds.'

'I don't suppose you remember the name of the gardening company.'

She shook her head miserably. It didn't matter, they probably weren't in business now, and even if they were, they wouldn't have employment records from back then. And this man could have been casual labour.

'Did he have any tattoos or any distinguishing features?' He recalled the tattoos on Ashford's knuckles in the photograph he'd seen in his flat.

'Not that I remember.'

Ashford might have had the tattoos done later. 'Was he Doyle's flatmate or just visiting?'

'I don't know.'

Horton had a picture of Ashford on his mobile phone. He showed it to her.

'It's like him, but I couldn't say for certain. It's just a blur.'

'That's all right.' Horton put his phone back in his pocket. 'I'll need you to come into the station to make a statement. Perhaps you could do that tomorrow?'

'I will.' She showed him to the door. 'What will happen to the coins?'

'We'll try to locate Mr Howe's son. He's the rightful owner.'

She gave a timid smile. He left her knowing those awful memories would continue to torment her. He hoped she would confide in her husband, who he felt would be understanding and provide her with comfort and reassurance. It had happened fifteen years ago, but even so, Horton knew it could still feel like yesterday.

CHAPTER TWENTY-FIVE

'The electoral roll will give us a list of people living in that house at the same time as Doyle,' Cantelli said after Horton had reported back to him. 'But this man Judith that saw could have just been visiting, and that could have been Ashford — he lived in Southsea fifteen years ago and worked for Mowlem's for the council. He could have come across Doyle and teamed up with him, and he could have been moonlighting in Mr Howe's garden.'

'From what Judith said, and I believe her, this man was very vindictive, and although I don't know Ashford, it doesn't sound like him to me.'

'I'll see if I can find Norman Howe's son. It will be interesting to know if he remembers the box and coins, and if so, why he didn't report them missing, although given what you've told me it seems he hardly saw his old man.'

Horton reached into Walters's desk drawer and found a packet of chocolate biscuits. He took one and offered the packet to Cantelli. 'They'll only melt if we don't eat them.' Biting into one, he continued, 'I think Doyle took Mr Howe's house key from Judith at some time without her knowledge and had it copied. It would save him having to break in. But instead of quietly slipping in and out, his twisted little brain

227

came up with another idea, the one you said when you were in the hospital, with his counterpart who may or may not be Ashford. Doyle liked to play games. He was manipulative and cunning. He took great delight in getting others into trouble and getting off scot-free, laughing and gloating at them.'

'You sound as though you knew him well.'

'Unfortunately, I did, at school. He was a bully, like Wenham, but in a more subtle way. Doyle had a kind of magical power over people, Judith Brindley included. She's coming in tomorrow to make her statement. Can you see her?' Horton knew Cantelli would be understanding. 'I'd like your opinion.' He reached for another biscuit. 'Shall I take them to Walters? He must be feeling faint if he hasn't eaten in the last half hour.'

'He's probably raided the vending machine.'

'Then help yourself.'

Horton retired to his office, where he made some notes on his interview with Judith while it was fresh in his mind. Then he checked through his messages, made a few calls and dealt with the urgent stuff. He needed to update Bliss and Uckfield on the Southmoor remains — neither knew yet that Lauder had confirmed murder and ID. Uckfield was in his office but there was no sign of Bliss, either in the incident suite or in her office. Perhaps she'd found an urgent meeting she needed to attend off the premises where the air-conditioning was still working. The heat was overwhelming. Trueman's five o'clock shadow had sprouted into a close-cropped beard. Dennings, in his office, was peering bleary-eyed at his computer. Seaton looked befuddled. Walters was drenched with sweat. Only Chawla looked cool, as though she could go another twenty-four hours without so much as a bead of perspiration.

'Better set up another crime board, Dave. We've got a fifteen-year-old murder to solve.'

He knocked and entered Uckfield's office. Wet patches were under the big man's armpits, his short hair was plastered to his head and his face flushed. The sweat was already running down Horton's back and he longed to be on his boat in the middle of the Solent, about the only place there would be a breeze.

'If you haven't got good news then you can bugger off,' Uckfield grumbled.

Horton briefed him about Doyle, Ashford and Judith.

'OK. Tomorrow, Trueman will start in and apply for Ashford's bank and mobile phone records. We'll also check if he's returned to his flat and lifted his passport. You were right about Wenham. He was practising fraud. It didn't take DS Webb of the Economic Crime Unit long to spot it. False invoicing.'

'The same as Marlene Arlett. Then why didn't Daniel Kettering, his accountant or his office manager pick it up?'

'That's being thoroughly investigated. The office manager is cock-a-hoop that she'd been right all along about Wenham being rotten to the core. Kettering is staggered. And who knows how the accountant will act when confronted, probably burst into tears. Aside from that, we've got nothing.'

'But it's enough to bring Kerris in for questioning.'

'When I've got the finer details from Webb, and after he's made sure that none of the other marina managers are in on it. Seaton and Walters haven't found anything to connect Kerris with the sailing club arson yet. If he did it then there must be a reason, but I'm buggered if I know what it is. I don't know about you, but I can't think in this blessed heat.' He rose and opened his door. 'Trueman, when are they going to fix the blessed air-conditioning?' he roared.

'Tomorrow.'

'It had better be.' To Horton he said, 'I'm going home. You can update Trueman about Doyle tomorrow. He's waited fifteen years, another night's not going to make a blind bit of difference, especially as it sounds as though there's no one missing him.' Horton followed Uckfield into the incident suite, where the Super bellowed, 'Let's call it a day before we all melt or have a coronary.'

Nobody needed telling twice, not least Walters. Horton had never seen him move so quickly. He turned to Trueman as Dennings emerged from his office and nodded goodbye.

'Best decision the Super's ever made,' Trueman said, shutting down his computer.

'Are they really going to fix the air-con tomorrow?'

Trueman threw him a glance. 'Who knows, could be next Christmas. I wish to God this awful weather would break.'

'Just remember that when it's howling a hurricane and peeing down with rain.'

'If only.'

'I'll give you the gen on the Southmoor murder tomorrow. Jamie Doyle's the victim, and Peter Ashford's the main suspect.' They made their way down the stairs.

'Wenham was on Hayling Island the Friday before he was killed,' Trueman said. 'But not at the golf club, he was at the Yacht Harbour. He'd been to see them about a possible quote for a dredger.'

The Yacht Harbour was the other side of the island from the holiday village, and the lake, although that only amounted to three miles. Horton returned to CID and collected his jacket and helmet. Cantelli had left. The air was heavy. He felt certain it would break in a thunderstorm and the sooner the better. It might help to herald in a brighter, fresher feel.

He thought about taking that night sail but the tide wasn't right. It was too hot to run and he didn't feel like a swim. Instead, he contented himself with a long cool drink on deck listening to the chatter of some people on a nearby boat and the occasional car on the road. He heard a child laugh. It was late for that, and it made him think of Emma on board Jarvis's superyacht, which always made his stomach clench. But he had to get used to the fact that Emma would be spending a lot of time with her future stepfather, and he had to find somewhere to live to make sure that she spent time with him too.

His thoughts veered to Harriet. He wondered if her brother would persuade the powers that be to declare his father legally dead. He saw again her expression on her father's yacht, and his thoughts turned again to whether she and her brothers would race it during Cowes Week in August. That in turn made him think of Kerris. He'd said he'd been involved in racing. Horton hadn't heard of him, but then he didn't know everyone in that field. In fact, he knew few people. He wondered if there was anything on him on the internet. There wasn't.

After another long cold drink and temperate shower, he lay on his bunk not expecting to get too much sleep. He managed it until four, then he went up on deck with a drink and sat for a while. It was the coolest part of the day. He considered again what Trueman had recently told him about Wenham and whether it was worth talking to the Yacht Harbour manager. Would he get more of a steer on Wenham? He wouldn't get anything there on Nick Kerris. And now that DS Webb had uncovered the fraud there was no need to try and unearth that. The Yacht Harbour hadn't yet negotiated or signed a contract anyway.

He finished his drink and went below. Surprisingly he fell asleep. It was gone seven-thirty when he woke. The air was even heavier, the sky a dull bluey-grey. It was stifling hot with no breeze. Despite his certainty in the early hours of the morning that he'd get nothing new at the Hayling Yacht Harbour, there was still that niggle that Preston worked and lived on Hayling and Preston had been involved with Wenham some years ago. But unless Preston kept a boat at the Yacht Harbour there was no reason for him to have been visiting there at the same time as Wenham.

He called Cantelli and asked him to brief Trueman about Doyle, then told him where he was heading. He didn't expect to be long.

It took him a while to track down the manager, but eventually Horton found him on a pontoon.

'Yes, Wenham was here last Friday.' Ken Turner straightened up from tying a small motorboat to one of the pontoons. The stout man in his mid-fifties swept his perspiring brow with the back of his broad hand. 'Why do you ask?'

'We're investigating his death. His body was found in a burnt-out car on Gosport.'

'You don't say! Bloody hell! You think it was deliberate? Kids? Hooligans?' He looked bewildered. 'But I'm not sure how I can help you. I only met him once.'

'Surely you must have used his company's dredgers before?' Horton gazed around the packed pontoons. He had never put in here, but he knew the small channel into this inlet regularly silted up.

'No. We have our own dredger, but its engine is busted and it's too expensive to fix. It'll be sent for scrap when I get around to it. So I've been forced to hire, hence contacting Kettering. Not a bad thing though because there are so many regulations nowadays with employing staff, not to mention the amount of red tape surrounding dredging and dumping. You can't just go ahead and shift the silt like you used to. You have to have it tested and analysed and then fill in countless forms to get a licence for it to be taken out to sea. Money for old rope if you ask me, can't see any harm in moving mud from one place to another, but there you go.' He shrugged his broad shoulders. 'I'll be glad to retire at the end of the season, then it's no more boats for me. It's golf.' He did a mock swing, almost tumbling off the pontoon. 'Wenham was a golfer, did you know that? When we found we had that in common I suggested we go to the club and talk over a glass of beer and sandwich.'

Horton's spine tingled. 'Which club did you go to?' As if he needed to ask.

'Hayling. Do you know it? Just off the seafront at Sinah.'

Oh yes, Horton knew it. It bordered that lake. 'And this was Friday?' He wanted to make absolutely sure.

'Yes.'

Why hadn't Seaton picked this up? 'You're a member?'

'Only a social one now, which means I get to use the bar, restaurant, and the clubhouse. The company pay for that. But come my retirement in October I hope to be a full member. I've got to be proposed and seconded by two

232

existing members of at least two years' standing, but that's no problem and I've been playing at the public golf course at Crookhorn and got a good handicap.'

Had Seaton concentrated on full members only? It was irrelevant now that Horton had found a connection. But just because Wenham had been at the golf club didn't mean he had seen or come across Preston. He'd probed a bit deeper.

'What time was this?'

'One-thirty. We were there for about an hour, maybe a bit longer.'

'Did everything go all right with the lunch?'

'Yes, fine.' Turner looked puzzled at the question.

'And you've not been asked about this already by the police?'

'No. Why should I have been? You're the first officer I've spoken to and I had no idea Wenham had been killed.'

'How was Mr Wenham's mood?' He tried not to sound too curious.

'Very bright. Hey, you're not thinking he topped himself?'

'No, that's been ruled out. Did he say anything you thought odd? Or did he act in a strange way at any time?'

Turner again wiped his forehead. 'Not that I remember, only . . .'

'Yes?' Horton eagerly prompted.

'It's probably nothing. But now that you mention it. We were upstairs in the bar on the balcony, it was blazing hot, but we had a bit of shade before the sun came round to the west side.'

'The side that overlooks the lake?' Horton said, disguising his excitement. This was it.

'Yes. Des was looking across to it when he said, "That's funny." I said, "What is?" He said, "I know that man."'

'And?'

'That was all, because I got called away by a member who keeps his boat here.'

Horton silently cursed but held on to his hope and patience. 'You didn't see anything?'

'No. I went inside the bar because I didn't want Des, or anyone else, earwigging my conversation with the member. He's a bit of a moaner. I took him off to a quiet spot. When I came out there was no one at the lake, leastways that I could see. Might have been someone fishing who Des recognized. I can't say I looked. There was just the water, some ducks, the boat and the concrete gun emplacements.'

'You didn't ask him about it?'

'No. He said he'd buy another round of drinks and we went inside. We talked golf and dredgers. He said he'd get right on to the estimate. I wondered why I hadn't heard from him because he seemed very efficient. Will someone from the company be in touch with me?'

'I'm sure they will.'

Horton returned to his Harley, his mind whirling. Had Preston been at the lake on that Friday? Had Ashford? His boss at Camplow said he'd had Friday off as well as Saturday, Monday and Tuesday. Horton was certain that one of them had been there, or perhaps both of them had. There was no connection that he knew of between Ashford and Wenham, but that didn't mean to say there wasn't one. Wenham had been murdered, like Doyle had been, and Ashford was missing. Aside from that there was that past association between Preston and Wenham.

He made his way to the holiday park but stopped at the angling club car park. Inside the gates he could see Preston's car. He pulled in. The gates were locked but luckily a member was just coming out. Horton showed his warrant card and asked if he knew where Mr Preston was.

'You'll find him over at the store.'

Horton made his way to it, where Preston, dressed in a T-shirt and casual trousers, was leaning over one of the two angling club boats. He looked up, his surprise turning to annoyance.

'Can't you ever leave me alone?'

'Not when there's a murder investigation.'

'How many times do I have to tell you that has nothing to do with me?'

Horton looked at Preston's arms. There was no sign of any burns as a result of the car fire.

'Where were you the Friday before last?'

'Why should I tell you?'

'Why shouldn't you? If you prefer, we can do this at the station.'

'Threats now, is it? You're arresting me for minding my own business.'

'I am quite prepared to caution you and take you in if it's the only way to get a straight answer from you. Where were you, Mr Preston?'

He ran a hand over his face.

'I was here. But only for a short while. Friday is busy at the park. I had to get back.'

'What time were you here?'

'I came over during my lunch break at about one-thirty and stayed for about forty minutes.'

The time Turner had said he was there with Wenham.

'And what did you do while you were here?'

'Peter and I talked about the state of the lake, and the safety of the fish. Then I walked about, examined some of the swims and left Peter here with Bosman.'

'Why was Christopher Bosman here?'

'He was taking water samples.'

'I thought he was doing that on the Tuesday the box was found.'

'He was. I was surprised to see him on Tuesday, but he said he'd had to return to get more samples because he wasn't happy with the ones he'd taken on Friday.'

'Was anyone else here?'

'A couple of members.'

'Their names?'

'Look, what's this all about?'

'Their names, Mr Preston.'

'Donald Copley and Aaron Watley.'

'Did they see Mr Ashford or Mr Bosman?'

'Probably. I've no idea,' he said with exasperation.

Horton was rapidly thinking. 'Where was Peter Ashford at the time?'

'Here. This is where we talked.'

Horton looked across the lake to the golf club. The balcony was clearly in view and Wenham could easily have seen them both. 'And Bosman and the other two men?'

'Bosman was in the boat, out on the lake, this one.' He indicated the small one in front of him. 'Donald was at Back Bay and Aaron at Little Island.'

'And they are where?'

'Just along there,' he pointed to his right.

'Show me.'

Preston set off at a brisk pace along the opposite edge of the lake to where Horton had been previously, at the stock pond.

'Aaron was at this swim and Donald the second one down from here.'

Horton crouched down as though he was sitting and fishing on the wooden platform. He did the same at the other swim. He felt sure that Wenham couldn't have seen either man, the foliage was too thick around both swims.

'Are you going to tell me what this is all about?'

'Did you see Wenham on that Friday?'

'No.'

'Did he drive round here and accost you?'

'No. I told you before I haven't seen him for fifteen years.'

Horton held Preston's hostile gaze. Was it a bluff? Preston had no alibi for the time of Wenham's murder. Perhaps they should take a look at the holiday park's books and Preston's bank account.

'Do you know, or have you heard, of a man called Jamie Doyle?'

'No.'

That had the ring of truth about it. Horton didn't see how Preston could have been involved with Doyle and Ashford in the theft of the coins. But he wanted his prints to make sure they didn't match the unknown ones that were on that box and said as much.

'I never touched that damn box,' Preston protested.

'Then your prints won't be on it. I'll follow you to Havant police station, we'll get them done now.'

With ill grace Preston returned to his car and Horton tailed him to the police station on the Harley. There, while Preston's prints were taken, Horton called Uckfield.

'You've only got this man Turner's word that Wenham saw anyone he recognized at the lake. And even if he did, it might not have meant anything. Wenham could have seen someone he knew on the golf course. He might have seen a colleague or an old fishing friend. He could have meant he knew the greenkeeper.'

Horton said he knew all that, but he was convinced this was significant and it tied in with Ashford's disappearance.

Caustically, Uckfield said, 'Well, when you find out how Wenham knew Ashford let me into the secret.' Horton suspected the air-conditioning hadn't been fixed. 'Anyway, you're wrong,' Uckfield continued. 'We've had a break-through on Wenham's murder. Jason Downs.'

Horton felt deflated, although he had suspected Downs from the beginning.

'He wasn't sitting on his boat all alone sulking after the row with his wife. He took off on it. We've got two witnesses, boat owners, who saw him go out, and what's more, he didn't go out of the harbour but up it. Dennings and Chawla have re-interviewed him and his wife. He says he just motored around the harbour, trying to calm down.'

'Then why did he say he was sitting on his boat contemplating his navel and his marriage?'

'Because he didn't think it would make any difference. And he knew Wenham. He's conducted marine surveys on Kettering's boats.'

Horton recalled he'd asked Dennings what kind of surveyor Downs was.

'He claims he only knew him slightly and is adamant he had no idea it was him in that car. The row he had with his wife was over an affair she's been having.'

'With Wenham?'

'She says not but is refusing to tell us who her lover is or was. We're bringing them both in to make their statements. She may change her mind under further questioning.'

Horton rang off. It certainly looked as though Uckfield had his killer. Downs had opportunity and means, and he might have a motive if Wenham had been his wife's lover. There was no need to detain Preston in connection with Wenham's murder, but there was still Ashford and that tin box. They now had Preston's prints and would compare them with those on the box.

'I hope this is the last I see and hear from you, Inspector,' Preston snapped as he was leaving the station.

'Aren't you interested in the coins?'

'Not anymore. You can keep them as far as I'm concerned, and so can Peter Ashford.'

CHAPTER TWENTY-SIX

'I've found Norman Howe's son, or at least the last known address we have for him,' Cantelli greeted Horton. 'Lives in Kensington, London. I've asked the Met to call round. Norman Howe died thirteen years ago. Primary cause pneumonia, secondary Alzheimer's. I doubt there's much his son can tell us, if he's there, but you never know.'

They would have to wait for Ashford to show up somewhere to get to the truth. Horton felt restless. It was the impending storm. The sky was growing darker and he caught the growl of thunder in the distance. But there was more to it than that. Although he had suspected Jason Downs from the start he felt uneasy about it. There were so many thoughts rumbling around in his head. OK, so what was bugging him? He sat and began to consider it.

If the sea wall had never been breached, Doyle's body would never have been found, certainly not for some time. Even then the remains could have been swept out to sea but for a stumbling dog walker. Ashford would have no need to move the box, no need to have been blackmailed by Wenham, who saw him do it, and no need to take off. But he hadn't been blackmailed by Wenham if what Uckfield believed was true. Wenham didn't know Ashford, he only knew Robin Preston, and if Wenham hadn't been blackmailing Preston or Nick Kerris, then Downs was their man for Wenham's murder.

So, who had killed Doyle? That must have been Ashford. He called up the article on Southmoor that he'd shelved in place of his visit to Judith. The reporter had given some background about the history of the moor taken from a comprehensive study carried out fifteen years ago by Allington Environmental. There was that time frame again. A lot seemed to have occurred fifteen years ago. The area was deemed to be part of a rare and internationally important coastal habitat with the remains of well-preserved archaeological sites. These included prehistoric forest, peat deposits, stone tools, Bronze Age settlement and burial remains. The last far more recent, he thought wryly.

It also yielded up Roman pottery — maybe Cantelli's fragment hadn't been from a local kitchen showroom after all. He smiled and continued scrolling through the report, finding it interesting but not relevant to his investigation. In the back of his mind, he kept coming back to something Ken Turner had said. Was it Wenham's comments on that golf club balcony? He couldn't grasp what it was.

He returned to the Southmoor report. There had been salt workings, Saxon watercraft and some modern shipwrecks. The coastline had been subject to much change and realignment due to reclamation, natural processes and hardening, and was historically an area of marsh and farmland. Southmoor was crossed by a number of small watercourses and had been used for growing watercress in the nineteenth century. Those watercourses were now being swamped by the incoming tide. Water and soil samples had been taken and analysed. The geology bore out what Marsden had told him. Something resonated with him — in fact, a few points did — and his pulse quickened.

He searched the internet for the original report, feeling certain it would be on there because the council would have been obliged to make the findings public and the journalist had got her information from somewhere. Yes, there it was in all its glory — the background, the history, the methodology, the report's authors and contributors. His brain scrambled with the information. And now he remembered what he'd seen on the golf club balcony when he was at the lake with Cantelli — a pair of binoculars on a stand. Excitedly, he made to call up the reports on the finding of the tin box when his phone rang. Seeing it was Dr Pooley, he answered it with eagerness.

'I've got a print from the knife,' Pooley cried triumphantly. 'And a match. Not on the fingerprint database but with two prints on the tin box. It's the ones we can't identify.'

Not Ashford's then. He hadn't killed Doyle. 'Are Jamie Doyle's prints on that knife?'

'No.'

He asked Pooley to check the prints against the recent ones taken from Robin Preston and call him back. While he waited with barely concealed impatience, he read through the reports of the police officers and that of Walters on the finding of the tin box taken from Preston and Ashford on the day, and the one Bosman had emailed over after they had met him at the lake, when Cantelli had decided to chew grass instead of his usual gum.

He also recalled who Preston had said had been at the lake on the day Ken Turner had taken Wenham to lunch, and Turner's conversation with him at the boatyard: *there are so many regulations nowadays . . . not to mention the amount of red tape surrounding dredging and dumping. You can't just go ahead and shift the silt like you used to. You have to have it tested and analysed.* Then there was Kerris's comment. What had he said? *The dredger's been on-site for two weeks, shifting silt out to sea.* That silt would have to have been analysed before the dredger was hired. *The lake is becoming more eutrophic with the silt build-up and the increased biomass.*

He rose and stared out at the dull grey sky, rapidly thinking. He just needed Pooley's phone call. It finally came. The prints weren't Preston's. Horton had suspected as much.

He grabbed his jacket and helmet. Cantelli wasn't at his desk and Walters was on the phone. He'd call through later.

He might be wrong, but as he weaved his way through the traffic in the stifling, humid heat of the late afternoon on to the Gosport peninsula he knew he wasn't. It all fitted, but to check his theory further he needed to visit Elizabeth Quay. He recalled Kerris's conversation: *I prefer to pit my wits against the weather and the sea . . . Racing. Now there's a challenge for you. You have to take risks. You're up against the elements, which are uncontrollable, but that's part of the fun.* And Gaye's words in the mortuary: *You wouldn't believe how competitive some dinghy sailors are. They'd do anything to win and don't much like it when they don't.*

Was Kerris into dinghy racing, not yacht racing? But he wasn't here to question Kerris about that. It could wait.

A roll of thunder rumbled in the distance. A flash of lightning struck far out over the Solent. Outside the office he alighted from his Harley and stared along the pontoon to the dredger.

He found Kerris in his office. He confirmed what Horton had realized. It wasn't Preston or Ashford who Wenham had recognized at Sinah Lake on Friday when he had been at the golf club, and it wasn't either of them he had attempted to blackmail. It was a man Wenham had met here on 20 June when he'd come to see Kerris about the contract for the dredger.

Having got the answer to his question he made to leave when he said. 'Do you play cricket, Mr Kerris?'

'Yes. Why?'

'You look as though you might be a good bowler as well as a sailor.'

'I am.' Kerris gave a cocky leer.

'And you like sailing close to the wind. A bit too close. One day you might get your fingers burned.'

Outside, leaving a ruffled Kerris, Horton called Cantelli. There was no answer. He phoned Walters.

'Look up Nick Kerris for me in relation to dinghy sailing.'

'I don't need to, guv. I've already got it. Dr Clayton has just told me. She was about the only member of Tipner Sailing Club me and Seaton didn't contact yesterday, aside from the Chief Constable, and I wasn't going to ask him if he had ever heard of Nick Kerris. Dr Clayton said that Nick Kerris caused an accident when he was teaching dinghy sailing in Wales through negligence, almost killed two sailors.'

'And knowing Kerris, he no doubt claimed he was innocent and it was the other sailors' fault. Well done. We'll deal with him later. Where's Cantelli?'

'He took Judith Brindley's statement and went out. Don't know where, said he had a man to see about a plant. Must be going to the garden centre.'

Horton didn't think so. 'When was this?'

'About forty minutes ago. Mrs Brindley came in with her husband.'

Horton was glad she had told him.

'Everything is there in black and white, just as you said.'

'Does she recall anything more about the man she saw at Doyle's bedsit?' Not that Horton needed it now, he knew who Doyle and Wenham's killer was.

'Hold on. Yes, she says he was slight, longish fair hair, thin lips.'

Horton called Uckfield and got his voicemail. He left a short message and set out for the address that had been on the statement that they had all blithely ignored.

CHAPTER TWENTY-SEVEN

Hollow House was a large shabby property set in its own grounds at the end of a curving lane on the northern side of Portsdown Hill. The massive housing estate developments to both the east and west hadn't reached there yet but Horton was certain they would, given time. The sky was dark and thunder rolled and grumbled in the background. The air was suffocating. It was with some relief that Horton couldn't see Cantelli's car. Maybe he *had* gone to the garden centre.

He made to knock on the door, when Christopher Bosman stepped round from the right of the house where there was a clump of trees set back from the road. He looked startled but tried to cover his anxiety with a smile that didn't quite come off.

'Inspector Horton, I didn't expect to see you.' His attempt at lightness rang false.

'Didn't you?'

'I hope Sergeant Cantelli is OK?'

'Perfectly, thank you. Fully recovered.' Horton's gratitude to this man had blinded him as to his part in a murder, or he should say murders. This was the man Judith had met in Doyle's flat, now older, with shorter fair hair and an auburn-flecked goatee beard accentuating that long thin face and hiding the thin lips.

'Then how can I help you?'

'You can tell me about that tin box and its valuable contents.'

'I didn't see much of it when Peter found it. But if I can help then I will. Come through into the garden. It's too hot inside the house, and although it seems a storm is on its way, I don't think it will reach here for a while. It'll be cooler under the trees.'

Of which there were many. There was also a small lake. It had dried out considerably since the drought — Horton could see the edges where its borders had been — but there was still a fair bit of water. There was also an upturned red boat on the dry grass this side of the lake and a paddle beside it. In the centre of the water was a small clump of bushes. The rear of the house looked as dilapidated as the front. The French doors were open.

'Do you live here alone, Mr Bosman?'

'Yes. My father died four years ago. It's far too big for me. I need to sell it, but I haven't got round to putting it on the market. It needs a lot of work. I'm not sure where I would move to either.'

Horton felt like saying how about a bedsit in Eldon Road, Southsea, like you used to visit to see Doyle. But he refrained.

'Can I offer you a drink?'

'No, thank you.' Horton wasn't convinced that Bosman wouldn't poison him. It was then he noted two glasses on the rickety table. One half full, the other empty. Had Bosman been expecting him? Or was there a guest in the house?

'Please take a seat.' Bosman waved an arm at the moss-spattered wooden seats to their left, under some shady ash trees.

Horton sat when Bosman had done so. He didn't look as nervous now. Perhaps he believed he hadn't been found out.

'Why did you move the tin box to Sinah Lake when you've had it here in your own lake for fifteen years?' Horton launched right in; this was where the algae on the box had come from. Would Bosman feign bewilderment? Would he deny it?

Bosman studied his slender hands, frowning as though they were dirty. And they were, thought Horton, very dirty, with the blood of two men on them. A rumble of thunder filled the air. Bosman glanced up and cocked his head. His mouth moved, counting. 'Ten, it's a way off yet. We need the rain. I moved it because I panicked.' His eyes alighted on Horton.

With a thrill, Horton could see he was about to get the truth. He thought he should caution Bosman, but before he could do so he continued. 'It was stupid of me, but then I wasn't thinking rationally. I knew the breach of the sea wall at Southmoor would get larger. In fact, I went there regularly to inspect it. I could see what was coming. The wave patterns were eating under the earth, eroding it, and its secret was eating away inside me. It would only be a matter of time before Jamie was exposed, unless the sea wall was repaired, and the council and the owner of that land had no intention of doing that.'

Horton again made to speak, but Bosman was too keen to get things off his chest. Whether he'd repeat them later when under arrest was another matter.

'Of course, there was nothing about Jamie's death to associate it with me. I should have left things as they were. That way two more men wouldn't have died, but it's too late for that now. It's played on my mind. I'm glad you're here, Inspector, and not unexpectedly. Sergeant Cantelli should have forewarned me.'

Horton tried to hide his surprise, but didn't succeed. 'You asked me if he was all right.'

'Yes, I did, didn't I?' He stroked his beard.

'He's been here recently then?'

'He came over to thank me, or so he said, but I knew that was a trick.'

Horton's blood froze. He stiffened with horror. His earlier suspicion had been correct. Why hadn't Cantelli called him to say he was coming here? But then why should he have done so? The sergeant didn't know Bosman had committed three murders — by what Bosman had just said, Horton was assuming the third death was Ashford. Unless . . . His eyes flashed to the glass. My God. Not Cantelli. But where was his car? Maybe he had been and gone. But Bosman's words about it being a trick filled him with dread.

'Where is Sergeant Cantelli?' he demanded.

It was as though Bosman hadn't heard him. 'You haven't brought anyone to arrest me, I see. I'm glad of that too, unless they're following.'

'They are, Mr Bosman,' Horton said stiffly, thinking of Uckfield, when he picked up the message he'd left. 'When did Sergeant Cantelli leave?'

'He hasn't.'

Horton went rigid. 'He's in the house?'

'No.'

Horton watched Bosman closely, but his expression remained calm and composed. It was as though they were talking about the weather. Horton's mind raced. Two glasses on the table, one half drunk. The other almost empty. 'You've poisoned him and put him in the lake.' He could barely speak for fear.

'No, but it's where you'll find Peter Ashford.'

'Then where . . . ?' Horton's eyes fell on the boat. He dashed a glance at Bosman then rushed towards the boat and threw it over. There, hunched, in the foetal position was Cantelli. Swiftly, Horton felt for a pulse, his own racing fit to burst. He felt sick with dread. Cantelli was alive. Thank God. He reached for his phone, half expecting Bosman to rush him or pull a knife, but the man just stood there, half smiling.

'Ambulance,' Horton barked into his phone, and quickly he gave his name, rank, phone number and the exact position. He prayed silently and heartily that they'd be there in time. 'What did you give him? The same as at Sinah Lake?'

'It grows very freely around my lake.'

But Bosman must have given Cantelli a larger dose and perhaps the more poisonous root. There was no visible sign he had been sick, which was bad. How much time did he have?

'But why? Sergeant Cantelli's done you no harm.'

'He came to arrest me, as you have.'

'No, he came to thank you. *I've* come to arrest you, and I'm now formally cautioning you.' Where was that ambulance?

Bosman's hand came out of the sleeve of his long safari shirt, and in it was a long sharp knife. Horton wasn't afraid of that. As Bosman came for him, Horton's training and instinct kicked in. Swiftly and easily, he disarmed the man and wrenched his wrists behind his back with more force than perhaps he should have done, but he didn't care. If Cantelli died . . . If this man had killed him . . . Into his head flashed Charlotte and Barney's kids.

'Now you can have a real set of police handcuffs on,' he hissed in Bosman's ear. 'And they're not coming off until you're in custody.' He pushed him forcefully onto the chair, noting the burn scar just above his wrist. 'Move one inch and I'll thrash you and say you tripped while resisting arrest.'

He crouched down over Cantelli. Bosman sat and looked disinterested.

'Hang on in there, Barney,' Horton said. 'Help is coming. You'll be all right, just hang on.' Should he stick his fingers down Cantelli's throat to make him sick? Why wasn't that blessed ambulance here? It was taking an age. He'd lift and carry Barney to the car, only he didn't have one. He was on his bike. He could take Cantelli's car, but where was it? Then Horton knew. Bosman had come round to the front of the house from the clump of trees just off the right-hand side of the property. Horton would find the Ford there.

He half made to go when the sounds of a vehicle screeched to a halt outside, then another, not the ambulance though. Uckfield's squat figure strode round into the garden with DI Dennings beside him and two uniformed officers behind them. Uckfield made straight for Horton.

'Bloody hell, is he—'

'He's alive. The ambulance is coming. Bosman's poisoned him. You'll find Cantelli's car the other side of the house, and Ashford's body in the lake. You can charge Bosman with the murders of Jamie Doyle, Desmond Wenham and Peter Ashford.' Horton didn't even like to think he might have to add Barney to the list.

The siren of the ambulance came as a massive relief. A minute later it screamed to a halt and the siren was silenced. Horton swiftly gave the paramedics instructions about the poison. They would start to pump out Barney's stomach immediately and get a drip in him. Horton watched as a lifeless Cantelli was taken into the ambulance. He felt sick with fear of what might be. The first drops of rain began to fall as the thunder rolls drew closer. A flash lit up the sky. Bosman, who was being led away by the two uniformed officers, looked up.

Uckfield came off the phone. 'Chawla and Seaton are coming over, as are SOCO and Clarke. We'll take the house apart and drag that lake. Dennings will stay here and oversee things. You'd better come back and update me.'

'Later, Steve. I'm following the ambulance and I need to tell Charlotte.'

Uckfield nodded. 'Bosman can wait then. Do him good to brood on what he's done. Is he mad?'

Horton shrugged. He followed the ambulance to A&E, where he repeated to the nursing staff and then a doctor what had happened. Then he phoned Charlotte. After a moment's silence she said, 'I'm on my way.'

He waited until she arrived, by which time Cantelli's stomach had been pumped dry, he was on a drip and he'd been given anticonvulsive drugs as a safeguard. It had been touch and go. If Horton hadn't taken that trip to the Hayling Yacht Harbour, if Ken Turner hadn't told him about Wenham, and if he hadn't made the connection in time and gone straight to Bosman's house ... if instead he had followed proper procedure and returned to the station to report in, and they had planned the arrest, Cantelli would be dead. Horton felt sick when he thought of it. With huge relief that Cantelli was out of danger and would make a full recovery, Horton finally left the hospital.

CHAPTER TWENTY-EIGHT

It was raining heavily when Horton reached the station, the thunder rolling around overhead, the lightning flashing almost continually. Bosman had been booked in, stripped of his clothing and put in a disposable suit. The team were still at his house.

'We found Ashford's body,' Uckfield said, as they made their way to the interview room. 'No marks of violence on him. Looks as though he was poisoned and then dragged to the lake and left to die.'

The fate that would have befallen Cantelli. Horton thought of Ashford's two sons and felt immensely sad for them.

Bosman was sitting hunched over his plastic beaker of weak tea. He waived the right to a solicitor. 'It seems pointless now,' he said. 'I'm glad it's over. It's a relief really. I've lived with it for fifteen years. I'm sorry about Sergeant Cantelli. Will he be all right?'

As if you care. 'Tell us what happened, right from the beginning when you were friends with Jamie Doyle — or was it more than friends on your part?' Horton said tersely.

Bosman smiled. 'He was an amazing man, so funny, so alive. He made me feel alive too.'

'How did you meet him?'

'I was doing a part-time gardening job to get some money while I went through university.'

'You worked on Mr Howe's garden,' Horton said.

'Yes. How did you know? Oh, I suppose that girl told you. The one with the terrible skin. She thought Jamie loved her, the fool. I soon put her right on that.'

Horton felt like wiping that grin off his pathetic face. He forced himself to remain calm. It took an effort to do so and to hide his contempt.

'You were in Mr Howe's garden,' he prompted.

'Jamie came over to me. She went inside to do something for the old man. We started talking. We got on like a house on fire.'

Yes, because Doyle had recognized a weak soul like Judith and had cultivated Bosman in case he could use him. Knowing Doyle of old, he was probably already working out some scheme to rob the elderly man and thought Bosman would come in handy for that, either helping him, or putting him in the frame for it, just like he had Spider Baxter. No doubt Doyle could see that Bosman was hero-worshipping him.

'Doyle persuaded you to help him steal a valuable horde of coins.'

'It was a joke.'

'I'm not laughing. Are you, Inspector?' Uckfield said, puzzled. 'I must be missing something. Give us the punchline, Mr Bosman, then we might all have a good laugh, including the three men who are dead.'

Bosman's face flushed and he looked angry for a moment, but it soon passed. He glanced down at his cold tea, then back up at them. 'I didn't mean to kill them.'

'Now that is a joke,' Uckfield sneered.

'It all went wrong,' he whined, plucking at his beard.

Horton said, 'Doyle came up with the idea of how to rob Mr Howe.'

'No, it was my idea. It *was*,' he insisted, as though seeking praise. 'I was chatting to Jamie in the old man's garden, and I told him how my father was almost conned by some rogue gardeners who knocked at his door and said they'd only charge four hundred pounds for clearing it up. He agreed and let them in, but I returned home before they had started and told them to clear out.'

'And yet you still contrived to con a vulnerable elderly man,' Horton said with distaste.

'We were going to put the box back. We just wanted to see if we could get away with it.'

'Oh, come on!' Horton cried incredulously.

'It's the truth. It's what Jamie told me.' He scowled.

'But he tricked you.'

'I went along with his scheme because when I stood up to those men it made me feel good. Jamie made me feel the same way. He believed in me. He made me feel more confident. He made me feel valued.'

Horton knew exactly what Doyle had done. 'It was a test of your loyalty to him, or was it your love?'

Bosman twitched nervously and smoothed his beard.

'He said if you really loved him, you'd do as he asked. It would prove to him how much he meant to you.'

'It would bind us together for ever.'

Uckfield coughed and cleared his throat noisily.

Bosman seemed oblivious to it. 'Jamie said there was a tin box containing valuable coins. He didn't want the box or the coins, but if I would help him take both from right under the old man's nose it would be something for us to share. Not the contents but the experience.' Bosman reached for his plastic cup then changed his mind. 'I came up with the idea that I would pose as the police officer and arrest Jamie in the act of stealing the box. He could easily break into the house.'

'But he didn't have to. He had his girlfriend's key, or a copy of it.'

'Yes. I'd bought two sets of handcuffs online. Mr Howe had met Jamie a couple of times, but we doubted he would remember him, given his Alzheimer's, but if he did, I was to say that we, the police, had had our eye on him for some time and were just waiting for the right opportunity to arrest him. My heart was hammering fit to bust. It was so exciting, and I was so nervous. I didn't think I'd be able to go through with it, but I did.' He lifted his chin, his lips twitched and his eyes glowed. 'Mr Howe fell for it completely and Jamie was perfect. He should have been an actor. Mr Howe didn't recognize me because I'd been working in the garden, and although he came out with cups of tea, he didn't take any notice of me, and I wore a cap. Anyway, he was confused enough to think he'd be wrong.'

Again, that smirk. Horton wanted to feel pity and empathy for one of Doyle's victims, as he had for Judith, but he couldn't for someone who had murdered to save his own skin and could also have killed Cantelli in the process.

'I couldn't believe we'd get away with it. Jamie got in with the key he'd had copied and left the door unlocked for me for me to slip in. He made a lot of noise so the old man would find him. Then I entered saying I had been watching Doyle and had followed him there. He was a crook, well known to the police. He'd left the door open for a quick getaway. I handcuffed myself to Jamie, and the box to his other hand, saying I had to take away the evidence, including the key to the padlock, and I'd return it once we'd finished with it.'

'And Mr Howe smiled trustingly and said, of course.' It made Horton sick to think of it.

'It was always part of the plan for me to return the box and coins.'

Horton widened his eyes. Uckfield snorted.

'It was,' insisted Bosman. 'It's what Jamie said.'

'He lied,' Horton said flatly.

'I unlocked our set of cuffs in the car, leaving only the one attached to the box, and drove away. It was my father's car, but he had stopped driving by then. I thought we were going to Jamie's flat, but he said it was too public and it was best to go somewhere private and open the box. I asked him why we needed to open the box if we were going to return it. He laughed and said surely I didn't believe that. I had. He said we would open it and divide up the spoils. I told him if the coins were that valuable, we'd have trouble selling them. Anyone buying them would be suspicious and could report us to the police, so too could Mr Howe.'

'And the girl?'

'Oh, Jamie had ditched her by then. She had no idea what we had done.'

'So, the scales fell from your eyes,' Uckfield said with heavy sarcasm, 'and you saw Doyle in his true light.'

Bosman made no comment.

Horton said, 'You had been working on the survey at Southmoor for Allington Environmental. Your name, among others, is in the report. And you suggested going there. Had you already planned to kill him when you drove there?'

'No, I . . . I didn't know what I thought. My head was hurting fit to bust after all the excitement. I just needed space and some time to try and reason with him. It just came into my mind that it was the right place to go. As you say, I had been working there. That day had been the final one of the survey. I knew at that time of night no one would be there. It was summer and still light. At Southmoor Jamie said let's go for a walk and discuss this.'

Horton thought that rang true. Doyle hadn't committed murder before and maybe he hadn't intended to then. Perhaps he wanted to give Bosman a hiding as a warning to keep his mouth shut. Or he would see that Bosman would meet with an accident.

A large clap of thunder overhead made Bosman jump. His eyes darted around the room as though someone was coming for him. Tiny beads of perspiration pricked his brow. The room was stifling. The air-conditioning was still not working, but Bosman's sweat wasn't solely caused by that. His demons were coming for him.

'What happened next?' Horton prompted, seeing Doyle's spiteful, cocky face close to his own frightened one all those years ago, hearing those cruel taunts about his mother, hissing them over and over in his ear until Horton had turned and hit the larger boy, for which he had taken a severe beating. He'd told his carers at the home, and his teachers, he'd fallen off his bike. They didn't believe him. But he'd got his own back on Doyle in another fight. After that Doyle had left him alone.

'I locked the box with the cuffs still on them in the boot of the car,' Bosman said. 'We walked along the path. We'd gone so far when Jamie stopped and pulled a knife on me. He said our friendship was over. I was horrified, deeply hurt and afraid. I knew I was fighting for my life. We wrestled. I grabbed his wrist and before I knew it the knife had pierced his chest. He struggled for breath. He fell. He was dead within minutes. I didn't know what to do. I couldn't confess, and neither could I be found out. It would ruin me and destroy my father.' He gulped in some air as another crack sounded almost overhead. 'There were some dense shrubs close by. I dragged him into them. The ground was quite wet from the rain. I cleared what I could with my bare hands and then with a plank of wood I had found. I covered him with more brambles, cutting my hands to shreds almost. I knew the brambles would quickly do the rest and cover him completely. I just hoped no dog would sniff him out. Even if it did no one would be able to put him with me. I made sure there was no ID left on him. I drove home in a daze and threw the wretched box with its handcuffs on it into our lake and tried to forget it had ever happened. It was like a bad dream.'

There was a short pause filled by another deafening clap of thunder. Bosman gave a cry and chewed his lip as his eyes fled to the ceiling.

Horton said, 'Most of what you say is probably true, except Doyle didn't pull the knife on you. It was the other way round. When you locked the tin box in the boot of your car you took out a knife you kept there, perhaps for work purposes. You stuffed it up your sleeve and you rammed it into him. Your prints are on the knife that we found beside Doyle's body.'

'They would be because, as I told you, we struggled for it.'

'Then Doyle's prints would be on it, and they're not.' And the prints on the box matched Bosman's, which had been taken when he had been brought in.

Horton continued. 'When you could see that Doyle's body would be exposed by the breach in the wall, you worried that someone might connect you with him being buried there.' Bosman bit his nails. 'You moved the box to Sinah Lake, far away from where you lived, and it was convenient because you had been commissioned to take water samples by Peter Ashford, the pond manager, on the Friday before the box was found.' It was why Ashford had had the Friday off work. Preston had confirmed that. 'You saw it as the perfect opportunity to get rid of the incriminating evidence for ever. You were out on the lake in the angling club's boat the day Desmond Wenham happened to be having lunch with a prospective customer at the golf club. Wenham saw you behaving furtively and he watched as you lowered the tin box into the lake. Perhaps he wouldn't have got curious — after all, he had seen you at Elizabeth Quay taking silt samples on the day he'd gone there to give them a quote for the hire of a dredger.' Kerris had verified that on Horton's earlier visit. 'Then he saw you taking some samples and putting them in your usual silver case, the one you had used at Elizabeth Quay. What Wenham couldn't work out was why the box he saw you lower into the lake had a set of handcuffs on it. There's a pair of binoculars on a stand on the balcony.' And when Turner had left to pacify the grumbling boat owner, Wenham had peered through them and watched Bosman closely, probably with a smirk on his face, working out how he could use such information to his advantage. 'He could see that you were up to no good, and he'd make something out of it.' That would have been typical of Wenham's behaviour given what they had learned of him.

'Yes,' Bosman breathed.

'Louder for the tape,' rapped Uckfield.

'Yes, you're right.'

Horton had also asked Kerris if Wenham had contacted him on that Friday, or over that weekend, to ask the name of the man who had taken the silt samples at Elizabeth Quay. He had, and Kerris had given it along with Bosman's mobile number, thinking that it was probably work related.

'When did Desmond Wenham contact you, Christopher?' asked Horton. Thunder split the air again but not quite as loud.

'Saturday. I tried to fob him off. I told him I had been lowering the box to monitor the nutrient level in the water, but he said it hadn't looked that way to him, not with handcuffs on it. Were the fish violent, he joked. He would ask the secretary and pond manager. I couldn't let him do that, so I agreed to meet him on Sunday at Fareham Quay. He said he'd keep quiet about seeing me dump the box in the lake if I paid him. He wanted two thousand pounds. I told him I couldn't possibly pay that, and besides, it wasn't worth it. Again, I tried to tell him it was all part of the analysis.'

But Wenham knew it wasn't and he smelled fear. He knew he had Bosman, a timid man, in the palm of his hand, one he could manipulate and exploit.

Bosman continued. 'He said in that case he'd tell the angling club and the police. I capitulated, knowing it wouldn't be a final payment. He would be back for more. I said I needed some time to get that money and agreed to meet him again at Forton Lake on Tuesday night.'

'Did you suggest that venue?'

'No. He did. But I went there to look it over before the meeting.'

'And that's when you thought you could arrive and depart by boat.'

Bosman nodded.

'For the tape, please.'

'Yes.'

'You trailered your small boat on the back of your car to the Gosport Hardway.' The same boat he'd used to hide

Cantelli. 'I saw your car had a tow bar on it when we were at the lake.'

'Not there. From Wicor Marina,' Bosman corrected him. 'They're used to seeing me launch my boat. I have an outboard motor I fix to it and often go around the harbour.'

And it was closest to where Bosman lived. Horton cursed himself for not checking that out more thoroughly. 'Before that, you returned to Sinah Lake to retrieve the box in case Wenham told anyone or decided to take the box and sell the contents himself, or so you reasoned.'

He ran a hand over his face. 'Yes.'

'But you had planned to kill him so he wouldn't tell anyone,' Uckfield insisted.

'I couldn't think straight. I just needed to get that box away. It has haunted and tormented me all these years.'

Horton again. 'You told Peter Ashford you needed to return on Tuesday to take further samples because you weren't happy with the first ones.'

'Yes.'

And Preston had also told Horton that he had been surprised to see Bosman because he thought he'd already got everything he needed in the way of samples on the Friday.

Uckfield said, 'What happened then?'

'I was very nervous.' He wrung his hands as though reliving the memory. 'Was anyone watching me? Would I manage to get it?' He rubbed his bloodshot eyes. 'I did, and I wanted to clear out as quickly as I could, but I couldn't leave because Preston was doing something by the gates. I hurried back to the boat and took it further east of the lake until I came to the stock pond area that had dried out. I could get ashore there and take the path that leads round to the golf club. I could leave it in the undergrowth there and collect it later when no one was around.' As he and Cantelli had speculated. Bosman seemed to have dried up.

Horton took it up. 'But there again you were unlucky. You heard someone coming. Peter Ashford.'

'Yes. I didn't know it was him. I quickly hid the box in the clump of weed and hemlock water dropwort in the middle of the dried-out patch, and then hurried back to the boat. I had no idea that Ashford was going to start clearing that area or that he would find the box.' Bosman was almost crying now. His eyes had welled up and his cheeks were hollows in his drawn, pale face.

Horton could see in front of him a weak-willed, isolated, lonely man, with faulty reasoning and a self-centred nature. Not an arrogant man, as was often the case, but one whose fear and guilt had driven him to protect himself at all costs.

He said, 'You returned to the lake and quickly took some samples, hoping Ashford wouldn't find the box. Then you walked back along the path to discover Ashford had found it and called the police. It wasn't as you had told us. You didn't tell him to call the police. By the time you told us this you had killed Peter Ashford, which was why, in your warped reasoning, he had to die, in case we checked with him.'

'Yes.'

'Then Preston arrived and you told them you couldn't hang around because you had another appointment. You didn't want to be there when the police showed up.'

'There was nothing I could do.'

'You could have owned up then,' Horton said, stiffly.

'How could I? Everything would come out.'

'Like it has now,' Uckfield snarled.

'I didn't know that then. All I knew was that Wenham could say he had seen me with that box and I couldn't afford to pay him. I met him as agreed in the industrial unit car park.'

'You were already there, having arrived early by boat, which you hauled up onto the shore further up the creek,' Horton said, as he had earlier conjectured.

'Yes. There was no one about. I handed over what he thought was the money, but it was a package of paper. He said, don't mind if I count it, do you? I said go ahead. While he was bending over the rear of the car undoing the bundle I took my small paddle and hit him, twice. He fell forward and the rest you know.'

'Tell us anyway.'

Flatly, as though he'd lost all interest, Bosman said, 'I pushed him in the car and drove it down onto the shore. Then I got two rags from my boat and some petrol I'd put there in a can and set light to the car.'

Uckfield said, 'And burned your wrist doing so.'

'I was so frightened I thought I'd go up in flames too. I didn't realize the fire would take so quickly. But I managed to dowse my wrist, and though it hurt like hell I soaked it in sea water, which stung and caused me more pain, but I had to grin and bear it.'

What does he want, a bloody medal? Praise?

Uckfield said, 'And you had Wenham's blood on your shirt.'

'Yes, but you won't find it, I burned it,' he declared triumphantly. 'Wenham was a horrible man.'

Quietly, Horton said, 'That was no reason to kill him. And Peter Ashford was a hard-working, kind family man who had never done you any harm.'

'But he could have done, don't you see that?' he urged. 'That's why I had to kill him. He called me Tuesday afternoon to say he'd been thinking about that box and asking if I'd seen it before. He said he'd seen me around that area before he'd set to work clearing it. That I must have spotted it, I should tell the police.'

'No,' Horton corrected. 'Turn that the other way around. You got to thinking he must have seen you place that box and you called him. You had his number because, being the pond manager, he'd arranged for your company to take the water samples. You asked him to meet you at your house, said you wanted to discuss the finding of the box with him. Ashford came in all innocence. You offered him a drink, the same one you'd given Sergeant Cantelli, only no one got to Ashford on time. Three men murdered all because you thought stealing from a vulnerable elderly man was a prank, and it would make you look powerful in the eyes of a man you hero-worshipped, but who despised and pitied you.'

Bosman blinked and swallowed hard. 'What will happen to me now?'

'What do you think?' Horton said scathingly.

'I couldn't go to prison. I couldn't be shut in. I didn't mean to kill Jamie. It's that box. It's cursed. It's evil.' His eyes darted about the room.

Uckfield raised his eyebrows.

'You must understand that I was only protecting myself.' He began to weep.

Horton scraped back his chair. Uckfield rose more slowly. To the constable outside Horton said, 'Take him back to his cell and give him another cup of tea.'

He fetched a strong black coffee for himself and for Uckfield.

'I don't know about you, but I could do with a double whisky,' Uckfield said.

'I don't drink.'

'No, I forgot. But that scenario is enough to make anyone want to. How people fool themselves.'

Yes, thought Horton. 'Wenham suggested the unit by Forton Lake because he'd met Kerris there previously in order to blackmail him. Kerris is the sailing club arsonist.'

'He's confessed?'

'No, but he knows I know. I asked him about Bosman taking silt samples when Wenham was negotiating the contract with him. He'll probably not admit to the arson, not now that Wenham is dead, unless we hold back on the arrest of Bosman for murder and make out we think Kerris killed him. He might cough up to the lesser charge. Wenham recognized Kerris the night he was with Suzanne Edley at Tipner.'

'And we can charge him with fraud.'

'That's probably how Wenham extracted payment for his silence. Kerris started working for Elizabeth Quay in March. He used the workboat to motor up the harbour to the sailing club. He might have targeted more sailing clubs if it hadn't been for Wenham. Kerris has a big chip on his shoulder where dinghy sailing clubs are concerned. He was teaching at a sailing club, or school, off Wales, and his cavalier approach and big-headedness nearly cost two sailors their lives. I don't have all the details, but it was enough for the clubs round here not to want him as a member. He's the sort who will never accept he was at fault. He moved here and took the Elizabeth Quay job, which he hates. He needed his adrenalin fix and he became embittered and resentful towards dinghy sailors and clubs and thought he'd take revenge.'

'Sounds as warped in his thinking as Bosman.'

'Fortunately, he only got as far as targeting one, with no one hurt. The fact he's involved in the fraud means he'll either have to say he went in with Wenham willingly and face the charges, or admit he was forced into it through blackmail, which means he'll have to say why and admit to arson. He'll weigh up which will be the lesser crime of the two in terms of punishment.'

'You'd better get him out of bed and bring him in.'

'I will. But first I've got something I need to do.' He collected his jacket and helmet and, on the way out, called Charlotte. The thunder had passed, leaving a steady rain and sticky humidity. Charlotte was at home. She reassured him that Cantelli was doing well and on the way to his second recovery.

He saw that he also had a message from Harriet, who had heard that Cantelli had been taken to hospital. News of an officer down always travelled fast. He messaged her back saying that Barney was out of danger and would make a full recovery. He hesitated for a moment before adding, *I'll call you tomorrow.*

Horton rode to the hospital. It was late but his warrant card permitted him entry. Cantelli had a small room to himself. The lights were subdued and the room silent, as was the corridor, with just the rain lashing against the darkened window. Horton crossed to the bed. Cantelli was sleeping.

Horton's gut twisted in agony at the thought of what might have been, and there was a lump in his throat. He took a long deep breath and slowly exhaled.

'What would I have done without you, Barney?' he said quietly. 'Got to have someone to keep me under control, buy me bacon butties and tell me I'm mad.'

As he left, he could have sworn Cantelli had smiled.

THE END

ACKNOWLEDGEMENT

With grateful thanks to Jonathan Smith, senior forensic scientist; Ian Snook, treasurer of the Portsmouth and District Angling Society and the Hayling Golf Club.

THE JOFFE BOOKS STORY

We began in 2014 when Jasper agreed to publish his mum's much-rejected romance novel and it became a bestseller.

Since then we've grown into the largest independent publisher in the UK. We're extremely proud to publish some of the very best writers in the world, including Joy Ellis, Faith Martin, Caro Ramsay, Helen Forrester, Simon Brett and Robert Goddard. Everyone at Joffe Books loves reading and we never forget that it all begins with the magic of an author telling a story.

We are proud to publish talented first-time authors, as well as established writers whose books we love introducing to a new generation of readers.

We have been shortlisted for Independent Publisher of the Year at the British Book Awards three times, in 2020, 2021 and 2022, and for the Diversity and Inclusivity Award at the Independent Publishing Awards in 2022.

We built this company with your help, and we love to hear from you, so please email us about absolutely anything bookish at: feedback@joffebooks.com

If you want to receive free books every Friday and hear about all our new releases, join our mailing list: www.joffebooks.com/contact

And when you tell your friends about us, just remember: it's pronounced Joffe as in coffee or toffee!

Milton Keynes UK
Ingram Content Group UK Ltd.
UKHW010816241123
433194UK00004B/323